Skeleton in a

Dead Space

Skeleton in a Dead Space

by

Judy Alter

A Kelly O'Connell Mystery

Turquoise Morning Press
Turquoise Morning, LLC
www.turquoisemorningpress.com

Turquoise Morning, LLC
P.O. Box 43958
Louisville, KY 40253-0958

Skeleton in a Dead Space
Copyright © 2011, Judy Alter
Trade Paperback ISBN: 9781937389253
Digital ISBN: 9781937389260

Editor, Ayla O'Donovan

Trade Paperback release, August 2011
Digital Release, August 2011

Turquoise Morning Press
www.turquoisemorningpress.com

Dedication

To Fred Erisman, who always said I could write a mystery and helped me do it.

With thanks to....

I owe so much gratitude to so many people for their interest in my writing and my career, but for this novel I specifically want to thank a few:

—First, my two oldest granddaughters. With some changes, Madison, now thirteen, and Eden, now eight, are Maggie and Em. I wrote the first draft of this novel so long ago that they were then the ages of my fictional girls, and I had them in mind as I crafted Maggie and Em. I hope Maddie and Edie know how much I love them.

—All my children and grandchildren for showing me often how proud they are of me and how much they love me: Colin and Lisa, Morgan, Kegan; Megan and Brandon, Sawyer, Ford; Jamie and Melanie, Maddie, Edie; Jordan and Christian, Jacob.

—Fred Erisman, years ago my major professor in graduate school, still my friend, advisor, and mentor; Fred read this manuscript until I'm sure he knows it by heart, and he counseled me about it over many enjoyable lunches.

—Peter, owner of the Old Neighborhood Grill, for once signing permission to use his restaurant in the book on an imaginary piece of paper in the air and then suggesting the Grill, mentioned often in the book, as a perfect site for book signings. He serves the best breakfast in town and a pretty mean meatloaf at night.

—Donatella Trotti, for allowing me to mention, always with praise, her wonderful small country Italian restaurant, Nonna Tata.

Praise for Skeleton in a Dead Space

An endearing sleuth, a skeleton behind the spice cupboard, and a fistful of subplots that will keep you guessing. A nicely done debut by an author to watch.

—Susan Wittig Albert,
author of the China Bayles mysteries

Award-winning historical novelist makes a fine debut in the mystery field with *Skeleton in a Dead Space*. Alter gives readers a twisty plot, excellent use of setting, and a very likable protagonist. I hope this is just the first of many novels about realtor/detective Kelly O'Connell!

—Livia J. Washburn
author of the Fresh Baked Mystery series and
the Literary Tour Mystery series

Skeleton in a Dead Space is a must-read for cozy fans. Kelly O'Connell is an engaging realtor with adorable daughters and a talent for trouble. Alter's mystery debut stands on a lasting foundation of sinister clients and suspect houses. Location, location, location—for murder!

—Charlotte Hinger,
author of *Deadly Descent* and *Lethal Lineage*.

Skeleton in a Dead Space

Kelly O'Connell never thought real estate was a dangerous profession, until she stumbled over a skeleton in a
dead space in an early-twentieth-century Craftsman
house she was transforming into a coveted modern
home in an older urban neighborhood in Fort Worth,
Texas.

From that moment, she runs into teen-age gang mem-
bers, a manipulative ex-husband, a needy and single
pregnant friend, a cold-blooded murderer, and a policeman who wants to be more than her protector. As free-
spirited as the chocolate-peanut-jalapeño candy she
craves, Kelly barges through life trying to keep from
angering her policeman-boyfriend, protect her two
young daughters, pacify her worried mother a thousand
miles away, and keep her real estate business afloat. Too
often she puts herself in danger, and sometimes it's the
girls, not Mike, who come to Kelly's rescue.

Chapter One

I am passionate about a few things—my daughters, old houses, the neighborhood I live and work in, white wine, and chocolate. But certainly not skeletons. I could have lived my life without ever seeing a skeleton. And yet that's just what I saw one fall morning after I answered the phone at my real estate office. I had no idea of the twisted and scary road that skeleton would lead me down.

I reached for the phone hoping, maybe, for a new real estate listing or a buyer panting after one of the Craftsman houses I had redone. But not something dead, something dead a long time. It was an October day, with North Texas at its best—sunny, temperature in the 70s, a light breeze, and trees that were beginning to turn because we had a cold snap. The girls—Maggie, seven, and Em, four—had been laughingly happy when I took them to school. I was finalizing the details of a contract—a nice real estate sale that would boost my firm's income for the year, so when the phone rang, it was an intrusion.

"O'Connell and Spencer Realtors," I answered automatically, my tone somewhat terse. I admit I don't handle interruptions well, but I can't bear to let a phone ring unanswered.

"Miss Kelly, you come right now. Mother of God!" Anthony Dimitrios, the carpenter and jack-of-all-trades who renovates houses for me, yelled into the phone. He is volatile, given to outbursts of various emotions, from anger to joy, and I don't take any of that seriously. But this was different. This was panic.

"I'm on my way," I said, even as I heard the phone click dead. No chance to ask him what was the matter. Slipping my feet back into shoes and grabbing my purse and keys, I headed out the door. Where was Keisha? My office manager had disappeared. *She's probably gone to get lunch.* I locked the office, my thoughts tumbling. Whatever was the matter with Anthony, I had a bad feeling about it in the pit of my stomach.

****

I am the O'Connell part of O'Connell & Spencer—Kelly O'Connell—and my ex-husband, Tim Spencer, was the Spencer part. It's a small firm in the Fairmount neighborhood of Fort Worth. Though Tim left over three years ago, I hadn't changed the name. O'Connell Realtors sounded ordinary to me. I liked having the business to myself—well, most of the time. Tim was smart about real estate, but he wasn't so smart about people, and I found I got along with clients better than he did.

Anthony was working on a house on Fairmount Avenue, a wonderful red brick with a wide, roofed front porch held in by a three-foot solid brick wall and evenly placed round pillars reaching from the low wall to the roof line. The house had leaded glass bay windows, hardwood floors, and solid oak woodwork, once painted white but now painstakingly being restored to the original varnished state. It was a two-bedroom, or I'd have thought about moving the girls and myself into it.

Anthony stood on the front porch, wiping his forehead with a big handkerchief and running his hand through his hair, a nervous gesture. He was a big burly man of about sixty with dark curly hair just touched with bits of gray and usually laughing eyes His eyes weren't laughing now. *He's standing there so it can't be that bad.* "Anthony, what's the matter?"

"Wait till you see," he said, leading me into the house, through the living room and dining room and into the kitchen.

The kitchen was once redone, maybe not too long ago. It was now a galley kitchen, which didn't match the house at all. In the name of frugality, we decided against trying to puzzle out the original configuration, but one thing bothered both of us. On the left wall there was a deep cabinet—we decided to put pull-out drawers on rollers, so that the back space could be easily reached. Next to that, though, was a shallow cabinet with shelves no more than three or four inches deep, enough for spices or one row of canned goods but nothing more. Beyond that the oven and microwave extended much farther back. What was behind the spice cabinet? We laughed about that dead space, and then Anthony suggested we make the spice shelves swing out like a false door, so that the occupants of the house could utilize the space behind. I thought it was a terrific idea.

Today, he'd pulled out the spice shelves and the sheet of wood that held them, all in one piece. It leaned against the counter on the other side of the kitchen. But when I entered the kitchen, he pointed to the space behind where they'd been, and then he wiped his brow again. The space looked like an empty cabinet with nothing put into it. Whatever, I wondered, could be wrong with him? I looked inside the dead space, but it was too dark to make out much except a wooden box, sort of like an old orange crate only larger. "Pull that out," I said to him.

"Mother of God, no, not me."

"Well, give me your flashlight." I shined the light inside the box. A skeleton, a human form, was curled in a fetal position inside the box. I gasped and pulled back.

Anthony was no help. Some instinct told me not to
move the skeleton. What had I read in all those mysteries? Don't mess with a crime scene.

"I'm sorry, Miss Kelly." He always calls me Miss
Kelly, which irritates me a bit. I don't call him Mr.
Anthony. "I wanted to warn you, but..." His large
shoulders shrugged.

"Nothing to be sorry about, Anthony. You didn't
put it here." My heart was pounding.

He held up his hands, palms out, denying any
knowledge.

I wasn't sure what I felt—shock, surprise, fear. A
skeleton was once a living human being. How had this
person died, stuffed in a box? The horror of it made me
clasp my hand to my mouth, afraid I was going to be
sick. And a bit of me—not the better part, I admit—felt
repulsion. A skeleton is gross. I was also apprehensive,
dreading that this discovery would only lead to something worse.

Holding my breath, I looked closer. Mummified bits
of skin around the mouth pulled it back into a grotesque
grin. Bits of hair, faded now so that no color was dis-
cernible, clung to the skull, and scraps of fabric clung to
the bones. It was impossible to tell without touching—
and I didn't want to anyway—but I thought the fabric
was lightweight, maybe once even floral. Now it was
dirty gray. A woman, I decided, and, from the size, a
young woman. But for all I knew, it could have been a
young boy.

Digging in my purse, I handed Anthony my cell
phone and ordered, "Call 911."

He took the phone and went to the front porch. I
stood by the box, as though the poor creature needed
someone to watch over her—or him. Within minutes, I
heard the wail of sirens, and it dawned on me that
Anthony didn't tell them it wasn't a fresh body.

Two police officers rushed in, not quite with guns drawn but looking on the ready, checking out the situation. One was an officer I knew—Mike Shandy, who was assigned to the Fairmount neighborhood. I sometimes ran into him at neighborhood meetings and at the Old Neighborhood Grill on Park Place, where locals went for food and gossip. His wholesome, ex-Marine look—dark blonde crew cut, really blue eyes, and a nice grin—was appealing. I told myself I didn't notice such things, especially when I was standing over a skeleton.

"Hey, Kelly," Officer Mike Shandy said. "Didn't expect to see you."

"Hey, Mike," I replied. "We own this house. But there's no need to hurry. This one's been here a long time."

Shandy peered into the box and let out a loud, "Oh, my God!"

The other officer paled.

"What do you know?" Shandy asked.

"Not a thing, except that Anthony found this just now when he took out those shelves." I pointed to the shelves leaning against the counter. "We wondered what was on the other side of them." My voice was shaky at first, but as I talked it gained some strength.

"How long have you owned this house? Previous owners?"

"I bought it about four months ago from a young couple who'd lived here two years. I don't think they were ready to be urban pioneers once they found out they were going to be parents." Urban pioneers was what Fairmount residents often called themselves, living in a neighborhood where an updated home was likely to stand next to a run-down, paint-peeling, porch-sagging structure with a refrigerator on the front porch and cars parked in the front yard.

Things went along like all the police procedurals I'd ever watched on late-night TV, when sleep wouldn't come. The evidence team arrived, photographed everything, dusted for fingerprints—a huge waste of time, to my mind, since they'd find Anthony's and not much else, maybe mine. Then the medical people arrived. They quickly decided to take box and all to the morgue—transferring the fragile contents to a gurney presented insurmountable problems. I hung around because I felt I ought to... and because I was curious.

When all the technical people began to leave, Mike looked at me, and said, "Don't leave town." But he said it with a wry grin that I liked, the kind of grin that might be a slight bit of flirting. Then it hit me again—flirting over a skeleton, even if it was now gone out of the house? Couldn't be.

"Of course not, but I'm glad we found this instead of some new owner. Tell me, how does a living, breathing person end up a skeleton in a dead space in an old house?" I thought a minute and then added, "I think it's a she."

"So do I," he said. "But we'll get a medical report. It takes longer with skeletal remains."

"Can they tell how long it's been here?"

"From what I understand, that's the hardest part. They can tell age, weight, previous injuries—all that sort of stuff—but how long is pretty much a guessing game. If we had a clue who she—or it—was, we might try for dental records. But that's a long shot until we identify the, uh, body. When was the house built?"

"1916."

He whistled. "Wow. Almost a hundred years. Theoretically, we'd have to look through newspapers, missing person's reports, and all that since 1916. No telling how long it takes a body to get in that condition—if it was someplace really cold or really dry, you'd have a mummy.

But not in Texas. Varmints had something to do with turning the body into a skeleton. They can get into places we think are sealed tight."

There were rats and mice all over Fairmont, and I knew that, but the idea still gave me the creeps. I wondered if the body smelled at one point—enough to alert neighbors that something was wrong. Sure, skeletons don't smell—but dead bodies do after a few days, and from all the TV shows I've watched, the smell is pretty powerful and pretty awful. Didn't anyone notice? And who lived in the house at the time?

Mike Shandy was businesslike. "I'll let you know what forensics turns up. But it won't be quick." And then he added, "We'll have to tape off the house for a few days. Guess you'll have to stop work."

Swell. I want Anthony to finish this house so I can sell it, and now he has to stop work. Anthony sat perched on the wide, concrete top of the porch wall, smoking a cigar which he usually never did around me.

"Sorry," I said. "I should have told you not to hang around. You want to take a couple of days off? They're going to put crime scene tape around the house, and nobody's supposed to go in or out."

He grinned. "Yeah, I'd like that. I'll take my boys fishing in the river. I need to get away from this place for a bit. That…it spooked me." Anthony's much younger wife died of cancer a couple of years earlier, leaving him with three children to raise. Emil, I thought, was about seven by now, and Stefan was twelve. The oldest, Theresa, was seventeen. She sometimes babysat for me, and I worried about her because she was saddled with the care of the family.

"I'll go home now and tell them they can play hooky tomorrow," Anthony said, walking down the stairs.

I didn't remind him that the school system's attitude toward playing hooky, even with parental approval, was strict. Instead, I asked, "What about Theresa?" I asked.

He frowned. "She won't fish. She'll have to go to school."

Something struck me as wrong about that, but it wasn't my business.

****

When I finally left the Fairmount house, I intended to go back to the office and finish up that contract—until I glanced at my watch. I was already late to pick up the girls, a situation that was too chronic with me and always made me feel like a bad mother. I made a conscious decision not to tell the girls about the skeleton. It would just scare them, and I was still hoping that it would amount to nothing in our lives.

I went first to the day-care center where four-year-old Em wiles away the time until she is old enough for kindergarten.

"Hi, Mom," she said, reaching up for a kiss. "How was your day?"

It was such a solemn, caring question that I almost cried.

"It was okay, sweetie. How was yours?"

"Not so good," she said matter-of-factly. "I was ready to go home after lunch. But Miss Emily told me you couldn't come get me that early."

"She was right, honey. I was busy, but one day soon, we'll play hooky all day, okay?" I think I got the idea from Anthony. If he could do it, so could I.

That quiet, sincere voice again, "I'd like that, Mom." Em was my solemn child, and I often worried that she needed more laughter in her life.

Her sister, Maggie, on the other hand, was a blithe spirit, full of joy and laughter one minute and pouting the next. This afternoon she was pouting and not at all forgiving when I picked her up at the local elementary school where there was also an after-school program. "You're late," she said accusingly, "and that makes Miss Benson angry."

She's already acting like a teenager, angry and bored with adults, and she's only seven! I admitted to myself, however, that I only saw flashes of that behavior. Most of the time, Maggie was a love, a child who would run a block to give me a hug. Besides, she was right. The after-school day-care program director frowned at me when I straggled in after four o'clock, and I'd ignored the look. I wondered if she'd asked Maggie, in exasperation, "Where *is* your mother?"

Now I felt guilty about both girls. "I'm sorry, Maggie, I had sort of an emergency."

"Well," Maggie said in her determined voice, "Daddy was never late. I just hope I'm not too late for ballet."

I wanted to scream and ask her how she remembered that her father was never late when he hadn't seen the girls in three years. And besides, if he was never late picking her up, he was always late with payments, be they mortgage, car, or child support. Nowadays he wasn't even making the latter.

Em moaned. "Do I have to watch Maggie's ballet lesson?" This earned her a jab in the ribs from her older sister, which set Em to wailing.

"No, Em. You and I will go to the grocery while Maggie's in her lesson. And you're not late, Maggie. Your ballet things are right there in the back of the car where you put them."

"I didn't put them anywhere," Maggie said, "They're laid out in my room."

My instant thought was, "I told you this morning to put them in the car." But instead of making a deteriorating situation worse, I said, "Fine. We'll go home and get them. It will only take a second, and you'll still be on time."

And she was, but barely. One of the advantages of living and working in Fairmount is that everything is handy, even the school and the day-care. I raced into the house, grabbed Maggie's ballet clothes, and was back in the car before the girls could start fussing at each other.

After we'd walked Maggie into class—never let a child out of the car by herself is one of my rules—I said to Em, "Let's you and me rush to the grocery for a few things and then surprise Maggie with pizza." Keisha was always complaining that I fed the girls junk food, but when you're late and tired, pizza and frozen dinners sure are easy. I know better, and I am always resolving to make home-cooked meals, but I usually only manage one or two of those a week.

"Okay, Mom, pizza would be good. I like it."

I'd been a single working mom for three years. I loved my children, I loved my job, but I was getting tired of juggling. When Tim was there to share, it was a lot better—I couldn't believe that thought even went through my mind. But Tim loved his daughters—or had then—and carried his share of parenting responsibilities. It was just now that he'd dropped out of their lives like a stone dropping into deep water, and I knew Maggie missed him. She remembered the good times—and so did I.

For a long time, Tim and I were happy. We had all the things young couples want—and sooner than most couples. I later found out that was because Tim wasn't paying bills, but at the time I enjoyed the dinner parties we gave, the Christmases when Tim bought way too many presents, the vacations we took.

Sometimes I look back and think I was blind and dumb.

****

The pizza was a success. I got Em settled into pajamas in front of her favorite video, something about Dora, and I sat down at the dining table to help Maggie with her homework. By eight o'clock the girls were in bed, and I was exhausted.

Once I was in bed, my imagination took over and shock set in. That skeleton once was a person, someone with a life of her own (I was convinced it was a small woman), with joys and sadness, hopes and dreams, but she couldn't have expected to end up as dry bones hidden away in a box. Who was she? What happened and why? Was she dead when sealed up, or did death come slowly, locked in a dark box—too horrible a thought to contemplate, like Poe's "The Cask of Amontillado," which would give anyone chills.

A fantasy began in my mind. She was young, blonde, and beautiful of course, a schoolteacher, a churchgoer, an all around small-town girl come to the city. But she fell in love with a scoundrel who cheated on her; she confronted him, and he strangled her. I was so close to working out a novel in my head that I named the skeleton. Maybe it was those wisps of once-flowered material, but she made me think of Miranda from *The Tempest*. That, I decided was how I would think of her instead of "the skeleton."

Could the police solve a mystery all these years later? I assumed it was many, many years, and yet to let it go unsolved seemed barbaric. And the idea of rats and mice—I didn't want to think about that again either. It made my flesh crawl. At last I drifted into a troubled sleep, but the ringing phone startled me awake.

When I mumbled "Hello," a deep voice said, "Forget about the skeleton. Don't investigate or you'll be sorry." Whoever was on the other end slammed the phone down in my ear. I looked at the clock: three o'clock, and for me, sleep was over for the night. Who would call with that strange, threatening message? Who, besides me, could care about an old skeleton? And how did they know so quickly? Should I call Mike Shandy? No, he'd just tell me to lock my doors and let the police handle it. A hidden place deep inside me was scared, but I was also angry. Nobody was going to threaten me. I'd learned a lot in the three years I'd been single, and protecting myself and the girls was the biggest lesson. I got up to check them, but they were sleeping peacefully. Once back in bed, the endless questions played themselves in my mind. Who was Miranda? How did she get there? And how long ago? Why?

Sleep came again fitfully at dawn, less than an hour before the alarm went off. Sleepless though the night had been, I turned off the alarm and got right up. In that space of time before the girls were up, I sipped coffee and read the newspaper. Once, Tim and I employed an agent who never read the paper. I was almost firm with the woman about how important keeping current was. After all, the business section had lots about real estate trends and developments, and the general news was important. You couldn't talk to clients and say, "What hijacking?" when then news the day before spent six hours following the travels of a truck and its woman driver hijacked by a man she did not know. No, I was convinced it was important to know what went on in the world but also to know what went on locally. Besides, I loved reading the local news in the peace and quiet of the early morning. It was one of my favorite times of day.

On page three of the city news section, in the "Local Briefs" column, there was a piece about a skeleton being found in a house under renovation in the Fairmount addition. It gave the address of the house and said that the remains had been sent to the county coroner's office for possible identification, adding that authorities were not yet sure of the gender or age of the victim nor when the death occurred. I didn't learn anything from reading it, but I wished that O'Connell and Spencer Realtors were mentioned—anything for publicity. On second thought it occurred to me that maybe the omission was good—future buyers might be turned off by a house that held a skeleton for who-knew-how-many years. As it was, curiosity seekers would drive down Fairmount today, just to see the house where a skeleton was found. And they'd see the O'Connell and Spencer sign out front. The article could bring forth someone who knew something. It might work to my advantage and to that of the police. In the bright light of a Texas morning, a skeleton seemed more of a curiosity than a threat, worth only a mention in the local brief news. I decided not to tell Mike Shandy about that strange call in the early morning hours.

Chapter Two

I should have woken the girls up ten minutes ago. I'd gotten so absorbed in thinking about what that tiny news brief did or didn't mean that I lost track of time. I flew up the stairs, trying hard to be gentle even though I wanted to scream that we were all late and they better jump to it. They stumbled around, looking for toothbrushes and the clothes that we laid out the night before—I didn't exactly approve of the color combinations. Em chose an orange shirt and blue plaid pants, but I didn't object. I raced downstairs to pour cereal and milk into bowls and pack peanut butter and jelly sandwiches in lunchboxes. Maggie would say, "Peanut butter again?" Mental note: put lunch meat on the grocery list. While they ate their cereal, I went upstairs to throw on slacks and a turtleneck, topped by a blazer—my standard outfit. Maggie was at school in good time, but Em was a bit late. "That's okay, Mom," she said. "It's only pre-school and they aren't as strict." I hugged her. Then, frazzled before the day began, I headed to the office.

Keisha thrust a sheaf of pink slips at me as I walked in the office door. "You win the lottery or something?" Keisha was a young, large African-American woman—not fat but big-boned, large all over—and she dressed to take advantage of her size, sporting long glittering fingernails, a huge beehive hairdo, lots of makeup, and wearing sweeping loose clothes, even caftans. I blessed the day I called the school district's vocational program to find an administrative assistant. Keisha was much more—and she didn't even mind making coffee. She was also friend, confidante, and occasional babysitter.

"I think what happened," I said, "is that I lost the lottery—and a lot of other contests. All these this morning?"

Keisha nodded. "And if this phone don't stop ringing, I'm tearing it out of the wall."

"Be my guest," I said as I wandered toward my desk. Mostly Tim and I found it easiest to do business ourselves, without agents, and I didn't hire anyone after he left, so the room always seemed large and bare. But so far I was doing fine by myself, though I often felt pushed by too much to do. If I ran into the perfect agent, I'd reconsider. I riffled through the call-back slips. Joanie called. No choice there—I'd call Joanie first. She was must be worried about me after seeing that piece in the paper.

Joanie Bennett was maybe my best friend. We'd met when Tim and I first came to town, at an open house. Joanie was looking at houses she couldn't afford. But she was talkative, and I was always chatty on the job because that's part of real estate, so we hit it off. She seemed to bubble over with enthusiasm for life in general, and I liked that. We'd meet for lunch and gradually I found out that she was in advertising, working with high-dollar clients for one of the most prestigious agencies in town. She was also single and longing to be a wife and mother—but she never seemed to meet the right guy. Tim and I would include her and the current man-of-the-moment in our dinner parties, and I agreed with her—whoever he was, he wasn't the right guy. Joanie, I decided, wasn't a good picker. After Tim left, Joanie was great support for me, and I came to rely on her visits. We'd drink wine late into the night, and many times she fell asleep on the couch. The next morning we both felt awful.

Now, I assumed she was calling about the skeleton. "Joanie, it's Kelly."

"Kelly? I'm so glad you called right back. Thanks."

"It's okay, Joanie, I'm okay. Just sort of dazed. Finding that skeleton was bad enough, but seeing it in the newspaper and getting twenty phone calls by nine o'clock is a bit too much."

"Skeleton? What skeleton?" Joanie's tone was one of complete surprise.

Someone else who doesn't read the newspaper. "Isn't that why you called?"

"No. I called because I have a huge problem, and I have to talk to you about it right away. Not lunch. Not a restaurant. It has to be private." Joanie passed over the skeleton and went right back to her own problem, whatever it was that demanded privacy. Joanie's requests for advice—which she usually ignored—weren't that unusual. Neither was the oblivion to what was going on in someone else's life. It was just Joanie.

"Busy day, Joanie. I've got a stack of calls to make, got to check on a house I'm negotiating for...." I also wanted to start checking city directories to find out who lived in the house on Fairmount.

Joanie wailed. "I have to talk to you today. It can't wait. Kelly, this is big, really big."

"Okay," I relented. "Come by the house tonight, after the girls are in bed. About eight?"

A dramatic sigh on the other end of the line. "You can't do anything before that?"

"Nope," I said, my voice firm. Give Joanie an inch and she'd take a mile.

"Okay. Oh, and you can tell me about the skeleton. That's a disgusting thought."

"Thanks. See you tonight." I hung up, with more of a slam than I meant.

Next I returned a call from Christian, my friend at the title company. Christian was a good guy, willing to work with clients, and I gave him all the closings I could. We'd lunched a few times, during which he talked about his wife and baby and how wonderful they were. I sort of envied him that domestic bliss. But he was also a caring person, and I could hear concern in his voice now.

"Kelly," he said, "what's going on? What's this about a skeleton in that house on Fairmount?"

"It's true, Christian, and I need your help." He could do a title search that would turn up owners, deeds, wills, trusts, mortgages, judgments for the last thirty years. I had a sinking feeling that I would need to know about owners beyond thirty years ago—that was, after all, only the '70s. But what he could do was a start and maybe the title company's old card file would tell me more.

"Sure. What do you need? But, wait, are you okay?"

"Yeah, I'm okay. Just a little shaken. And a whole lot curious."

"I bet."

"Can you have your office do a title search? We may have to go back beyond the usual thirty years—the house is ninety years old, and there's not a good way of dating skeletons. But it's important to know who owned the house."

I heard him take a deep breath. "You give me your title business for the next thirty years?"

"Cross my heart," I said.

"Okay, Kelly, I'll see what we can find. But it will take some time. Can you be patient?"

'No, but I'll try. It will take time to do tests on the skeleton too. Meantime I've got to fight to keep publicity down. And I'm also going to check city directories, so we can compare title holders to residents."

He laughed. "In Fairmount in the last twenty years that could prove a puzzle. Take care and let me know how you're doing."

Fairmount is an inner-city neighborhood of homes, most built in the 1920s, most bungalows but also some spacious two-story homes and some architectural gems, such as original Craftsman houses. Starting in the '60s or maybe earlier, Fairmount began to go downhill; houses became ill-tended rental property. By the '90s that began to turn around—the neighborhood was close to the hospital district and to downtown, and young professionals found it convenient and charming. They began to buy the older, deteriorating houses and restore them. Then a neighborhood association stepped in, and the business streets—mainly Magnolia Avenue and Rosedale Street—began to perk up with new restaurants and boutiques. Some of the old-standbys remained of course, like the Paris Coffee Shop which has been a breakfast meeting place for people from all walks of life and all businesses for years. At noon, people stand in line for the pies. Tim saw the opening for growth in Fairmount early on. O'Connell and Spencer specialized in buying older homes and renovating them for sale. But these days I don't turn away an outright sale either.

What Christian meant about Fairmount proving a puzzle was that when Fairmount was on its downhill slide, becoming rental property, people moved in and out at a rapid rate, and nobody seemed to care about fixing houses up. It was not what you'd call a stable neighborhood. Checking occupants fifteen, twenty years ago, might well provide me a long list—and the people listed might be impossible to find.

I wadded up the slips that were calls from newspaper and television journalists and threw them in the wastebasket. Keisha was impressed by my aim and clapped every time one hit the basket. She frowned when I missed, because I didn't get up to pick the paper up and put it in the wastebasket—I'd do that later. One or two were business calls. I returned them, even getting an appointment to view a house for a new listing. Then I began to sift through the paperwork on my desk.

The phone rang almost immediately. Keisha forwarded it to my phone. When I answered it with "Kelly O'Connell" and heard, "Ms. O'Connell, Mark Sullivan here. *Fort Worth Star-Telegram.* We'd like to do a feature story on the skeleton you found yesterday—you know, play up the mystery aspects, interview people who lived in the house, and all that. You game?"

I tried to keep a tight rein on my temper and my tongue. The *Star-Telegram,* these days, was the only general newspaper in town, and it paid to have good relations with the newspaper. "No, Mr. Sullivan, I'm not game. I want to sell that house, so I don't want to spread the story far and wide about a skeleton being found in it. Too many people might think it's haunted."

Long silence on the other end of the line. Clearly that was exactly the aspect that Mark Sullivan planned to play up—a haunted house. "You sure? You might benefit from the publicity." He knew it was a weak hope; I could tell from his voice.

"I'm sure," I hung up the phone and looked across the room. "Keisha?"

Keisha shrugged. "I'm done taking those calls, Kelly. You're gonna have to tell them yourself."

"Thanks a lot. I'll treat if you'll go get lunch—a cheeseburger from the Grill with curly fries and lots of ketchup."

"You got a deal," Keisha said. "I'll go about 11:30, beat the crowd."

I worked steadily all morning, finishing the contract that should have been done the day before and clearing my desk so that I could spend the afternoon beginning to explore city directories. Should I begin in the present and work back or in 1917 and work forward? That skeleton had to be there say, ten years, but to start in the middle seemed risky.

Keisha brought me a salad. "You got to eat right," she said. "You feeding those girls the way you eat?"

"I fix healthy, balanced meals. And this salad is perfect. Thanks for adding grilled chicken to it." I tried to put indignation into my voice, but I know she caught the glimmer of a giggle. I wanted that cheeseburger.

I finished the salad, wrapped up the loose ends on my desk, and made a note of two houses I wanted to do a curb assessment on. I could tell from the curb whether or not I wanted to see a particular house. Tim knew the business and he taught me well. The marriage didn't do as well.

I still couldn't pinpoint where it went wrong, when it began to sour, except that it was right after Em was born. Our last year together was miserable. Tim never wanted to go anywhere, do anything. Gone were the days when we entertained and went to parties, out to nice restaurants, lived the life of the happy young couple. There was no affection—and no sex. Dumb thing that I am it took me a long time to realize he had a girlfriend, and a lot of those "calls" had nothing to do with real estate. I guess in some ways I'll always be Pollyanna.

****

I was about to head out the door when Keisha said, "Phone for you." I raised my eyebrows in a question.

"Nope," Keisha said. "You best take this one."

Emily Shannon, Em's pre-school teacher. Em loved the fact that she and "Miss Emily" shared a name. I didn't love what I heard now.

"Kelly, Em's been fighting. I'm afraid she's pretty upset, and you better come take her home."

Em fighting? Impossible. "I can't believe it," I said.

"Neither could I," Miss Emily echoed, "but Sarah said something that upset her. I'm sending Sarah home too. They were scratching and kicking and screaming."

"No biting?" Apparently biting was common in children, but I couldn't imagine it. *Not my girls.*

"No biting,"

I called over my shoulder, "I'm gone for the day. I'll have my cell phone on."

****

Em sat in the reception area, with a teacher's aide beside her. The aide held her hand and whispered words of comfort. But the poor child was sobbing. I knelt down and wrapped my arms around her. "Baby, baby, what is it? What happened?"

Em raised a tearful face. "Sarah said you had a skelton in your closet. She said her mom said that was bad. What's a skelton? Is it in the closet at home?"

Oh dear God. How was I to know I should have explained it to the girls? And how do you tell a four-year-old the difference between a real skeleton, awful enough, and a skeleton in the closet, that old phrase that Sarah's mother probably used jokingly. But just at the wrong time. And both little girls misinterpreted it.

"Were you sticking up for me, Em?"

"Yes, Mommy. I didn't want anyone to say bad things about you. And she kept repeating it, like she was singing a song."

"It isn't anything bad. The skeleton's not in my closet but I found one yesterday in the house Anthony's working on. And it was sort of scary. That's why I didn't tell you." I rose and held out my hand. "Come on, Em, let's go home, and I'll tell you all about the skeleton. Can you say it that way—skel-e-ton?"

Em nodded and repeated. "Skel-e-ton."

"Good girl. Let's go find Miss Emily so you can tell her you're sorry."

"Okay." Em hopped off the couch, hooked her backpack over her shoulders, and took my hand.

Over Em's head, I silently asked the aide if Sarah was already gone and was relieved that the answer was an affirmative nod of the head. I stuck my head in Em's classroom and said, "Miss Emily? Em would like to talk to you a minute."

The teacher came to the door and sent the aide into the room. "Em? Are you feeling better?"

Em nodded. "I didn't understand. I thought Sarah said something bad about Mommy. But Mommy's going to 'splain it to me. And I'm sorry I caused trouble."

Miss Emily hugged her. "I know you didn't mean too. And I'll see you tomorrow. Okay? We'll start all over again."

"Okay," Em said, clutching my hand.

In the car, I said, "Em, I have to drive by two houses. Can you help me decide if I should look at the insides or not?"

Em nodded, silent with responsibility.

The first was a two-story clapboard house with an uncertain shingle roof. Years of neglect showed in peeling paint, shutters that hung askew, a wood pillar that showed rot at the base. I detected cracks in the masonry of the exterior chimney, a sign of structural problems, though that wasn't unusual on the shifting earth of the neighborhood. Still, the house sat neglected too long. And it didn't have much basic charm to begin with. A plain-Jane house with evenly matched windows, plain pillars on a small front porch.

"What do you think, Em?" I already knew it wasn't a possibility.

"I don't like it, Mommy. It looks like lazy people live there. They don't even trim their bushes."

"You're right, Em. Thanks. I'll take it off my list."

"I'm glad I can help you, Mommy."

The next house was a craftsman-style bungalow, quintessential WWI period. The bushes weren't trimmed here either, but deliberately left to grow free. The house was brick, and someone apparently painted the trim within five years. The square pillars with decorative braces, wide porch, gabled dormer, low-pitched roof, and stone chimney hinted at the probability inside of wainscoting, beamed ceilings, a built-in buffet, and double doorways with visible braces. I didn't see any telltale rot at the base of the pillars, and the roof looked pretty good. Anthony could work wonders with this one. *Please, God, no skeletons in the closet.*

"Em?"

"I don't know, Mommy. The bushes aren't trimmed….." That must be her criterion for judging houses.

"But don't you think the house looks more interesting?"

Solemn agreement. "Yes, I think so."

"Okay. I'll make an appointment to look at it tomorrow. Now, you know what I think?"

"No, Mommy, what do you think?"

"I think you need a cone from Curley's Custard."

A smile lit up Em's face. "I think that's a good idea, Mommy. I'd like chocolate."

"Chocolate it is, and we'll bring some home for Maggie, so she doesn't feel left out."

That was just what we did, and the extra cone turned the trick. Maggie was the caring, loving, protective big sister, giving Em advice on avoiding children who were unpleasant, hugging her a lot, and telling her that she was proud of her. "I'd have done just what you did, Em," she said.

"Really?" Em asked, her tone somewhat awed.

"Really," Maggie confirmed.

The mood was marred by a call from Sarah's mother, who launched into a "your-child-hit-my-child for no reason" tirade.

I tried to stay calm, saying it was all a misunderstanding. "Em thought Sarah was saying something bad about me. You said something about a skeleton in my closet?"

"Well," an impatient tone, "that was just a joke. Everyone knows that."

"Four-year-olds don't," I said and hung up the phone. Then I gathered the girls together and explained about the skeleton.

"Oh, Mom, was it gross?" Maggie asked.

"No, Maggie. It didn't look like a person. But it was scary—and sad to think about."

"Now what do you do?"

With my fingers crossed behind me, I said, "The police will have to find out who that person was and how he or she got there. It's not up to me."

I fixed chopped steaks with brown gravy for dinner, one of the girls' favorites, and green beans and green chili rice. *Okay, Keisha, the rice is instant, but the rest of it is fresh and wholesome.*

The girls were tucked in for the night, Em worn out by her day and Maggie reading a book. I told Maggie she could read for fifteen minutes, but I knew she would stretch that out, and I would forget to check on her. The pattern of our lives.

When the doorbell rang at five minutes to eight, I wondered who it could be—but then I remembered. What with Em's "fight" and all, I had forgotten all about Joanie. Joanie and I often laughed that she shared a name with 1950s movie star Joan Bennett. Joanie said that was where she got her glamour, and I never reminded her that Joan Bennett's hair was dark, her look seductive. Joanie was blonde, with shoulder-length hair, and, no matter how hard she tried, she gave an impression of eager instead of seductive. She had blue eyes—friendly, open, inviting—and I swear she never met a man she didn't like. Since, at thirty-seven, she was five foot five inches and still shapely, all those men liked her equally well.

Joanie flourished a bottle of pretty good chardonnay.

"You eat dinner?" I asked.

Making a grand gesture, Joanie almost dropped the wine and said, "I couldn't eat. Not a bite."

If you drink much of that wine, you'd better eat. I went to the kitchen to trot out some cheese and crackers. Then I curled up in the big overstuffed chair, wine glass on the table beside me, but Joanie perched on the edge of the couch, clutching the wine glass as though she might splinter it in her hands any minute. I didn't have to wait long.

"I think I'm pregnant."

I didn't know what I'd been expecting but not that. I asked the logical question, "Are you sure?"

Joanie nodded. "I took one of those home tests this morning, and it was positive. That's when I called you."

"Gosh, Joanie, I'm sorry I wasn't more help right at the time." And then, remembering my own pregnancies, I said, "You can't drink that wine."

"Yeah, I can," Joanie said.

I thought I knew what she meant, but I wasn't ready to talk about it. Instead, I asked the obvious, "Who's the father?"

"Nobody."

"Impossible."

"Nobody that matters. A fling. Not someone I even want to tell about this."

I said the next slowly, hesitantly, "You don't want to keep the pregnancy, do you?"

To my relief she set the wine glass down. Joanie buried her head in her hands. "How can I?" she said, and now she was crying. "My folks would disown me. I'd lose my job. What kind of a future would I have? What kind of a future would the baby have?"

I took a deep breath. "You know your folks wouldn't disown you. They might be disappointed, but in this day and age I doubt they think you're saving yourself for marriage. This is just one of those things that aren't supposed to happen. I don't know about your job right now, but lots of single moms have good careers, Joanie."

I looked at her, head still buried in her hands. "Joanie, this calls for chocolate." I keep a hidden stash of exotic chocolate bars—milk chocolate with ground peanuts and jalapeño. They're addictive, and I have to watch myself or I'd be going all the way to our upscale store, Central Market, to buy them every day. Joanie knows that if I offer to share my chocolate, it's a big deal.

In the kitchen, I remembered how elated I was each time I discovered I was pregnant. What would it be like to have pregnancy as a threat? When I handed her the chocolate—she seemed to have an appetite for that and ate half of the big bar—I said, "I can't say one decision or the other is right for you, but I want you to think about it so you don't do something you regret later."

Joanie raised her tear-streaked face. "If I have an abortion, will you go with me?"

I didn't hesitate. "Of course." *Even if you don't agree, you support a friend in her decision.* I poured more wine. "Want something more than chocolate to eat now?"

Joanie nodded.

Just then the phone rang. Who could be calling at nine-thirty at night?

It was Anthony, and for the second time in as many days, I heard panic in his voice. "Miss Kelly, you come quick. The house on Fairmount—it's on fire. Mother of God!"

"I'll be right there." I slammed down the phone. "Joanie, I've got to go. My Fairmount house is on fire. Stay with the girls for me, will you?"

Joanie looked panicky. "What if they wake up? I...I don't know anything about kids. I'm no good with them."

As I grabbed my purse, I said, "If Em wakes up, wake Maggie—she'll take care of her. If Maggie wakes up, just tell her where I've gone. She'll be fine. Thanks, Joanie. I need you right now."

And I was out the door.

Chapter Three

The curious had already gathered in a knot across the street from the house. I parked at the other end of the block and threaded my way between fire trucks. Lights flashed, walkie-talkies crackled, and shouts rang out. Confusion at its worst, though I clung to the hope that it was more organized than it seemed.

"Hey, lady, you can't come in here. Get across the street with the others." An angry voice was followed by a strong hand grabbing my arm.

I pulled away indignantly. It was a policeman I didn't know. "I own this property. Where's the fire captain in charge?"

His attitude modified but only a little. "I'll take you," he said, reclaiming his grip on my arm.

I jerked away again. He wasn't going to drag me anywhere. "I'll follow you," I said, my voice as strong as I could make it. But then I saw an ambulance and, sitting at the open back door, Anthony, his head wrapped in a bandage. I ignored the policeman and ran toward the ambulance; the policeman stood there bellowing, "Hey!"

"Anthony, what happened to you?"

A rueful smile and a tentative gesture to his head. "I got a goose egg, Miss Kelly. Somebody decked me from behind. Felt like tire iron or something like that. Maybe a blackjack." Out of his coveralls, Anthony was wearing a plaid shirt and jeans that revealed more belly than the coveralls did, especially as he sat hunched over in the ambulance. He looked like somebody's kindly grandfather.

"Decked you? Why? Who?"

As Anthony shook his head, another voice said, "You tell us."

The fire captain. "He doesn't have any idea. Do you?"

"No," I said and then turned to Anthony. "Start from the beginning. What were you doing here at nine o'clock at night?"

"I left yesterday without my tools. Wasn't thinking. Today, I went fishing. Tomorrow, you don't need me, I work for a friend. I came back for my tools."

"And?"

Now a sheepish look. "I knew I shouldn't cross that yellow tape, but I snuck under it. In the back, by the kitchen. I keep a key hidden back there. Got the key, unlocked the door, and then—wham! Next thing I know I'm in the kitchen, on the floor, and I smell smoke. I ran outside hollering 'Fire, fire,' and somebody called the fire department."

"It's definitely arson," the fire captain said.

"Arson? Who would set the house on fire? Why?"

The fire captain remembered his manners. "I'm Captain Coconauer. Kelly Coconauer. And you're?"

"Kelly O'Connell. I own the house."

A grin on his Irish face, complete with wrinkles indicating too many years of fighting fires. "Same first name." Then the grin disappeared back into the wrinkles "You find a skeleton here yesterday?"

"Yes, sir." Yes, I was a bit intimidated.

"Seems like too much of a coincidence."

I agreed. "But what? Who?"

"Not my job," he said. "We got the fire put out. Now the police have to figure out who and why. But sounds to me like there's something someone didn't want found."

My three-in-the-morning caller didn't waste any time. I considered that for a moment, then switched gears. "How bad is it?"

"Thanks to Anthony here, we got to the fire early. Kitchen's pretty much gone—he tells me he can start over pretty easily. Rest of the house is untouched. But there's smoke and soot everywhere. 'Course we pulled the wiring first thing, and we pulled out some of the ceiling. Make sure it didn't spread in the attic. You wait a while; I can take you through it with a flashlight."

"I'll wait," I said. I fingered the cell phone in my pocket. The girls must be all right or Joanie would have called.

"I'll wait too," Anthony said. "Theresa's home with the boys."

As I turned toward the house, I found myself facing bright lights. Microphones were thrust into my face, and the questions came fast. Every TV station in the area must have sent someone.

"What happened?"

"What do you know about this?"

"Is this the skeleton house?"

"I own the house," I said, struggling to keep my voice steady and trying to avoid looking at the lights, "but I know nothing about this. I...I don't have anything to say."

"How about you, sir?" One bold reporter thrust a mike in Anthony's face, but he brushed it away, got up, and stalked off. I followed him, and the surly policeman held the reporters at bay.

About an hour later, Captain Coconauer took Anthony and me through the house. We'd spent that hour sitting on the curb, in silence, because there wasn't anything to say. In my confusion, I forgot about the middle-of-the-night phone call I'd received.

The captain led us through the now-open front door because the steps to the back were destroyed. Coconauer assured me that "his people" would secure the property before they left.

"Great. All we need is some homeless people to drift in and start another fire."

"Yeah. It could happen." His voice was rueful.

I never saw a house that had burnt before, and I was almost more dumbstruck by this than I was about the skeleton. The once-white walls were covered with black soot, and the stench was unbearable. We tracked soot around, picking it up on our shoes.

"Oh, yeah," Coconauer said. "Take your shoes off before you even get in your cars."

With a tentative finger, I touched touch the wall and left a smear; when I drew it away, my finger was stained black. The soot covered the woodwork as well, and I thought of the refinishing we were going to do and how much more difficult it would be now.

The ceiling was torn out, and large bits of insulation hung down.

I didn't know where Anthony would begin to restore the house, but the other Kelly seemed to sense that. "It was mine," he said, "I'd call Black Brothers, the disaster people. Matter of fact, they probably got a guy outside already. They're great fire chasers."

Black Brothers was a company that cleaned rugs and furniture but specialized in cleaning up after disasters— fires, floods, and the like. So it was no surprise a few minutes later when a man stopped me as I came down the front steps.

"Ms. O'Connell? Mark Anderson of Black Brothers." He thrust a card at me. "At your service."

"What do you do?"

"First thing, we'll tear out the walls…"

"I don't think so," I said. "They're the original pulled plaster."

"But, ma'am, they're covered with soot. That plaster's gonna smell bad."

"Find a way to fix it, and I'll hire you," I said and turned away. I was too tired to argue.

"You be in the office early, Miss Kelly?" It was Anthony. "I…I want to talk to you."

Surprised, I said, "Sure, Anthony."

"And I bet we can bleach those walls and maybe paint Kilz on them—or I'll look for something else that will do," he said. "Don't let them be tearing out those good plaster walls."

"Thanks, Anthony." I felt tears creeping down my cheeks and brushed them away.

The street was empty of curiosity seekers. When a man stopped me by touching my arm—why did everyone grab my arm tonight?—I almost screamed for Kelly Coconauer.

"Ma'am, I'm an insurance negotiator." He thrust a business card at me. "I can help you get a better deal from your insurance company. You know,"—he almost snickered as if it were a joke we shared—"fudge a little on the damage and repair cost."

"No thanks," I said, walking away. But the man reminded me that in the morning my first call would be to the insurance company.

****

The lights still burned brightly in my living room, and Joanie's car was parked in front. I eased the front door open. Joanie lay on the couch, sound asleep, her arms tight around Em, who was curled up next to her, snoring gently as only four-year-olds can. Both the snack tray and the wine bottle—a one-and-a-half liter one—were empty. No wonder Joanie slept. She didn't budge when I eased Em out of her arms and, whispering to my child, carried her upstairs.

"I had a dream, Mommy, and I wanted you."

"I'm sorry, baby. I had to go. It was an emergency."

More awake now, Em said, "Maggie told me that you would be home soon, and I shouldn't worry. But I was lonely, so I sat with Joanie. I guess we both fell asleep."

"I guess you did." I tucked her back into her bed. "Go back to sleep now, Em. I'm right here." I sat, stroking the child's hair until I heard that regular breathing again.

Gathering a pillow, sheet and blanket, I went back downstairs. "Joanie," I whispered, "you spend the night right there." I spread the sheet and blanket over her and tried to slide the pillow under her head.

"Kelly?" Joanie said, raising her head groggily. "Em woke up and cried for you, but Maggie helped me. And then we both fell asleep. She's so adorable, Kelly. I loved holding her."

Yeah, and you'd love holding your own baby.

****

No short mention in "Local Briefs" this time. The fire earned a picture on the front of the local section, complete with an 18-point. headline proclaiming, "House Where Skeleton Found Burns; Police Suspect Arson." Grateful that the picture only showed the massed fire trucks, I began reading. Fairly straightforward, the article suggested that the fire department claimed it was arson because of the coincidence of a skeleton found in the house the day before. They referred to the smell of kerosene in the kitchen, so that must have been where it had begun. Thank God Anthony got out all right.

When I flipped on the local TV news, things got a lot worse. The cameras caught me looking bewildered, scared, absolutely out of control. The way I remembered the moment, I was calm and collected and answered straightforwardly. That's not the way it came across on camera.

"Is that you, Mom?" Maggie padded into the kitchen in her PJs.

"Yeah, darlin', that's me."

"You look funny," she said. "Were you scared or something?"

"I didn't think so," I said, "but now I guess maybe I was."

The phone would ring all day, I knew that, but I didn't expect a call at home. It was Dave Shirley, my insurance agent and a longtime friend. "Kelly, we're gonna have to get an adjustor in that house first thing. When can you be there?"

"Whenever you say, Dave. After I get the girls to school. I'll be there by nine-thirty. Is this okay with the police?" There went the day, sitting in a burned-out house waiting for an insurance adjustor.

"Yeah. They said we could go in, but we got to leave the crime scene tape up."

Darn. That house is jinxed. I'll never sell it even if I get it fixed. And it will cost me an arm and a leg. Even if I sell it, I'll lose money.

Joanie came out of the downstairs bathroom, where she'd gone to "put on her face," a much more elaborate procedure for her than me. "Thanks, Kelly, for the talk…and the couch. I don't think you helped at all." She gave me sad smile.

"Sorry, Joanie." *Nobody can help. You'll have to figure this one out for yourself.* "Come back anytime."

I got the girls to school, on time for once, and then ran by the office to tell Keisha where I'd be and grab a handful of papers that I could work on. I forgot about Anthony and my promised nine o'clock meeting with him in the office. He came to the house just before nine-thirty. I was sitting on the porch on the collapsible chair I always kept in the car, staring off into space, enjoying the cool October breeze and being thankful it wasn't cool enough to drive me inside that smelly house.

"Miss Kelly? I got something to show you." He fished in the pocket of his coveralls and handed me a gold locket, with a delicate monogram: M.W.M., scrolled in elaborate letters. The points of the letters were heightened by diamond chips. The gold felt good in my hands. This was a valuable piece.

"What's this?"

"Found it in the kitchen. I didn't quite tell the truth last night. I rooted around in that kitchen, searched the corners of that dead space. Figured you were so intent what was in that box, we never looked any more. And this is what I found. Stuck it down in my pocket just before I got hit."

I opened the locket and found a picture of a woman on one side and a man on the other. The pictures were black and white, but I could tell that the woman was young, quite young, maybe early twenties. She was smiling slightly, and expertly used makeup made her eyes look large and mysterious—the whole effect was that she knew a secret. Her dark hair hung just below the chin, turning up in a pert flip while the top of it seemed teased slightly. I took a deep breath—the '60s. The hair was the '60s—not the rebellious side of the '60s but not every-body was a hippie in those years. I remembered pictures of my own mother, who was born in 1945 and came of age during that decade.

The man was older—thirty-five, perhaps—and wearing a business suit, white shirt, and tie. His eyes looked intently at the camera but I could tell nothing from looking at him—I saw no joy, no intensity, just a dark look. He was handsome, if you liked the almost perfect, wavy dark hair kind of good looks. I never trusted men like that—especially after Tim.

"It's evidence," I said, looking at Anthony. "Maybe important evidence."

"Yeah. You gonna give it to the police?"

"Not before I think about it."

"That's what I thought. You want me to start tearing out tomorrow?"

"I'll call you. There's another property you might go look at. Meantime, you got work?"

"Yeah, I got work. Don't worry about me."

"Anthony," I started, and then let his name hang in mid-air.

"What is it, Miss Kelly?"

I started to tell him about that threatening phone call because now I'd connected it to the fire—I just couldn't figure out why someone would care so much about the skeleton and that house. But I told myself there was no sense worrying Anthony. "Nothing," I said. "I thought of something to ask you...but it isn't important."

He gave me a puzzled look and turned to go. "You call me if you think of it," he said.

The adjustor was thorough, slow, and not talkative. I spent the morning on the porch—not wanting to follow him around inside where the smell was overpowering—and felt like I'd wasted the time. I went through the stack of paperwork, made the calls I could on the cell phone, and stared down the street until I'd memorized every house on the block.

The adjustor left about noon, taking with him a small spiral pad of notes that inspired my curiosity. But he said nothing, not even, "Sorry." I called the office to be sure nothing major happened, grabbed a sandwich from the Grill, and headed for the main public library downtown and the city directories.

Despite my resolve to be methodical, I started with the '60s, because of the picture in the locket. If I found a resident with the initials M.W.M., I'd have scored a hit, and I could give the locket to the police, along with information about the owner. I didn't think far enough ahead to figure out what I'd tell the police about having it in my possession without turning it over to them. But it didn't matter—I didn't find M.W.M.

Only two people lived in the house in the '60s, when Fairmount began to lose its solid middle-class footing, turning into rental property. I copied the names: Marie Winton and Lupe Chavez. Marie Winton apparently lived there in 1960, and Lupe Chavez and his family occupied the house in 1968. I backtracked to the '50s and found that Marie Winton moved into the house in 1957. I wished that Marie Winton's name had been Martin or Montgomery or McAdams. The M.W. fit but not a last name beginning with M. I guessed my next step was to check the City Hall tax rolls. Of course, if Marie Winton had married, those records would be of little help. Still, they might have a clue.

I had to pick up the girls or risk angering the day-care teacher again.

No ballet, no Scouts, nothing scheduled for the afternoon. I sank into the quiet of my house with gratitude. Maggie went off to do homework, complaining that second grade was much harder than first. "I'll look at it with you when you're through," I told her. Em sat watching a video. *She shouldn't be glued to the screen so much.* But I was too tired to object, too tired to think about dinner.

The next thing I knew Maggie was shaking me. "Mom, you fell asleep. What's for dinner? I'm hungry."

I shook myself awake. A moment's hesitation, then, "Hot dogs and custard at Curley's." The girls cheered and rushed around to gather shoes and sweaters, while I realized the last thing I wanted was a Hebrew National hot dog. But it was easier than thinking about defrosting in the microwave and cooking something. *Tim would accuse me of not taking good care of them.*

Curley's was basically a drive-through, but it had a small grassy area, nicely planted, with three picnic tables. Frozen custard was the specialty—in several irresistible flavors, though I always hoped for chocolate mint. But you could also get kosher hot dogs, one of the few non-custard items on the menu. The girls ate theirs plain with mustard; I added chili, onions, and pickle relish and then worried about indigestion. But I was surprised at how good it tasted, after my initial hesitation. The custard flavor of the month was pumpkin—appropriate but not appealing, so we all had chocolate. You never go wrong with chocolate, even without jalapeños in it.

It was still warm, the heat of the day lingering, but I could feel the slightest chill creeping into the air. Fall was here, and Texas would soon show us its changeable nature—warm one day and bone-chilling cold the next. We sat at a picnic table, eating with plastic forks from paper containers, and the girls telling me about their days.

"How was your day, Mom?" Maggie asked.

"Busy and boring," I said.

"Yeah," she said, "I have boring days too. But tomorrow will be better."

"Yeah, it will."

I got the girls in bed soon after we came home and settled down with that novel I was still trying to read.

****

The next few days were uneventful. Mike Shandy called to say that the police removed the yellow crime scene tape from the house, and Anthony could begin work again. "I'd do what Coconauer said and call Black Brothers first," he said.

"I will. I was just mad the other night that they were already there, like vultures—or ambulance chasers!"

He laughed. "I know. I saw the sparks in your eyes. Glad you didn't try to deck that so-called insurance mediator. I'd have had to arrest you for assault."

I remembered being alone when the sleazy man approached me. "How did you know about that?"

"I was watching you. Wanted to make sure you got to your car okay. But I didn't figure you'd want a police escort right at that moment."

"Thanks," I said, "You were right."

"Kelly, you call me if you need me. Got my card?"

"Somewhere."

"Thanks," he laughed again. "That makes me feel important. I'll drop another one off at the office."

So, Mike Shandy is watching out for me. Interesting. I should tell him about that phone call.

Good as his word, Mike dropped the card off later that day, when I happened to be out of the office. When I came back, Keisha said, "That cop, the one who's sweet on you, came by, left this for you."

I took the card and turned away so Keisha wouldn't see me blush.

The next day, I blanked the office out of my mind and went to City Hall to check tax records, only to learn records that old were on microfiche in storage and would have to be retrieved from their archives. I filled out a request form and was told I'd be notified when the records were available. There was a microfiche reader in the office, and I would have to read the film there. But the files would only be held in the office for one week— if I didn't read them within that time, they'd be returned to storage.

"I'll read them," I said with determination.

Back at the office, I found myself doodling, writing the initials "M.W.M." over and over on my notepad.

Who was Marie Winton, and did she know M.W.M.? She lived in the house from 1957 to 1968. She was beautiful, and she looked sophisticated. She must have been single. How did she support herself? By then, Fairmount wasn't an expensive place to live, but still...

A client called wanting to know why her house didn't sell. I bit my tongue to keep from saying, "Because you refuse to fix it up, and it's over-priced for its current condition." I asked for a meeting to talk about lowering the price. The woman was now near enough desperate I could reason with her, I figured. Being extra pleasant with clients usually worked—my mother taught me that a teaspoon of sugar caught more flies than a cup of vinegar—but some people tried my patience. Tim, I know, would have been a lot blunter. Then another woman called wanting to buy an old house in Fairmount but one in good condition. "We have very few of those on the market," I said, "but I'd be glad to meet with you and take your information." Her name was Claire Guthrie, and, just over the phone, I got the impression of sophistication.

By the time I finished both phone calls, I was almost late—again—for picking up the girls. As they got into the car, each complained about being cold. An early norther came through, and the temperature dropped dramatically, as it can do within minutes in North Texas. "We'll go get sweaters, and then we'll go to the Grill for turkey burgers. How's that?" In truth, I was once again too tired to cook—but then, when wasn't I? *I've got to get better organized so I can feed them at home. Keisha would have a fit, except that turkey burgers are better than hamburgers.*

The Grill is a wonderful, comforting place. For long years, it was a bar called The Locker Room, but Peter, the new owner, had transformed it into a friendly, down-home café. You ordered at the counter, where a blackboard listed the day's specials, and then a wait person brought your dishes to you. We were regulars, so Peter and his crew knew us and greeted us, always with a special word for the girls. It was sort of like going home to your mom's kitchen.

The girls split a turkey burger and ate every last one of the fries, while I forced myself to be content with a grilled chicken salad. Maggie chatted about second grade and the boys she thought were cute—*omigosh, already?*—and Em talked more solemnly about the project she was working on, "a s'prise for Mommy." They were so good and so dear that I drove them by Braum's for ice cream cones on the way home.

It was dark when we pulled onto our street. We arrived to confusion. A police car in front of the house, a knot of neighbors outside, and a shattered front door.

Chapter Four

Mike Shandy greeted me as we pulled into the driveway. I was so angry at this violation of my home that I shouted at him, "What happened?"

"Neighbors saw it," he said, unruffled by my anger. "A car drove by, and a guy fired a shotgun blast at the front door." He shook his head. "Not even dark yet. They get bolder and bolder."

I couldn't believe it. This wasn't the skeleton house; it was my home; the home where I kept my daughters safe, or so I thought. Why would someone target this house out of all those on this street? Something told me my house was the specific target, and that both scared me and heightened my anger and determination. No one was going to scare me. "What did the neighbors see?"

He shrugged. "Old car. Indeterminate model. Looked like three or four guys inside, teenagers or young men." He hesitated a minute. "The shooter for sure was Hispanic."

"Gangs? Why would some gangers shoot up my house?"

"No reason at all that I can think of," Mike said. "But it wasn't random vandalism."

"Thanks," I said wryly. "I figured that out. But why my house?" I wished I'd told him about the threatening phone call. Maybe this was all linked to the skeleton and the Fairmount house, but how could that be? How would people even know where I lived? Indignation mixed with confusion, and I thought seriously about screaming.

He looked straight at me. "Yeah, I didn't want to scare you. But all this is no coincidence."

So then I told him about the call. "All this over a skeleton? It makes no sense. But it makes me mad. The shooter could have killed the girls."

"And you," Mike said. "Kelly, this is getting serious. I tried to find you this afternoon to talk about last night. Now it's urgent. We have to talk"

The girls were in the backseat, Em crying for her mother and Maggie asking over and over, "What happened to our front door?"

"Mike, I've got to get them settled. They're scared."

"For the time being, there'll be an officer on duty 'round the clock. I'll take the first shift. You get the girls settled, and then we'll talk."

A policeman guarding my house? What kind of insanity was this?

The girls had questions. "Who did this, Mommy?"

"Why would anyone want to tear up our front door?"

"Mommy, what's happening to us—everything seems wrong. There was the skelton"—Em reverted to her own pronunciation—"and then you left last night. Now…." She raised her hands in that age-old "I-don't-know" gesture and for just a moment I smiled.

"I don't know what's wrong, girls, but I know one thing: you're safe. You go to sleep. I'll be here, and so will a police officer. No one will hurt you."

"Is someone trying to hurt you, Mom?" Maggie asked, hugging me tightly.

"I think they're trying to scare me, Mag. But I promise I'm not scared."

Just as I was tucking them in, the phone rang. Joanie. "Hi, Kelly? What's going on? I was kind of blue, and I thought maybe…."

I know my voice was too short. "Not tonight, Joanie. We've had a bad night. Someone blasted the front door with a shotgun."

"Omigosh." Her astonishment was loud in my ear. "Why would they do that?"

"I don't know," I said, "but the police think it has to do with the skeleton in that house I'm redoing. I…I just can't think right now, Joanie, and the police are waiting to talk to me."

She sounded let down. "Okay. We'll do it another night."

"Yeah, we will." But I knew I didn't sound enthusiastic. It had nothing to do with Joanie—and I wanted to support her right now—but I was just too confused by what was going on in my own life.

Tired, so tired, but after I got the girls tucked in bed—they both insisted on my bed, of course—I opened the door and waved to Mike Shandy, who was parked in front of the house next door in a battered and old Honda Accord. I waited while he came up the walk to the house.

"Everything okay with the girls?"

"They're scared. And I'm angry."

"Good. You should be. Somebody's out to get you. Somebody doesn't want the truth found out about that skeleton—and they know or at least they suspect you're looking into it." He paused a minute. "You aren't trying to do police work, are you? We can take care of it."

I wanted to say, "Yeah, while my house gets shot up, my girls terrified, and my work on the Fairmount house stopped. And besides, who's worrying about that skeleton that deserves identification and a decent burial. And maybe family notified." But I didn't say any of that. Instead, I asked, "Coffee?"

"If it's made, I'd love it."

"I have a single-cup coffee maker. I can make it in no time. Black?"

He nodded. Going to the kitchen to make coffee gave me time to think, but thoughts tumbled in my head. Carrying Mike's coffee into the living room, my hand shook.

"Why would gangers be interested? That makes no sense."

He leaned back, comfortable on the sofa, coffee cradled in his hands. "Somebody's got connections and hired people to do their dirty work. The question is, how did they know about everything so quickly? Whoever is so worried about the secret of that house isn't the kind for drive-by shooting. I can't figure why it happened, but I know it wasn't a case of mistaken identity. So maybe someone has hired some gangers to frighten you—or worse." His voice dropped.

Mike's theory held true if the skeleton was there a long time—years ago the families in Fairmount were upper class, respectable, and they would want a secret kept. But if it only been there since the '60s, no telling.

I took a deep breath. "I have something to show you." I went to my briefcase and pulled out the locket. "Anthony gave this to me this morning. I was going to call you about it in the morning." Okay, a small white lie.

"Like the phone call you didn't tell me about. You were right. I would have dismissed the phone call as a wrong number, but now I'm sure it wasn't." He shook his head.

"I...I went to check city directories this afternoon. I thought I might find something that matched."

"Kelly, you've got to start telling me everything. You can't solve this...and it's dangerous for you to try."

"Nothing dangerous about city directories. I was saving your guys some time. I'm going to check titles at City Hall too."

He rolled his eyes. "Kelly, if whoever's behind this finds you're even scratching the surface, it will make them more determined."

"Mike, there are a couple of things here. One is…oh, I don't know…compassion, whatever. I don't want that woman to go to a nameless grave, and I'm afraid it would be too easy for you guys to let that happen." I took another deep breath. "The other is pretty crass and commercial. I want to sell that house. I don't want any potential buyer thinking it's jinxed or dangerous or whatever."

"I think the first one is what's bothering you."

I shrugged. "You may be right." Then, "Look in that locket—there's a picture of a woman that I'm pretty sure was taken in the '60s. Hairdo, makeup."

He opened the locket and looked. "Yeah, I expect you're right. Looks like my mom."

"Mine, too," I said. I told him what I'd found in the city directories, even dragging out the notes I'd made, which he copied into a small spiral that he carried.

"I'll check it out, but I don't expect much. It's the worst kind of cold trail. I don't suppose you'd take the girls and go somewhere?"

I shook my head. "No, but I'll do whatever it takes to keep my girls safe."

"You have an alarm system?" he asked.

"Yeah, but I never use it. I guess I better start setting it at night."

"And get an emergency alarm button that you can keep in your pocket or someplace handy all the time."

"Yessir," I replied. I was tempted to salute, but I didn't think he'd find it funny.

"We'll keep all of you safe," he said, but I wondered how he could be sure.

****

Tired as I was, sleep wouldn't come. The shattered door kept reappearing before my eyes and so did the skeleton in its box. And then, as I slept fitfully, the skeleton walked through the shattered door, trailing a chiffon-like gown in a floral pattern, bony hands pushing at the broken panels of the door. This time the brown hair was in an upsweep, as though she were going to her senior prom. I woke in a cold sweat.

"Mom?" Maggie cuddled close to me. "You were making a funny noise."

Guilt. Now my children were scared. I threw back the covers. "I had a bad dream." As I drifted off to more peaceful sleep, I thought, *This is the way it is—the three of us against the world.* Little did I know.

When I went to get the paper, I gave a sort of half-wave to the man who sat in front of the house in a car, this one a new Toyota Camry. He didn't even look my way. I supposed being invisible was one of the police-man's responsibilities. Or maybe he wasn't police but someone else watching the house. I was getting paranoid. Settled in the kitchen with coffee, I busied myself with the paper. Drive-by shootings often make the news but only if death was involved. Shattered front doors don't make it, and I was relieved that there was no mention of the incident.

The phone rang. A tentative, "Hello?"

"Kelly, what in the world is going on down there?"

"Hi, Mom. How are you?"

An indignant voice. "Well, I'm worried about you. My goodness, I told you not to stay in Texas once what's-his-name left. You should have come back to Illinois, where it's safe."

Sigh. No sense pointing out that crime was a lot worse in suburban Chicago than inner-city Fort Worth. My mom has been a worrier since the day I was born and before. When she fretted that I would "take cold," my dad always said, "Let the child be." As a youngster, I longed for brothers and sisters, just to take some of Mom's attention off me. Now, at thirty-six, I still had her full attention, especially since Dad died ten years ago. "How did you know something was going on, Mom?"

"That neighbor of yours, the one I liked so much— I can't remember her name…."

I could see Florence Dodson, the eighty-something-year-old who lived three houses down the street and complained that the girls picked her flowers, when I knew that my girls were too well trained to do that.

"Did Florence call, Mom?"

"Yes, she did, and it's a good thing. I can't rely on you to tell me a thing."

"There's not much to tell. We found a skeleton in a house, and then someone set the house on fire."

"And shot up your front door. Florence called early this morning."

That's an understatement—it's barely after seven now.

"And she told me you had policemen outside your house all night."

If Florence Dodson recognized the policeman, so did the bad guys. So much for their cover.

"Mom, it's nothing. It'll blow over in a day or two."

"Nothing, my foot. I'm getting the first plane reservation down there I can."

My backbone stiffened. "Mom, you can't do any good, and you might only make things worse. I don't want you to come. Wait till Christmas when you can enjoy the girls." Cynthia O'Connell, alone at sixty-eight and bored with a widow's life, was always looking for some diversion. Too often, she looked to me, an only child. Tim's leaving sent her careening to Texas in a disaster of a visit, Cynthia crying all the time until the girls were edgy and tearful and I was so irritable that I became short with both the girls and my mother. Since then, in spite of begging, I never took the girls back to Chicago, and my mom visited only twice. But this year, she was scheduled to come for Christmas, a visit that loomed big on my horizon until the last two days.

I used to be afraid to make Mom worry, especially if she took to her bed with a headache. But since I'd flown the nest and then I married Tim, I'd gotten more independent. These days, I stood up to her. I didn't want her worrying over me, and I didn't want her scaring the girls.

"If you're still alive by Christmas," she sniffed.

In the end, I prevailed, as I usually did with my mother. "I'll keep in touch, Mom. Don't worry, and don't listen to Florence. She needs to get a life." *And so do you.*

The phone rang again, just as Maggie wandered into the kitchen. I know my, "Hello," was short in tone.

"Kelly? What's going on?" It was Tim.

Tim's voice was friendly, caring, and for a moment I was taken back to the days when a call from Tim was the highlight of my day. I remembered how he could make me laugh, how I treasured his concern, how pleased I was when we planned things together, from a special dinner out to a much-anticipated bedroom rendezvous. Then I told myself, *that was then, this is now.*

"I'm fine, Tim," I said in a careful voice. "How are you?" I couldn't resist adding, "Where are you?"

He laughed. "I'm in northern California. But this isn't about me, Kelly. It's about you. What's going on?"

Caution crept into my mind and my voice. It was what? Five in the morning in California? Why would he be awake, let alone calling? "What do you mean?"

"I hear you're having trouble—arson in one of your houses, our own front door shot up. I'm coming to Fort Worth. I'll bring the kids back to California, so you don't have to worry about them."

The idea of Tim taking the girls to California sent cold fear into my heart. They were *my* girls, and I wouldn't be separated from them. Besides, Tim could hardly be called an ideal father. No, there was no way that would happen. I'd make sure of it. If he once got them to California, I might never get them back.

"No, Tim, they're safe. And they're in school. They can't just leave. You don't need to come. Believe me, they're safe." *And it's not our front door, it's mine.*

His voice turned cold. All the charm was gone. "Kelly, they're my kids too, and I don't want them in danger. I don't know what stupidity you're in the middle of, but I won't have the girls involved. I'll go to court and get an order."

That ripped it. "Go on and go to court, Tim. It will cost you money. Money that you should be sending to your children. No judge in Tarrant County will give you custody, even partial custody. You left. You haven't called or anything for six months, and you haven't paid child support." The strength of my voice surprised me, but I was angry, really angry.

Dimly I was aware that Maggie crept out of the kitchen, as though she didn't want to hear. I cursed myself for talking so loudly—and Tim for causing me to.

He slipped back into his charming role. "Kelly, Kelly, I'm just trying to help."

"Don't try," I said. "You will make things worse for me."

"I'm coming to Fort Worth," he said and hung up.

How do I tell the girls that he's coming? What do I do? My thoughts were almost desperate, and there was no one I could turn to for advice. I could have called Joanie, but she had her own problems—and she was preoccupied with them. Well, I guess that wasn't fair—an unexpected pregnancy is a major problem. Besides, her advice usually wasn't practical. But still I had no one to call.

Somehow I managed to hide the anger and the fear as I got the girls ready for the day and off to school. Maggie was subdued, casting looks at me as though she were wary of something, but at the school, she kissed me lightly on the cheek and said, "Have a good day, Mom." When I walked Em into pre-school, the child said, "Mommy, something's bothering you. Can I kiss it and make it better?"

I smiled. "Yes, Em, you can kiss it right here," and I pointed to my right temple. "It's a thought in my brain that I don't like, and a kiss will make it disappear."

"Okay," Em said, standing on tiptoe as I bent down. She planted a big smack on my forehead.

"Thanks, Em. I know it will be a good day now."

As I drove away from the pre-school, I wished I believed that.

When I walked into the office, Keisha took one look at me and turned back to her desk. But when I muttered, "Morning," she turned and asked, "You want a doughnut? Might do you good."

I considered. "No, I want a Starbucks latte and a Danish."

"You got it," Keisha said, picking up her purse. "You look like you need it."

I nodded. "Take some money out of petty cash."

At my desk, I tried to marshal my thoughts. I made a "to do" list, topped with replacing the door. Replacing the door. Of course, I had to find Anthony. One glance at my watch, and I knew that if he had a job today, he'd be long gone. I dialed his home, not expecting an answer.

To my surprise, Theresa answered.

"Theresa? What are you doing home? Why aren't you in school?" Then I recovered a bit of common sense. "This is Kelly."

"Yes, ma'am, Miss Kelly. I recognize your voice. I wasn't feeling well today, and Dad said I could stay home."

"I'm sorry," I said, relieved at the simple explanation. "Has your dad left?"

"Yes, ma'am. He went on a job for a friend, about eight this morning."

"Do you know where the job is?"

"Yes, ma'am. He always tells me in case we need him. This is another house in Fairmount—1916 Sixth Avenue."

"Thanks, Theresa. I'll find him."

Action, I decided, was better than waiting around. I went to Sixth Avenue. The house was one of the wood ones so common in the area. Right now, windows boarded, front porch sagging, it looked pretty hopeless. I wouldn't have bought it, and I wondered about Anthony's friend.

"Anthony?" I stood outside and called. After three shouts, Anthony appeared around the side of the house.

"Miss Kelly, what you doing here?"

"I need a new front door, Anthony. Someone shot mine up last night."

"Mother of God!" His hand flew to his head and started raking his hair, though I doubted he realized he was doing that. "Shot?"

I nodded. "What do I need to do to get a new one?"

"I'll go now and measure and then you go pick out the door. You know where you want to go?"

"Yeah. Old Home Supply on College. I want one that fits the house." Old Home Supply was a wonderful store where you picked your way through everything to find the treasures. Want some old French doors? They have them to fit hundreds of openings. Old sinks, faucets, chandeliers, glass doorknobs—all of it in a jumble that leaves you bewildered unless you have patience. I once walked by an antique metal couch in front of the store that had a Texas star in the middle of the back and a running horse on either side. I chewed on the thought all afternoon and then called back and asked them to deliver it. It was wonderful on the patio, though I did add a cushion. Old Home Supply was where you found almost whatever you needed for an old house.

He smiled. "Of course. Let's go."

We climbed into my Camry—a good serviceable car for driving clients around, though I would much have preferred a Volkswagen bug convertible. "Can you leave your job?"

He shrugged. "It's a friend. He bought the house for himself. I told him it wasn't worth fixing, but he's determined. I'll work for him when there's nothing more important." Clearly, I was more important.

We were at the house in three minutes. Anthony tsk-tsk-ed over the shattered door, now covered by plywood, and took measurements that he wrote on a piece of paper. He handed it to me.

"Want to go with me to pick the door?"

"Yeah, I'd like to do that. I trust you, but I gotta see that it would work."

On the way to College Avenue, a short drive, I said, "Tim called."

"The husband? Don't mess with him, Miss Kelly. He's no good."

"He's heard about what's going on—the skeleton, the fire, the front door—and he wants to take the girls to protect them."

"No," Anthony said vehemently. "You must not let him. Does he care about the girls?"

I shrugged and thought a minute. "Yes, I suppose he does, but only as long as they don't interfere with what he wants to do. Would he use them to get at me? Yeah, I think he would."

"Your children," he said, "are God's blessing. You got to protect them. How did he know about all that so quick?"

I looked at him. "I've been puzzling on that this morning. I don't have any idea. There are a few people that might have called him—and they might have seen the pieces in the paper about the skeleton and the fire, but they wouldn't have known about the front door." Florence Dodson? I doubted that. Mrs. Dodson didn't much like men. Dave Shirley, the insurance agent? I hadn't even called him about the door yet. One of Tim's old drinking buddies might have seen the skeleton and fire in the newspaper, but the front door....

He made a fist and rubbed it. "You need me to talk to him, I will."

I smiled. "Thanks. I'll keep it in mind. But you don't think I'm putting the girls in danger, do you?"

Anthony shook his head. "About that, I don't know. I'm afraid for you, and if you're in danger, then those precious girls are also. Why don't you talk to that cop—Mike what's-his-name? I think he's sweet on you."

"Anthony, just because we're both single and about the same age, don't go matchmaking. Mike's posted a guard at the house...."

"Guard? I didn't see no guard just now."

"That's by design. They don't want to be noticed."

"Oh, okay. But you talk to him anyway. Tell him about Tim. You never know if your ex-husband will do something crazy. I didn't like him. I got a bad feeling from him."

"Me, too," I said. *But I used to feel so good about him. How do people change so much? And which one of us changed?* I switched the subject. Just talking to Anthony strengthened me. He was, I decided, one of the most rooted and stable people in my world—and the other might just be

Keisha. They were the ones I should have called last night instead of feeling sorry for myself alone.

"I'm sorry Theresa isn't feeling well today. I was surprised when she answered the phone a bit ago."

"Theresa at home?" There was no denying the surprise in his voice. "She went to school this morning, like she should."

My heart stopped for a second. I owed Anthony the truth. "She told me she didn't feel well, and you told her to stay home."

He put his head in his hands. "Miss Kelly, I don't know what to do with her. She's...she's running with some friends I don't like, maybe even gangers, and she don't listen to me anymore. I'll take a strap to her when I get home."

No one ever took a strap to me in my life, nor could I imagine doing it to the girls, let alone a seventeen-year-old. "No, Anthony, don't do that. Talk to her. Find out what's going on. I'll help any way I can. Maybe she'd come stay at the house a few days, think things through." I realized that was a lame offer—if Tim didn't' think my home was safe enough for the girls, why would Anthony let his daughter stay there?

He shook his head. "Okay, no strap. I'll talk. I'll let you know what happens."

We picked a classic door, twelve panes, beveled glass, good and thick.

"This will look great when I get it painted," Anthony said. "What color you want?"

The old door was brown, to blend with the cream brick of the house. "Turquoise," I said. "Beautiful, bright turquoise."

Anthony smiled. "You got it. I'll get paint today."

Temporarily, both of us put the troubles of the day aside.

I went back to my office.

"Your latte is cold, and your doughnut is hard," Keisha said without looking up. "Don't send me on a fool's errand again."

"Sorry," I muttered. "I had to find Anthony in a hurry."

"He fix that door?"

"He's fixing…Keisha, how did you know about the door?"

"Mr. Spencer called." She waved a phone message at me.

I wondered again how Tim knew about everything—the skeleton, the fire, the door? I read the brief message, "Arriving 9:00 flight. Will come straight to the house."

"What's that sorry excuse coming back here for?" Keisha asked scornfully.

Boy, there was a side to Tim I didn't see when he was in the office. The people who worked for him didn't like him. Aloud I said, with some irony, "He's going to protect me and the girls."

"Yeah? You best get yourself a gun—and use it on him first."

I called Dave, the insurance agent, who said, "What? Again? Kelly, this has got to stop."

His voice told me he didn't know about the door, so he wasn't the one who called Tim.

"Someone's trying to scare me, Dave. I can't help it if they do property damage."

"They do too much," he predicted, "and the powers that be will pull your insurance. It isn't my call. Meantime, I'll take care of this one. Send me the bill. The deductible applies, of course."

I knew he didn't mean to frighten me, but he had.

I made some other calls and then called for an appointment to see the Craftsman house Em and I checked out before.

"You want to come now? It's not very clean, but I can tidy up before you get here." The owners were Mr. and Mrs. Adolph Hunt, and Mrs. Hunt sounded both pleasant and anxious to please.

"How about thirty minutes? Would that give you time to tidy up?"

"Yes. That would be fine. I'll see you then."

I went to Nonna Tata, a nearby small and intimate Italian kitchen, ate pasta with pesto, and wished for a good glass of wine to wash it down. Then I appeared right on time at the house for sale—and was immediately charmed. When Em and I made our curbside inspection, I didn't see the curved brick path that led to the front door—no concrete here—nor the antique rose bushes that lined the path. The landscaping was low key, not showy but natural. That explained what Em saw as untrimmed bushes. The main creed of Craftsman architects was to live in harmony with the natural woodwork and landscaping.

Inside, the house was amazing, preserved almost intact. The oak woodwork was still natural—paneling, pocket doors, mullions between long narrow window panes topped with small austere squares of leaded glass. Built-in cupboards in the dining room and the external brackets on doorways gleamed with polish and care. The walls were bare of artwork, which emphasized the beauty of the wood. A tiled living room fireplace was flanked by bookshelves with small leaded glass windows over them; the tile was a rust color that blended with the walls. But decorative, multi-colored floral tiles were inset on either side of the fireplace opening. The hearth was also rust-colored tile. Anthony wouldn't have to do anything to this house. I could sell it as is.

Mrs. Hunt watched me. Finally, she said, "It's old-fashioned, I know that."

"Old-fashioned," I breathed. "No, it's wonderful. You've kept it just as it was when it was built—and we don't see that in many of these houses in this condition any more. May I see the kitchen?"

"Of course. Someone will want to redo this, I know."

"Why?" I asked as we walked through the dining room.

'There's no place for the refrigerator. It's on the porch outside."

Typical of Craftsman houses.

The kitchen was updated. I half expected to see a porcelain sink on legs with no storage underneath. The double sink was porcelain, but it had enclosed storage underneath; still it had the traditional double windows over the sink and the built-in cupboards had been retained, with multi-paned glass doors, so that the homeowner was almost forced to keep dishes in neat rows. I thought of my ongoing argument with Tim and now saw his viewpoint—well, just a bit. The stove, a marvelous Aga, European and cast-iron, fit right in with the look of the house—and I knew that real cooks, gourmet cooks, prized those stoves. There was no dishwasher, but I didn't give that a second thought. I was in love with this house.

We toured the three bedrooms, one of which was now a comfortable TV/office, mostly because of the addition of built-in bookshelves, stained to match the original wood of the house.

Back in the living room, I sank into an overstuffed dark leather couch. Mrs. Hunt offered coffee, which I declined though I did ask for a glass of water. When we were both settled, I said, "The house has been immaculately maintained. Can you tell me its history?"

"I grew up in this house. So did my mother. My grandparents built it. We never saw any reason to change it."

I smiled at the comforting tradition those words hinted at. "Why," I asked, "do you want to sell it now?"

She shook her head sadly. "I don't. I'd like to live here until they carry me out, but Adolph...he wants to go to the Hill Country where his family is. He says we're old and we need someplace small." She shrugged. "I don't know what we'll do with all this stuff." Her encompassing gesture took in Oriental rugs, massive furniture, books everywhere. "You think anyone will buy it?" Mrs. Hunt's voice was tentative, doubtful.

The idea that forming in my mind suddenly sprang forth from my lips. "Mrs. Hunt, I'd like to buy it. Not to sell but for me and my daughters to live in. I'll pay a fair price, and if you want I'll take some of the furnishings." In my mind I was selling a lot of the furniture in my house at a garage sale. This gem of a house, which called out to me, wouldn't have reminders of Tim—and I could get rid of some of the furniture he'd selected, which never fit into our old house. Someone once said to me, after viewing the modern furniture, "The house isn't happy." And I knew it wasn't. Moving would be like starting life anew. The sale of my house would bring enough to cover the switch to this smaller one.

"You want to live in it? Why?"

"Because I think it's the most wonderful house I've ever seen," I said honestly.

Mrs. Hunt breathed deeply. "Then I want you to live in it."

At my insistence, we would make arrangements for another realtor to handle the sale. I didn't want any suspicion that I was taking advantage. I would, however, sell my own house myself—and I envisioned a wonderful garage sale as I discarded furniture that reminded me of Tim. For a moment, I regretted the expensive front door I'd just bought that day.

I floated out the door. For an hour and a half, I'd forgotten about skeletons and fires and shot-gunned front doors and Tim's immediate threat. I envisioned the girls and myself in this house. I'd have to tell them about not scarring the walls and all, but then they were past the age of writing on the walls with crayons. *Life*, I thought, *is good.*

Chapter Five

By the time I brought the girls home, the new front door was in place, gleaming bright turquoise.

Maggie forgot her frequent determination not show any excitement about things. "Oh, Mom," she said, "it's beautiful."

Never wanting to be left behind, Em echoed, "It's beautiful."

"I like it too," I told them. "I think it brightens the house." Impulsively I asked, "Girls, what would you think if we moved to a new house." Even as I said the words, something in the back of my mind told me this was a mistake.

"I like our house," Maggie said. "Why would we move?"

"We could live in a smaller house. And I found one that was lovely. You've heard me say that a house reaches out and touches you."

Maggie nodded grudgingly.

"This one touched me."

"Is it the house we found, Mommy?" Em asked, clapping her hands in delight.

"Yes, Em, it is."

"Em's seen it and I haven't?" Maggie's jealousy was almost tangible.

I bent to Maggie and hugged her. "The day Em came home from school because of Sarah and their fight, she and I drove by. She hasn't been inside, but I'll take you both inside... maybe tomorrow."

After supper, I got the girls bathed—Em still need-ed help—and in their PJs. I didn't mention their father's

72

anticipated arrival, though not doing so made me feel like a coward. The doorbell rang a little before eight, and I realized a disadvantage of the wonderful front door. If Jack the Ripper came calling, I had no place to hide. This time, it was Mike Shandy.

"Kelly, I've got news. Mind if I come in?"

"Actually, Mike, I'm glad to see you. Want coffee, a beer?"

"I'm on duty," he said, "so coffee. Thanks."

While the single cup was brewing I came back into the living room. Mike stood by the fireplace, hands clasped behind his back. "We heard from the coroner today. Your skeleton—"

My skeleton?

"—was a female, between twenty and thirty, about five foot six, probably not overweight." He paused. "Here's the surprise: she was about six months pregnant. And, she was shot in the head, almost execution style."

I sank down on the couch. *Pregnant. Someone killed a baby as well as the mother.* "Why would anyone kill a pregnant woman?" Then I remembered a line from a mystery I'd read—love, hate, and greed. Those were the reasons for killing someone. And which was it here? "DNA won't be much help will it? I mean you could get DNA from the fetal skeleton, couldn't you?" I hated those words even as I said them.

"Not really. DNA won't show us much, though we'll run it. The victim's DNA might help us identify her, but DNA wasn't much used in the early '60s, so it's unlikely hers would be on file. What we need is a lucky break to identify her and then match the DNA to something she wore or used or touch. As for the guy who did this, there isn't anything left to take DNA samples from that might indicate identity—you can shoot a person from a distance, and that wouldn't leave DNA. And suppose there was something—semen, or whatever—if the killer had a DNA sample on file, which is unlikely, the DNA was run years after this event, so we'd have to identify the person first. Long story short, it isn't going to help us." Almost as an afterthought, he added, "She didn't have a wedding ring on. We'd have found that."

"So you think the father of the baby killed her?"

"It's a place to start. But we haven't any idea who he was."

"How do we find out?" I asked.

"*We* don't." His tone was firm, and so was the look on his face. "Homicide does. I'm just a patrol cop, and you're a civilian. We're both out of the loop from now on. And I want you to remember that. You've already been threatened, Kelly, by someone who's not afraid."

"They're not afraid of what? I think they're afraid of what we might find out, and that's making them desperate. It makes me all the more anxious to find out what's going on so this will be over. I want that skeleton identified and given a proper burial…and I want to finish that house and sell it."

"I know you care about the skeleton, Kelly, but you've got to detach yourself. And the sooner you let us handle it, the sooner you can sell that house. I don't know why a forty-year-old murder means so much to someone today, but since it does, you've got to let professionals handle it. Believe me; it's dangerous—for you and the girls."

I thought about the door, and the girls, and Tim swearing to keep them safe. "I don't want any part of danger," I said, as though that concluded it. But I didn't tell him about my request for tax records. What if homicide requests the same rolls and finds out there's a prior request? I'd cross that bridge when I came to it, but I made a mental note to check the next day and see if the microfiche records were in the office.

Mike finished his coffee and took the cup to the kitchen. "I best be going. I've got patrol tonight. Anything else, Kelly?"

I shook my head.

"Why do I think something's bothering you that you should tell me about?" He smiled at me, and for an instant I thought the smile was almost paternal, as though he knew more about me than I wanted him to. Then again, a big something was bothering me—a something named Tim.

"It's not your problem. My ex-husband is flying in from California tonight. He wants to take the girls and protect them. Said he's coming straight here from the airport."

He moved back into the room but not too near where I sat on the couch. "And you don't want him to?"

"Of course I don't. He hasn't seen them in over a year, hasn't paid child support…." My voice was sharp and ugly in my ears, and I hated myself.

"Will he take no for an answer in a polite way? In other words, do I need to alert whoever's on guard?"

"No," I sighed. "I don't think he's violent. Just angry and manipulative. Trying to scare me with words will be his tactic."

"You get that alarm installed?"

"I reactivated it right after you told me, and got that little hand-held thing. Let me go see if I can find it."

His voice was exasperated. "If you don't keep it near you, it does no good. Let me see the control panel." I led him to the kitchen, where the panel was on a wall, at a point midway between the front and back doors.

"You know how to call the police on this thing?"

I nodded. "The technician showed me." I pawed around in the drawer under the counter and held up the panic button.

"Good. Keep that with you all the time, and don't hesitate to use it. This is the last night of the patrol—we don't have the manpower to guard you for long. But I'll come immediately if you call for help. And I'll tell the guy on watch tonight to be a little more obvious—like right in front of the house. Okay?"

"Yeah, thanks," I said. I was grateful that the girls and I were safe, but I felt dependent on other people, in a way I hadn't felt even when I was married. I wanted to take care of the girls by myself. It made me angry to have to deal with police and alarms and all. Life had once been simpler.

As he turned to leave, Mike said, "Oh, another good thing to do. Sleep with your car keys beside your bed. Where do you park your car? Garage?"

I laughed. "The garage is too full of Tim's stuff. I couldn't get the car in there. It's in the driveway."

"Good. Your keys should have a panic button. You get scared, you can always hit that and it will alert someone, even if it's just the neighbors, and it'll scare whoever's around. Lights flashing, horn honking, all that."

Mike left, giving me a smile and a salute. "Cheer up, Kelly. We'll find out who your pregnant lady was."

"I hope so," I said as I closed the door.

It was nine o'clock. Tim's plane would be landing. He would be here in an hour. I went upstairs and found that both girls were asleep, Em next to Maggie in her bed, the video still playing in the next room, Maggie's book thrown on the covers next to her. I leaned down and kissed each of them, praying to God to keep them safe. *They are so precious.*

A glass of wine in hand, I was watching out my bedroom window when a taxi deposited Tim in front of the house shortly after ten. Almost disconnected from the scene, I watched him come up the walk, key in hand.

Does he think his key will work? Incredible. When I heard loud, angry knocking, I went downstairs. Tim stood outside the door, gesturing.

"What the hell? You changed the front door and my key doesn't work." he stormed as he came inside.

"Well, you knew the door was shot up. Why'd you think the key would work?"

"The color of that door is all wrong for the house," he said, not answering the question. He was wrinkled and disheveled, as people are after a long flight. But he was also tanned and trim, in much better shape than the last time I'd seen him. I'd thought he was going to fat just a bit. His attitude, though, got to me. He was self assured, confident ...and condescending. I felt like the wife who'd been left behind, and without asking I knew there was another woman, had been all along. I looked out the door—the taxi was waiting.

Pulling my thoughts back to the door, I said, "I like it. And I live here."

He shrugged as though it didn't matter to him. "You've moved the furniture around. Doesn't look as good. Why is there a man parked outside just sitting there?"

"He's a policeman, guarding us."

"I knew you couldn't take care of the girls by yourself."

"Tim, let's not play games." I was direct. "You came to get the girls, and you're not getting them, so go away and call your lawyer."

He put his hands up, palms out, in an appeasing gesture. "I want to at least see them. I mean, I've come all the way across the country...."

"Tim, it's past ten o'clock. They're both asleep, and tomorrow is a school day. Go away. I'll see that you get some time with them tomorrow."

"Hi, Daddy." The voice, timid and small, came from the stair landing, where Maggie stood. Em hovered behind her.

"Maggie, my darling. Come to Daddy."

She came but as though she wasn't sure. Em made a beeline for me, grabbed one leg, and held on fiercely. Maggie was embraced in a hug, but she didn't hug back. She just stood there. After a minute, Tim straightened and looked at her.

"Did you miss me?"

Fair enough. "Yes, I did. But you didn't call or write."

He waved his hand, as though to brush away that small matter. "I've been busy, baby, but I've missed you a lot. Now run upstairs and pack your things so you can come with me."

"Where?"

"Oh, probably to California."

I clutched the panic button. Maggie came to stand by me. "I don't want to go to California. I like it here. We're going to get a new house and…."

"A new house," Tim exploded. "What the hell is wrong with the house I bought you?"

"You don't own it now, Tim. I bought you out, and I'm making huge mortgage payments. That's part of what's wrong with it. But the girls don't need to hear this. They need sleep."

"They're coming with me," he said and took a step toward me.

"Not tonight, they're not. Not ever, unless you get a court order." Em was squeezing my leg so tight that I thought I'd lose circulation. Maggie grabbed my hand, not the one with the panic button, thank goodness.

Tim took another step toward us.

I held up my hand. "See this? It's a panic button. I push it and that cop outside will be in here in seconds.

You better just go." I bent to the girls, "You run up-stairs, right now. Both of you. Get in my bed."

Tim looked confused and angry, but he turned to-ward the door. "I'll be back with a court order," he threatened.

With the girls safely out of earshot, I said, "Tim, I'm getting a restraining order first thing tomorrow. You may see the girls, but only in my presence."

He slammed the door, and I was thankful for the heavy beveled glass.

The girls slept in my bed again that night; each curled tight on one side of me, and it was hard to quiet them. Maggie sobbed, her heart broken by the father she'd once adored, and Em was afraid. "He's a bad man," she said.

"No," I said, "he's not a bad man. He just has some bad ideas. I think he loves you and wants to protect you." *How do you let a child think her father is a bad man, tempted though you are?*

"I don't want to go to California," Maggie whim-pered.

"You won't have to. Ever. I promise you that."

I lay awake between them all night, but the girls slept soundly. I didn't wake them the next morning—school be darned. I was keeping them with me all day.

****

We went to Ol' South Pancake House for break-fast—pigs in a blanket for Maggie, a waffle—mostly untouched—for Em, and eggs and bacon for me. Ol' South is a Fort Worth tradition, offering everything from standard eggs and bacon to elaborate Dutch babies (pancakes rolled with sugar and lemon) and blintzes. Well after ten o'clock, I dragged the girls into the office, situated Maggie with a book—thank heavens she'd decided that reading was fun—and gave Em with colors and blank paper. Em sat close to Keisha, who talked to her, loved on her, and promised her ice cream.

I called my lawyer. Karen explained the procedure for filing a request for a restraining order, said it would take at least a week for a judge to issue even a temporary order—and that wasn't good until it was delivered to the person named. "I can fax the form to you, you fill it out, send it back to me by courier," —I wondered why I couldn't just deliver it to the office, about a mile away; lawyers, I decided, made things complicated— "and I'll file it this afternoon."

The form, when it came, was intimidating, asking for evidence of abuse, photos, and all that sort of stuff. I had none. I had only my word that Tim threatened me, never paid child support, and hadn't seen the girls for over a year. I filled it out with a sinking heart—I wasn't going to get a restraining order in time to prevent Tim from taking the children. I was sure if I let him take them even to lunch, I'd never see them again. I called Karen back.

"I think you may be dramatizing, Kelly," the lawyer said bluntly. "The chances of him getting away with them are slim. The divorce decreed that he had visitation two weekends a month and we can't get that changed in the blink of an eye. I'd say try to work with him right now."

That is easier said than done. I considered a new lawyer, but I knew that would be shooting the messenger.

There was no way I could concentrate on work. I managed to call Alan, a colleague with his own realty firm. He knew the Fairmount area and whistled softly when I told him about the house I wanted to buy. "You'll steal it at any price," he said. I told him I wanted to pay fair market value, and he promised to contact

Mrs. Hunt right away, get an appraisal, and move things ahead.

I collected the girls and went to the Fairmount house, where Anthony was supervising the work of Black Brothers. Workers were spraying something on the walls and then wiping them down. It looked to me like a lot of the soot was coming off, but the burnt smell was still overpowering. Anthony opened all the windows, and the October air blew in, but I thought it would have to blow a lot to get rid of the smell. I gave the girls chalk to make a hopscotch, and they skittered off to the front sidewalk, Maggie saying, "It stinks in there, Mom."

Anthony looked at me as we stood on the front porch watching the girls. "Miss Kelly, something's very wrong. What?"

Anthony was one of the people I trusted. I told him about Tim's visit and my inability to get an instant restraining order. "I'm afraid he'll take them to lunch and they'll end up in California," I said.

"Miss Kelly, I have a solution for both of us. I talk to Theresa last night. She's lonely, she misses her momma, and, yes, she's running with a bad crowd. She admits it, but they pay attention to her and that's what she needs now. I want to take a strap to her, but I remember what you said. So I talk, I talk about how I love her, how you think she's a good girl, how whatever she does now can make a big difference in the rest of her life. For right now, she listens. But," he shrugged, "who knows? Why don't I send her to you as a nanny. We give her responsibility for the girls, and they don't go nowhere without her. I'll pick her up in the mornings for school and bring her back in the afternoons."

I was surprised he knew about such an idea. "And she'd be glued to the girls, every minute?"

"Yeah. She's not scary, but Mr. Spencer might not want to have to deal with taking a seventeen-year-old or beating her to get the girls away or something like that. She change the balance. And she be away from those friends."

I hugged him. "Anthony, I think it's the best choice we have. Is she at school today?"

He shook his head. "No. I left her at home. I pray to God she's still there."

"I'll go get her. Do you want to come too?"

"No. I stay here and watch. I don't trust these people. They take shortcuts when I'm not watching. And I'm looking—who knows, we may find another locket."

It was lunchtime when I collected a sullen Theresa. "Your dad will bring you some things," she said. "I need you to stay with the girls."

"What about school?"

"You can go to school while the girls are in school. Otherwise I want you with them like glue. I'll explain later."

When Theresa and the girls were back in the car, I said, "How about lunch?" I named one of those pizza places with various rides and games and puzzles but not very good pizza, groaning inwardly even as I said it.

Theresa just shrugged, but the girls both shrilled in excitement. Theresa seemed to brighten and went off with the girls to try out the entertainment. The girls loved the video games and simulation things—cars they could drive in place, etc. They had a sea of plastic balls that kids could dive into, and I shuddered every time the girls did, thinking how dirty those balls were. The only food they served was pizza and what was supposed to pass as a salad. While the girls played, I chewed on pizza that tasted like cardboard. On the way home, Em fell asleep in the car, and Maggie looked drowsy. Once home, I carried Em upstairs and urged Maggie to climb in her bed with her book. Not twenty minutes later, both were sound asleep.

Maggie came downstairs about four. "Mom, you said you'd take us to see that new house today."

I'd forgotten. "Mag, we went to lunch instead."

"I want to see the house," the child repeated.

"Okay, I'll call Mrs. Hunt and ask if we could maybe come in an hour. Em ought to wake up by then. Where's Theresa?"

"Upstairs watching TV."

Probably something I don't want the girls to see. I'll have to see if I can get her interested in reading.

Mrs. Hunt was cordial and said anytime at all, but I didn't want to land at the house at dinnertime. "My youngest daughter is asleep, and as soon as she wakes up...."

"I'm awake, Mommy," Em said, coming downstairs.

"Oh, she's awake. Okay if we're there in about twenty minutes? We won't be in your way long."

"That's fine, dear," Mrs. Hunt said. "You stay as long as those girls want to."

Inside the Hunt house, Theresa stood, unsure of herself and her role. Em walked right in as though she lived there, testing the overstuffed leather chair, feeling the wood paneling, peering out the paned windows. Maggie was silent as we walked through the rooms, until we got to the bedrooms.

"Which one will be mine?"

"You and Em will share that big one," I said as lightly as I could.

"Share a room with Em? No way."

"Maggie, you practically share a room with her now. It won't be that different...and it's a big room. We'll figure out a way to make it work."

Maggie crossed her arms in front of her, frowned, and said, "You get two rooms."

"Well, I need an office...." I began to rearrange in my mind. I didn't need much of an office. Maybe I could have a desk in a corner of the living room—a wonderful old roll top, as though I could find one and afford it when I did. I resorted to that age-old phrase, "We'll work it out, Maggie."

I thanked Mrs. Hunt, who looked a little uncertain, and we left. In the car, Em said, "I love it, I love it. Mommy, it's the perfect house for you."

"Yeah," I admitted. "It is for me. But what if it isn't perfect for you girls?"

Quietly Theresa said, "It's a good thing I won't be with you too long. Only until you don't need a nanny any more. There's no place for me."

Stunned, I said, "Theresa, there's always a place for you. Don't even think that." If I hadn't been driving, I'd have grabbed the girl and hugged her.

I wanted a glass of wine as soon as I got home, but the phone was ringing.

"Kelly," Tim said, "I want to take the girls to dinner. Nothing fancy, and I'll have them home whenever you say."

Here it is—the test. Keeping my voice as natural as I could, I said, "Sure, Tim. They'll be ready in half an hour. I'd like to have them home by eight—they missed school today and can't do it again tomorrow."

"No problem," he said.

"Oh, and Tim? They have a nanny who goes with them. That's the deal."

"A nanny? How the hell can you afford a nanny?"

"It's Anthony's teenage daughter, and it's too long a story to go into now. But Theresa will be going to dinner with you too."

"Anthony," he fumed. "Never did like that old man. I suppose he can't control his daughter, so he's given her to you."

"Tim, do you want to take the girls to dinner or not?"

"Yeah, I'll be there."

He was only twenty minutes late to get the girls. Em protested, but Theresa carried her, saying softly, "I'll bring you back to Mommy real soon. I promise."

Tim gave them both a disgusted look and held his hand out to Maggie, who refused to take it but walked along beside him.

My heart was in my mouth. Should I call Mike Shandy? Joanie? The airlines to check flights to California? I poured myself a glass of wine instead, went for my secret stash of that chocolate with jalapeños, and sat, hands shaking, in the living room.

Chapter Six

When the phone rang a little before eight, I jumped. I was on the couch with my second glass of wine and no food. I thought about my advice to Joanie the night she'd come over, and I knew I should eat but my nerves made my stomach say no to food.

"Hello?" My voice was tentative, because I was scared down to my toes, sure that it was Tim saying they were boarding a flight for California, and I would hear the girls screaming for me in the background. *Kelly, get a grip*, I told myself.

"Kelly, its Joanie. I have something big to tell you. Can I come over?"

"Not right now, Joanie. It's a bad time. Tim took the girls to dinner, and they're due back any minute."

"Tim? What's he doing here?" Was I imagining it or was there an odd tone, maybe a moment's hesitation, in Joanie's voice?

"Too long a story to tell right now, Joanie. I'll fill you in later."

"Okay, but I really have big news, and I want to share it with you."

I sighed. "Not now. Maybe after the girls are home and in bed. I'll call you."

"Promise?"

My head was beginning to pound from stress, wine, and no food. "Yeah, I promise."

Tim was only fifteen minutes late bringing the girls back, but to me it was an eternity. I was ready to start checking airline departures for California, calling the police, running out in the street and shouting, when suddenly there was his car. He didn't come in. Through the door, I saw Maggie reach up on tiptoe to kiss his cheek and Em allow him to hug her. He nodded at Theresa, who thanked him for dinner, holding out her hand. He ignored it. Then the girls came in, and Tim left.

"Hi, girls." I tried to sound casual.

"Hi, Mom," Maggie flopped on the couch. "Dinner was so good. We went to Joe T.'s."

Mexican food, Fort Worth's classic restaurant. It's on the North Side, where cowboy culture vies with Hispanic for the local tourist trade. You can sit outside on a flower-filled patio, on a nice night like that, and the prices are reasonable—except you can't pay with credit cards. I wondered if that was a problem for Tim.

I should have known Tim would take them there—the owner considered him a friend and always greeted him with a personal handshake. "I'm glad you liked it," I said, "Joe T.'s is always good and fun."

"I didn't like it," Em said, crawling into my lap.

Maggie was scornful. "You just didn't like Daddy's girlfriend."

My stomach catapulted again, but I waited.

"She was okay," Maggie said. "She didn't fuss over us, but she didn't ignore us. I didn't exactly like her, but I didn't hate her."

"I did," Em said solemnly.

Theresa chimed in, "Em, you mustn't hate people. You can dislike them."

"Okay, I dislike her."

I guessed since we were long divorced, Tim had a right to bring another woman to dinner—but overnight visits would be another matter. I wanted to ask for a description—height, weight, hair color, all that, but I refrained.

"Theresa, did you enjoy dinner?"

"Yeah, sure, it was all right." Theresa wasn't going to loosen up overnight.

"Okay, everybody upstairs to bed," I said, pulling myself off the couch.

"Me too?" Theresa asked, her sullen expression back.

"No, of course not," I said, "but would you get the girls into their pajamas. I'll be up right away to tuck them in."

They all trooped up the stairs, and, my conscience bothering me, I called Joanie. "They're home. Why don't you come over in half an hour?" I did not want to wait for Joanie and sit up half the night listening to her. I wanted to crawl into bed and pull the covers over my head.

"I'll be there," Joanie said.

I went up and kissed the girls goodnight. Then I stuck my head in Theresa's open bedroom door to say goodnight.

"Miss Kelly?"

"Yes, Theresa?"

"I don't trust your husband. He's no good."

I tried to pass it off. "Thanks for the warning. I think I figured that out myself, too." But inside I wondered what made the girl join the chorus of people who were saying negative things about Tim. *Had love blinded me that much?*

****

Joanie arrived even a little before the half hour, bearing a bottle of white wine. "For you," she said. I didn't want to tell her I'd already had enough wine for one night. "You want some?" I asked.

"Nope," Joanie said. "I'm not drinking. I brought some mineral water." She whipped a bottle out of her bag. "But I'd take ice and lime if you have it...or lemon."

"Sure." I fixed her drink, poured myself just a bit more wine, and cut some cheese for us to nibble on. "So what's this big news?"

"I'm going to have a baby." Joanie cried.

I was stunned. "You're going to have it? No abortion?"

"Absolutely not. I thought about a lot of things, including some of the things you said to me the other night, and I can't destroy this child."

The next question came slowly. "Will you raise it or give it up?"

Joanie raised her chin. "I'm keeping my baby. I've told my folks, and they say they'll love their grandchild. That's *all* they said."

I leaned over on the couch and gave her a big hug. "Joanie, I'm so glad...and so proud of you." To myself, I wondered if Joanie hadn't gone from one extreme to the other a little fast. She was like a person who has found religion at a revival and is devout for three months. Would the decision last or six or seven months into the pregnancy or, when it was too late, would she regret it?

Joanie pulled away. "I didn't know you had an opinion. I mean, I thought you just listened."

"I tried to," I confessed, "but I wanted you to keep the baby. I can't explain all the reasons...and I know all the arguments people would give you against it, but I think you're doing the right thing for your baby...and for yourself." I paused. "I'm proud of you, Joanie. It won't be easy." I would, I vowed to myself, be supportive, no matter what else was going on in my own life. I thought about the woman whose baby never made it to life, but this wasn't the time to think about Miranda, the skeleton.

It was midnight before Joanie left, and I crawled to bed, exhausted. I'd checked on the girls, and they were sleeping. Theresa, too, was asleep, with the guest room

TV still on. I turned it off and went to bed, where I collapsed in a deep sleep.

The phone woke me at four. When I mumbled, "Hello," a male voice—obviously Hispanic but trying too hard to disguise its youthful qualities—said, "Forget about the skeleton. Quit talking to that cop about it."

It gave me cold shivers. Then, I got out of bed, paraded barefoot down the hall, and looked at Theresa, sleeping in her bed. She looked young, innocent, like a seventeen-year-old should look. Was she connected to the call? No, that was a foolish thought.

From four to six, I went back and forth in my mind—should I call Mike Shandy? Should I forget it and hope it would go away?

At six, I knew there would be no more sleep. Sliding my feet into slippers, I padded downstairs and into the kitchen, where I turned on the early news, read the paper, and sipped coffee. *What I need right now is a loyal dog who would lie at my feet and tell me with his eyes how wonderful I am. Maybe he'd be a guard dog.* Followed by, *a dog? All I need is one more living creature to take care of.*

I woke all three girls at seven, urging them to hurry, fed them breakfast. *Okay, Keisha, it's eggs and toast with jelly, plus orange juice—that's healthy.* Theresa seemed in good spirits, almost hand-feeding Em her eggs and smiling at me. When Anthony came to pick her up for school, Theresa gave him an affectionate peck on the cheek, and he, surprised, hugged her.

The girls were on time, and in spite of the fact that I felt eighty years old from lack of sleep and too much wine the night before, I was optimistic—Tim brought the girls back, Joanie was going to keep her baby, and Theresa was lightening up. Life looked good. I could go back to worrying about who Miranda really was and who killed her. I was being stubborn, and I knew it, but that skeleton had a hold on me, as though it was calling out to me for justice. I couldn't bear to think of a young woman, about to have a child, shot to death and hidden away so coldly. If I didn't help find out who killed her, I wasn't setting an example of compassion and responsibility for my girls—and I wasn't living up to who I liked think I was. The police? I thought they'd forget about it in a few days, and I couldn't let the murder lie unsolved as it had all these years.

At the office I found a message that the tax records I requested were in the city clerk's office for review. I answered a few phone messages and then, as I headed for the city clerk's office, told Keisha I was out for most of the day.

"So what else is new?" Keisha asked with a grin. "I'll keep the business running. Don't you worry."

I threw a wadded up piece of paper at her and left.

The tax rolls were dull and pretty much corresponded with what I found in the city directories. The same people owned the house lived in it until up to the mid-1980s, when it seemed to have become rental property. From 1984 until 2004, it had had a succession of owners, though I remembered an even more rapid turnover of tenants. But then in 2004, the Whiteheads, the young couple I bought it from, had purchased the house. So that was the record of ownership. The only interesting thing it told me—and I chewed on this—was that from 1957 to 1968, the house was owned by Martin Properties, Inc. What was Martin Properties? Forty years later, it wasn't an existing player in the real estate market in South Fort Worth.

I had a red flag. I just didn't know what to do with it. After scribbling notes, I thanked the clerk and told her I would not need the records any longer. At least not now.

Then I left, arriving early to pick up Maggie. I sat in the car and pondered how I'd find Martin Properties,

Inc. Even if I found the company on other deeds, there would be no personal information, no way to track anyone involved. And to find that, I'd have to comb thousands of records. I could try Google, the city phone book, and old city directories, but I held out little hope for either. Somehow I suspected Martin Properties didn't want to be found, and a company like that—one existing only as a paper front—could easily hide its existence. At least from me. Maybe some high-powered, expensive private investigator could trace them, but I couldn't and I doubted the police would.

****

That night I made cheeseburger meatloaf, mashed potatoes, and green beans, and the girls ate heartily. "This is really good, Miss Kelly," Theresa said. "My dad, he cooks for us, but he uses so much Greek spice…I get tired of it. I like plain food."

"Thanks, Theresa. I'm glad you like it."

"I'll go get the girls ready for bed," she volunteered, "and I can help Maggie with homework, if you want."

"Thanks," I said. "That would be great. I'll do the dishes, and we can all turn in early. But if you have homework of your own, I'll work with Maggie."

"I did mine this afternoon," she said.

It should take longer than that to do the homework of a senior in high school, but I wasn't about to raise that issue. *Choose your battles, Kelly.*

The three of them went cheerfully upstairs, and I cleaned the kitchen, laid out cereal bowls and glasses for o.j. for breakfast, got things ready to assemble the girls' lunches, and felt quite efficient. Maybe having Theresa with us was a good thing.

Pretty soon, Em straggled back downstairs. "Mom? Did you forget that it's almost Halloween? I don't have a costume, and we don't have a pumpkin."

Halloween. Of course I forgot. "Oh, Em, I did forget. But I'll take care of it tomorrow. I'll get the pumpkin, and... do you remember the year Maggie was a princess? I bet that costume would fit you—I'll find it and see what shape it's in."

"What will Maggie be?"

"Let's go ask her."

Maggie's answer was instant and emphatic. "I want to be Hermione from *Harry Potter.*"

I hadn't read the Harry Potter books and had no idea what would be required to transform my darling daughter into Hermione. "What would the costume consist of?"

Maggie had thought this all out. "I could wear jeans and a plaid scarf—it has to be plaid—and v-neck sweater—I might have to borrow from you, but then I'd need a Hermione cloak, and a wand and a lantern."

"Not just any wand and lantern?" I thought I had the plaid scarf, but the wand and lantern were definitely not in my closet.

A firm shake of the head. "No. Hermione. I'm sure you can get them."

I sighed. Shopping endlessly for specific items is not one of my favorite things. To my mind, it's wasting time. "Maybe I can get them at a drugstore," I said with a faint hope.

As it turned out, I spent three hours locating the items and standing in line. *Next year, I'm going to plan ahead.*

The next morning, when Anthony came to pick up Theresa, she was cheerful and greeted her father affectionately. Over the girl's head, Anthony smiled at me. Aloud he asked, "You come by the house later?"

"I will," I promised. "I want to see how you're doing."

"I have something to show you."

I smiled. Anthony could always improve on my plans. In a day when skilled carpenters were hard to find and harder to afford, he was a real jewel.

The girls were cheerful when I dropped them at their schools. "Remember, I have ballet this afternoon. Theresa reminded me to pack my things. They're in the car."

And as I walked Em into her classroom, the small hand clutching mine, I said, "Have a good day, Em."

"You too, Mommy. I think this is a good day."

I was smiling as I walked into the office. "You win the lottery again?" Keisha asked.

"Almost. All three girls are happy, and I think things are going to improve."

Alan called a few minutes later, with the appraiser's report on the house. "I'm going to give it to the Hunts right now. I'll let you know what they say."

Waiting, I put pencil to paper, figuring what I'd clear on my house, what moving would cost, and how much I could pay for the Hunt house, calculating monthly mortgage payments, insurance, and taxes. I figured I could afford the appraiser's estimate plus more if I had to—and still bank some. I was anxious for Alan to call, but he didn't—and I had a house to show at 10:30.

"If Alan calls, be sure he has my cell," I said as I left.

The client, Claire Guthrie who wanted a house in good condition, seemed to like the first house, a two-story that had been one of the earliest Fairmount houses redone, but it now needed remodeling again. It was in what I thought of as Lower Fairmount, where the neighborhood begins to edge into the more fashionable Ryan Place.

"I like it," Mrs. Guthrie said, "and I think my husband will. But three bedrooms. We did want four so each of the girls could have her own room and we'd still have an office that could also be a guest room. Do you have any two-story four-bedrooms to show me?"

I thought a minute. I'd just put the sign up in my yard, and I hadn't straightened this morning—breakfast dishes were still in the sink. Honesty, I decided, was the best policy. "I do have one," I said, taking along breath. "It's my house. But I didn't straighten up this morning, didn't even do the dishes. I wasn't expecting to show it so soon."

"Oh, bother the dishes. I'd like to see it. If it's good enough for a realtor, it must be a good house. Why are you moving?"

"I'm moving to a smaller house." No need to add, "And more charming."

I took her through the house, room by room. Even with unmade beds and messy girls' rooms, the house showed well. And I knew how to point out its strong points—privacy in the master suite with its redone, spacious bath and its built-in office space. Claire Guthrie quickly saw that she could make another use of her guest room, and said, "I've wanted a separate place to put all my knitting supplies. This would be perfect."

In the kitchen I pointed to the warming drawer, the separate bar area Tim insisted on, the trendy glass-front cabinets, and the spacious work counter.

"I'm a cook," Claire gushed. "I'd love to cook in this kitchen. And we'd have to redo that other kitchen. How much are you asking for your house?"

I knew my price from my calculations earlier in the morning, and I gave her a figure, saying, "It's non-negotiable, and it doesn't include agent's fees."

"When could we have possession?"

"As soon as I hear from the agent who's handling the purchase of the new house, I'll be able to tell you."

We made arrangements for Mrs. Guthrie to bring her husband back at five that evening. After she left, I flew around the house, straightening the kitchen, making beds, fluffing pillows on the couch. Then I went and bought bouquets of fresh flowers to put in the living room and the kitchen. *If they don't buy the house, I'll still enjoy the flowers.*

When my cell rang, I answered it eagerly. But it was Christian, saying he'd fax the title search to me. But he read it, and I knew he'd pretty much found was what I'd about the house on Fairmount. "I think," I said, "Martin Properties, Inc., holds the clue. Ever hear of them?"

"Nope."

"Know where to look?"

"Nope."

"Big help you are," I teased. "And I was about to have a closing for you."

"Kelly, don't hold out on me," he said. "What house?"

"Mine."

"Yours? I haven't seen an MLS listing for it. You're not leaving, are you?"

"No. I'm buying the most wonderful Craftsman-style house you ever saw. At least, I think I am."

"You got a buyer for your house already?"

"Keep your fingers crossed. I'll know tomorrow."

Almost as soon as I hung up, the cell rang again, and this time it was Alan. "The Hunts want to sell it to you at the appraised value," he said, satisfaction filling his voice.

"Oh, Alan. I'm prepared to pay more. I figured it this morning, and I can go higher." I was blabbing, and I could feel my heart racing.

"Kelly," his tone cut me off. "You don't raise the asking price. Never. I won't allow a client to do that."

"Okay," I said.

"Want me to draw up the papers? Any specifications?"

"Yes, draw up the paper and no, no specs, except that the Hunts are welcome to visit whenever. Can I call her and arrange to go through the house with her again?"

"Sure, you call. I'll bring the papers by tonight for you to sign."

"Did she say when they wanted to close?"

"Standard thirty days," he said.

I figured that would give me time to clean out my house and, I hoped, sell it.

My evening was getting crowded. I remembered Anthony and hurried over to the house on Fairmount.

"I thought you forgot me," he said.

"Never. But I think I just bought a house...and sold mine." He had looked at the Craftsman house but didn't know I'd made an offer nor that I'd found a possible buyer for mine, so I told him the whole story.

"Terrific, Miss Kelly!" He grabbed me and danced me about the empty living room, laughing all the while. Then, abruptly stopping, "Now, my find." Leading the way to the kitchen, he said, "I find this in the bedroom closet, behind a fake panel." He handed me a small leather-bound book, with a gold-leaf page ribbon running through to mark a page. A gold clasp held it closed, and there was a place for a key—but no key. I pressed the clasp, and it sprang open.

I stared at Anthony, who was grinning. Then I leafed through the book—pages of neat handwriting, dated entries. It was Marie Winton's diary!

"You gonna give it to the cops?" he asked.

"Not until I read it," I answered without hesitation. "And maybe not then. We'll see."

I clutched the book to me, as though it were worth a fortune. "Thank you, Anthony. What made you look there?"

"I sometimes get tired of working on the kitchen, and I explore the house, getting ideas for what I can do to other rooms. I'm going to make these closets bigger, easier to get too—so I was testing the walls, and I found...." He looked sheepish. "Another dead space."

I wanted to rush home, lock myself in the bedroom, and read every word of the diary, but I had to pick the girls up and then the Guthries were coming. When I had Maggie and Em both in the car, I said, "We have to go right home and straighten things up. People are coming to look at the house at five."

Em asked, "What people? Why are they looking at our house?"

Just as I was about to say, "Because they might want to buy it," Maggie interrupted with, "Mom, I have ballet today."

I'd forgotten entirely. Ballet was from four to five. My mind raced. Maybe I could drop her off and find another mother—one I knew and trusted, of course—to bring her home. But when I got to the ballet studio, the only mother I saw was Sarah's—mother of the girl Em tangled with. No, that wouldn't do. I searched my brain—and then my purse for my notebook with Mrs. Guthrie's number in it. Frantic, I dialed.

Claire Guthrie answered with her usual enthusiasm. When I explained, she agreed it would be no problem to move the appointment to five-thirty. In fact, it might be more convenient for Mr. Guthrie. *That's what she called him, Mr. Guthrie. I never ever referred to Tim as Mr. Spencer.*

Rather than get more flustered by rushing around, I sat and watched the lesson. But Em squirmed and wiggled, clearly bored. "Mommy, I have to peepee." I took her to the restroom. "Mommy, I'm thirsty." I got her a paper cup of water from the dispenser. "I didn't want water. I wanted juice."

"Em, please be quiet. You're disturbing the lesson. If you're good for this and the Guthrie's visit, I'll get you whatever you want—well, almost."

I hustled the girls out the door and into the car, and we were home by five-ten. I rushed around, straightening things that I'd already straightened once that day. But when the door chimes rang, I felt I was ready. The girls were settled in the kitchen, with Theresa helping them bake cookies. I thought that bit of domesticity might add to the charm of the kitchen for the Guthries. Besides the smell of baking was famous as a subliminal factor or whatever in selling a house.

The walk-through went well. Claire Guthrie was so eager to point out the amenities to her husband that I sat back and let her take over. He seemed impressed, though I found him hard to read—inscrutable was the word that came to mind.

"May I offer you a glass of wine?" I asked, and both nodded their acceptance.

We settled in the living room, and I asked if they had any questions about the house, its history, its upkeep. Mr. Guthrie—I thought his name was Jim—asked about utility bills and all those practical matters, while Claire said, "You know, Jim, this just feels right to me."

I was seeing a sale within my sights and could barely contain my excitement. But just then the front door flew open, and Tim Spencer burst into the room, his face red with anger. "You cannot sell this house," he yelled. "I put too much into it. You cannot sell it."

The Guthries sat shocked, staring at him, and out of the corner of my eye, I saw Em peek around the corner.

I said the only thing I could think of. "My ex-husband does not come with the house," I assured them. I thought it was clever, but no one laughed, and Tim said, "Quit trying to be smart, Kelly."

"Maybe we should finish our talk another time," Jim Guthrie said, rising and looking at Tim.

Feeling foolish, I performed the introductions, and the two men shook hands perfunctorily. Claire looked as though she'd rather touch a snake.

Just as they started toward the door, which Tim had left open, Mike Shandy, in full uniform, appeared in the doorway. He looked at the strange assortment of people, looked again at me, and said, "Sorry. I'll come back another time. I just wanted to tell you that the detectives think they've got a lead on the identity of that skeleton."

While Tim roared, "Skeleton?" the Guthries left without another word. I watched them go with sinking spirits. There was a sale gone sour.

"Sorry," Mike said. "Did I interrupt something?"

I tried to smile at him, but it didn't work. "Nothing that was going very well. Mike, this is my ex-husband, Tim Spencer."

Mike, ever friendly, held out his hand. "Mike Shandy. I'm the neighborhood patrol officer. Been keeping an eye on Kelly and the girls."

"I'm sure you have," Tim said, ignoring the proffered hand. "What the hell are you talking about—a skeleton?"

I knew this was an act for effect, and Tim knew about the skeleton—I remembered that he mentioned it in that first phone call. But now I was too stunned to think clearly.

Mike said, "I guess Kelly will have to tell you that. Kelly, there's no more surveillance, but you if you need me you have my number." With a telling look at Tim, he asked me, "Okay with you if I go about my business now?"

"Sure, Mike. I'll be fine. Thanks. Maybe we can talk about the report in the morning."

"Sure," he said. But then, "Why don't we have dinner tomorrow night? I'm off, and we could talk about the whole case." His look at Tim was calculated, and Tim responded, looking indignant.

"I'd like to Mike, but the girls...."

"Theresa can keep the girls."

"I can take the girls to dinner," Tim said. "You two just go on and solve your mysteries." His voice dripped sarcasm.

My heart sank. I didn't want the girls with Tim, but until the courts settled things, I had no choice. "Okay, thanks, Tim." That was an effort to be gracious. "Theresa will have to go with you, of course...."

"Of course," Tim said sarcastically. "I can't see my girls alone. You'd think I was a pedophile."

"Tim," I said, "that's not it, and you know it. I want them to have the comfort of someone familiar."

"I'm familiar, for God's sake. I'm their father."

"Em doesn't know you, and she's scared of you. Theresa will go, and they have to be home by eight because it's a school night. And before you go, I need to know where you and your friend,"—my voice lingered on the last word—"are staying."

"The Worthington," Tim said curtly, naming one of Fort Worth's nicest hotels, and stalked away.

He must be doing better than I thought.

When Tim was gone, Mike said, "I didn't mean to make trouble."

"It's trouble that's there anyway."

"Are you really afraid he'd kidnap the girls, Kelly?"

"I'm terrified," I replied.

"Let's have dinner in. I'll bring something, maybe from Nonna Tata, and you provide the wine. That way, that jerk will know I'm on the premises and waiting for him to bring those girls home."

"Thanks, Mike. That would be great. I'll have a pinot ready."

He left, and I turned to see both girls peering out the kitchen door and Theresa standing behind them, the look on her face dark.

As I bent to hug the girls, Theresa said, "He's evil, Miss Kelly. I know the kind. He's evil."

I tried to cover the girls' ears. I knew Theresa meant Tim, not Mike, but I didn't want them to hear that.

Chapter Seven

The girls were upset after Tim and Mike left. Maggie balked at doing homework, and Em wouldn't leave my side. Theresa, upset in a different way, retreated to her room and refused to come out for dinner. I gave the girls waffles and bacon, sent them to early baths, and tried to tuck them in early. Both wanted to sleep in my bed, and I thought that was okay. They needed security after seeing their father behave so badly. I read to them until Em was asleep and Maggie seemed comforted.

As I got up to leave, Maggie whispered, "He'll be sorry, Mom. He's not like that. It's just …well, he told me he wants us to grow up in this house."

Curious, I sat back down by Maggie. "What else did he say to you, Mag? Did he say again that he wants you to go back to California with him?"

"Oh, yeah, but I told him no way. I live with you." She yawned widely.

I leaned down to kiss her nose. "You ready to go to sleep?"

"Yeah," Maggie said. "I don't think I'll have bad dreams."

Theresa was sitting at the small table in the guest room, busy with pencil and paper.

"Homework?" I asked.

The girl quickly put her hand over what she'd been working on. "No," she said hesitantly, "I…I'm keeping a journal." Then, defiantly, "You can't see it. Neither can my dad."

Mildly, I said, "I'm sure neither of us would think of asking to see your journal." Then I felt guilty, because I knew I was about to look at Marie Winton's journal. But to Theresa, I said, "I don't know why you say Tim is evil, and I don't think I want to know—I have my own opinions on the subject. But I do want you to make sure he doesn't take the girls off to California some night when I just think he's taken them to dinner."

"I understand that, Miss Kelly, and I can do it."

"He'll pick the three of you up at five tomorrow night. I told him the girls have to be home at eight because it's a school night."

"Okay," Theresa said impassively. "I'll go and eat his food. I hope he takes us some place really special this time."

I smiled. "Maybe I should suggest Bistro Louise?" It was one of the more expensive restaurants on the southwest side of Fort Worth.

"I've never even heard of that," Theresa said dreamily. "Is it good?"

I nodded. "It is. But I doubt you'll go there."

She shrugged, and I leaned down and hugged her. Somewhere inside this girl was a really sweet child trying to come out of a protective shell.

I looked in at the girls, but they were sound asleep. I was free to put on my robe and read Marie Winton's diary, even though it made me feel like a voyeur or worse. Some pages did make me feel worse, for Miss Winton had been a young girl carried away by passion, and she wasn't hesitant about committing that passion to words, words she never thought anyone else would see. She was in love with a man named Marty, but there was little description of him, except that he was married. As I read on, I became increasingly frustrated. Although Marty was mentioned a thousand times—and by then I could have identified him from some pretty personal physical details—there was no indication of his full identity. There was mention of a wife and daughter, but only in passing.

Marie had not begun the diary when she first moved into the house. Indeed she only began to keep it in early 1959, and it stopped abruptly on September 12 of that year. But the last entries were fascinating. Marie confirmed in June what she suspected. She was pregnant. She reported that Marty was overjoyed and promised her they would marry before the baby came. She asked about his wife, and he told her not to worry. He would take care of everything. What happened between 1959 and 1967 when the house was sold? Obviously, the skeleton was the pregnant Marie Winton. By then Marie had replaced Miranda in my mind. Indeed, I began to feel like she was an old friend, a girlfriend that I wanted to lecture as I had Joanie, for she was as foolish as Joanie.

Marie filled her days decorating the second bedroom as a nursery, buying baby clothes, thinking up children's names—she favored Rebecca for a girl and William for a boy, because she thought it sounded strong. Apparently Marty was generous and allowed her to spend lavishly on the nursery. I also noted wryly that, like me, she didn't appear much interested in making baby clothes or knitting for the infant.

But in late August, the tone of the entries changed. Marie reported that she saw a strange car outside the house several times, always the same car—a black Cadillac—and when she went onto the porch, it drove away. She told Marty about it, but he told her not to worry. Then one day, he brought a suitcase to her house and announced he left his wife and was moving in. Marie wrote of it with great joy, but she said some nagging fear wouldn't leave her alone. She didn't know what it was, but something was wrong.

And then, September 12 was the last entry, a brief happy note anticipating the baby and the family she would soon have. "I wonder when we will be married," she wrote. "I guess Marty will surprise me."

I closed the diary and found that great big tears were streaming down my cheeks. I cried for a young woman who had so many dreams and never lived to see them come true. What would I do with the diary? For the moment I tucked the small volume up high on my closet shelf. I wasn't ready to turn it over to anyone—it was too personal.

I was sound asleep, a child pressed into either side of me, when the phone rang at three o'clock. I should have learned by now not to answer, but, sleepily, I muttered, "Hello?"

The same young voice as before said, "You haven't stopped investigating that skeleton. We know you've been checking tax records and ownership stuff. If you don't give it up, you could be putting your daughters in danger." The line clicked, and, now wide awake, I stared at the phone. Putting my daughters in danger! I looked at them sleeping so peacefully, and my heart twisted. I would quit searching for answers, I vowed. The police would have to handle it. I would stick to renovation and selling real estate. But the same old question niggled in my mind: how could anyone so young care that much about something that happened forty-plus years ago? And particularly someone who I suspected was a gang member with no connection to that forty-year-old skeleton?

I lay wide awake, clutching the sleeping girls to me, rethinking everything I knew about the Marie Winton. Tomorrow, I vowed, I'll tell everything to Mike Shandy and give him the notes I'd made. If I thought that resolution would bring sleep, I was sadly mistaken.

****

The next morning at breakfast I told the girls that their father was coming to take them to dinner. Maggie took the news with equanimity but Em wailed, "I don't want to go. I don't like him."

Theresa was up like a shot, her arms around the child, saying soothingly, "I'm going too, Em. It will be all right. Maybe he'll take us for pigs in a blanket."

"At Ol' South?" Em asked.

Theresa nodded, and Em said solemnly, "Okay, if I can hold your hand, Theresa."

"You can, Em."

I marveled, less at Em than at Theresa. The girl could go from light and sunshine to dark and back again without any warning. I sighed. If that was a symptom of all teenage girls, I had some rough years ahead of me.

I was dispirited as I dropped the girls off and went to the office. I had, I knew, lost the sale of my house—and it was all Tim's fault. Well, maybe a little Mike's. What a time to arrive talking about the skeleton. I was sure he spoke before he thought.

At the office, I had barely dug out all my notes on the skeleton when Anthony called. "Mother of God!"

I wished he'd stop saying that. Among other things, it scared me.

"The house," he yelled, as if I was hard of hearing. "They trashed it. Graffiti on the brick walls, paint everywhere on the inside…Miss Kelly, I don't know how many times I can keep fixing this house. I don't ever get to remodeling, because I'm always fixing damage."

"I'll be right there, Anthony, and I'll call the police." I dialed the non-emergency police number and reported the damage and then headed to the house. What greeted me was appalling. Bright yellow paint splashed all over the red brick walls, not in the front of the house, but on the sides and the back.

"They didn't anyone to see them in front," Anthony said. "Punks." He spat in contempt.

"What's inside?"

"Come. I show you."

It looked like someone had a paintball fight in the house—bright colors were smeared all over the walls and floors. I reached out to hold on to Anthony and keep myself from falling in shock.

"It's not as bad as it looks," Anthony said. "We hadn't painted the walls yet, and we can cover that, use Kilz if we need to. And we haven't refinished the floors. But it's the idea that someone did this. Why did those punks do it?"

"How do you know it's punks?" I asked.

"Didn't you say before that you had phone calls from someone who sounded young?"

I hung my head. "Yeah, and I had another phone call last night. The caller warned me to leave the mystery of the skeleton alone. But why do young punks—your word, not mine—care about whether or not we solve the mystery of a skeleton forty years old?"

"Because somebody is paying them," Anthony said sagely,

I told myself if I stopped investigating, the vandalism would stop and the girls would be safe. Simple solution.

The police were perfunctory. "Hard to catch people like this. Best you can do is secure the house."

I thought we had. But after the police filled out their report and left, Anthony and I huddled. I called the electrician we used and arranged for motion sensitive floods all around the house. Anthony described the doors that should go on the house and went off to Old Home Supply to buy them and then to Home Depot to buy deadlocks. And he bought enough plywood to cover the windows—from the inside, where it couldn't be pried off.

"We finish," he said, "this place be like a fortress."

"Thanks," I said, feeling exhausted. I wondered if anyone would miss me if I snuck home and took a nap at noon. I got in my car to drive, reluctantly, back to the office.

"Phone message," Keisha said, handing me a pink slip.

It was Claire Guthrie. With trembling hands, I dialed the number. Of course, they didn't want the house—with a belligerent ex-husband and a policeman who arrived talking about skeletons.

"I want your house," Claire said, "but Mr. Guthrie is uncertain after everything that went on last night. Can we meet for lunch, and you can explain it to me? I think I can persuade him."

I grasped the phone. Haltingly, I managed to say, "Lunch would be great. What's a good day for you?"

"Have you had lunch yet today?"

"No."

"Let's meet at Bistro Louise in half an hour. Will that work for you?"

I tried to be nonchalant, though my heart was racing. "Sure. I can do that."

"Okay. See you there."

Bistro Louise, owned by a chef, was a high-toned restaurant that specialized in French haute cuisine. I ate there once years before, when Tim was spending money. I remember being appalled that I ordered Dover sole and later found it cost $45.

Claire and I met as though casual friends over lunch, and I managed to hide my agitation. I ordered the Salad Niçoise, and Claire ordered the sautéed flounder. I admired her panache. After five minutes, it wasn't hard to forget my agitation. I liked her.

"Okay," she said bluntly, "tell me what all that was about the skeleton."

I did my best to tell the story, leaving out the vandalism at my house and making it sound as though everything revolved around the house being remodeled. As for Tim, I shrugged, said I was getting a restraining order, and he'd probably eventually go back to California. "He wants the girls," I said, "but he's not getting them. He doesn't really care about that house."

"My goodness," Claire said, "you do lead an exciting life. But I have to tell you I've been through it too. I know all about it. Not the skeleton, of course, but the ex-husband. I have one who's nasty, nasty." And she was off telling tales that honestly did include a kidnapping attempt. "He went to jail," she said complacently. "Now, let's talk about happier things. How did you get into your business, and where are you moving?"

So I told her about my love of old houses, and I dwelt on the Craftsman house I was buying until I was afraid she'd want it for herself. But she didn't. Instead she switched the talk to old houses in general and then antiques and we chattered away all through lunch, our talk punctuated by frequent laughs. *I could be friends with this woman.*

Finally, she said, "About your house," the words I was afraid to hear, but her eyes twinkled with amusement. "I know I can persuade my husband. Can you write a contract I can give him tonight?"

"What do you want written into the contract?" I asked, trying to keep hesitation out of my voice.

"We want all light fixtures to remain," Claire said, "and we want some minor repairs done—the light switch in the master bath moved away from the shower, the furnace vents cleaned and inspected. Of course I guess the regular inspection would catch things like that."

"Yes, it would," I said with a sigh of relief. "Do you have a realtor?"

"No. I just consulted you. How soon can you close?"

"Thirty days," I said. "That's pretty standard, and that's what the seller asked for at the house I'm buying."

Claire sighed. "We hoped to have possession sooner—Christmas coming and all that. I don't suppose you can move it up?"

Holding my breath, I said, "I really can't." I'd forgotten all about Christmas coming up. Besides this was only mid-October—Christmas wasn't that soon.

Claire said, "Well, I guess if we want the house, we'll have to wait. Maybe we can come through, make plans between now and then?"

"Any time. Just give me a call so I can be sure to be there. You have my numbers." I took a breath. "I'll write a contract and present it for your consideration. You're free to make changes, requests, whatever—the inspection is a regular part of the procedure." From just one meeting, I was quite sure Jim Guthrie would try to negotiate the price, even though I had said it was non-negotiable. But I didn't mention that.

When the check came, Claire insisted on picking it up. "Lunch was my idea," she said.

I thanked her and assured her she would have a contract in her hands by four o'clock that afternoon.

"Aside from real estate," Claire said, "I enjoyed the lunch. We must do it again soon."

I made a mental note, as I told her goodbye and thanks, to take her to Nonna Tata.

I hurried back to the office. With Keisha's help, I had the contract ready to deliver before three o'clock. I sped to the schools, picked up the girls early, and said cheerily, "We have to go to Ridglea to deliver a contract."

"Ridglea?" Em echoed. "Is that someplace fun?"

"It's just a neighborhood," Maggie said loftily, "like Fairmount. Mom's working, and we have to tag along."

"Did you have something else you wanted to do?" I asked solicitously.

"My homework," Maggie replied.

"I'll get you home as soon as I can. I know you have to do your homework before you go to dinner with your dad."

Maggie yawned. "Maybe he'll help me with it."

I pushed the limit on the west freeway and turned north on Ridglea Boulevard. The Guthries lived in Old Ridglea, a more prestigious area than Fairmount by a long shot, but theirs was a sort of medium house, not one of the large and expensive ones. My house would be a step up for them in size and charm, if not in prestigious neighborhoods. I liked Claire even more for making that choice, and then I grinned about her sure belief that she could get that grumpy husband to do whatever she wanted. She hadn't seemed at first like the urban pioneer type, but I guess I misjudged her. I was pretty sure her daughters went to private school, so local schools weren't a factor.

I left the girls in the car while I ran up the stairs and rang the doorbell. When Claire invited me in, I said, "I hate to thrust these papers at you and run, but my girls are in the car, and I have to get them home to go to dinner with their father."

Claire gave me a look of faint amusement, as though she couldn't believe I would let that man take my children to supper. I stammered a bit. "They have a nanny who goes with them. She'll see that he doesn't put them on a plane to California."

"Good," she said. "I'll have these at your office in the morning," she said.

Once home, I gave the girls a snack, settled Maggie at the kitchen table with her homework, and asked brightly, "Em, can you help me set the table?"

"Just for you, Momma?"

"No, darling. Mike Shandy is coming for dinner."

"Oh," the child said. "I like him. I'd rather stay here with you." She had about her an air that said the matter was entirely settled.

"No, Em. You're going to dinner with your father."

"I don't want to." She began to pout, and I knew tears were next.

Maggie jumped in, getting up to hug her sister and saying, "Remember, Em? We're going to get him to take us to Ol' South so you can have pigs in a blanket, and Theresa is going to hold your hand."

Em looked unmoved. "I'd rather stay here."

"Em…." I gave her a long look and then a smile.

"Oh, okay," Em said. "But I won't have fun."

She's too young to tell her that life—or even dinner—isn't always fun.

When Tim came promptly at five, Em greeted him with, "We want to go to Ol' South."

Taken aback, he said, almost harshly, "Wait a minute. I'm taking you to dinner. I get to say where we're going."

Maggie gave him her sweetest smile. "No, Daddy, we're going to Ol' South."

Over their heads, Tim gave me a dark look as though I'd put them up to this. All I could do was shrug and explain, "They want pigs in a blanket."

I stood in the door and watched them go down the walk, Em's hand firmly clasped in Theresa's, the other woman waiting in the car. I felt a momentary twinge for Maggie, who held no one's hand.

Mike arrived at six, bearing veal scaloppini, a wonderful fresh salad, crisp garlic bread, and a bottle of pinot grigio. He explained the dinner demanded a light white and could we save my pinot noir for another night. I readily agreed. The table was set, though I avoided candles, thinking they were too obvious and instead slightly dimmed the chandelier over the table. Lamps gave a soft glow to the living area of the room. Miraculously, as least to me, I managed to change into black stretchy pants and a soft ivory silk shirt, with my turquoise hishi necklace with its Navaho fetish symbols draped around my neck. It was a treasure from my only trip to Santa Fe, and I saved it for special occasions. Mike whistled softly, almost under his breath, and I blushed slightly. Actually I felt awkward about this encounter.

"I have some good seasoned goat cheese," I said. No need to tell him I'd taken the time to make a trip to Central Market. And I'd gotten some more of my chocolate bars while I was there. Hmm. Would I share those with Mike? "Shall we have that and a glass of wine before dinner?"

"Sure," Mike said. "Give me glasses and a corkscrew, and I'll pour while you get the cheese."

When we were settled, we talked idly of nothing, breaking the ice. I learned that he grew up in East Texas on a farm. "Not the dirt poor farm you always think someone's going to tell you about," he laughed. "Dad was quite prosperous, but still I couldn't wait to get away. I studied law enforcement at East Texas State University. Dad always thought, to his dying day, that I'd go on to law school, but law enforcement is what I want to do."

"On patrol?" I asked curiously.

"Oh, no. I'll move up to detective someday, but I'm in no rush. I really like working here in Fairmount."

In turn I told him sketchily and briefly about growing up in suburban Chicago, where my dad was a lawyer and my mom a housewife. "She never had any interests outside the house, but my dad was my best friend. He encouraged whatever I wanted to do, including some hair-raising athletics. He'd be proud of me today." And I told him how it broke my mother's heart that I decided to go to the University of Texas—"the University at Champagne/Urbana is perfectly fine," I mimicked. Then I recounted meeting Tim, moving to Fort Worth, and going into real estate. I didn't go into details about the divorce.

Over dinner, Mike said casually, "Your girls are lovely. I'm sure raising them alone is hard."

"No," I replied, "It's a lot better having them to myself. I guess in a normal marriage that wouldn't be true, but it is in my case."

He was silent, cutting his veal, rolling the pasta against his spoon expertly—a skill I never mastered and much admired. My last comment must have stumped him, so finally I asked, "Mike, what did the detectives find?"

He swallowed and looked relieved. "Seems a woman named Marie Winton lived in the house from 1958 until 1967. They think she's probably the skeleton. They're tracking relatives right now to find out if she really disappeared. If she did, they'll get something for DNA tests."

I wasn't sure how to proceed, but the word cautiously came to my mind. "I know about her from city records," I said. "And during the time she lived there, a company named Martin Properties, Inc. was the owner on the tax records." I certainly wasn't going to tell him about Marie Winton's diary, and I didn't feel a bit guilty—well, maybe a smidgeon. But I figured whoever made those midnight calls had no idea the diary existed, let alone that it was in my hand.

"Kelly, you've been doing what I told you not to," Mike's voice was stern, but he didn't explode.

"Just investigating old records. I'm surprised your detectives didn't do it sooner. But I've sworn off. I'm leaving it up to the police." And the story of that last call, threatening my girls, came tumbling out.

"Kelly, these people mean business. You not only have to quit prowling around, you have to watch your every step and take extra precautions with the girls. I don't want them scared, let alone hurt. I'm not even sure Theresa is enough protection. I don't trust your ex one bit." He looked so serious, I almost defended Tim.

"Mike, he's the girls' father. And he says he came here to protect them. He won't let anything happen." I wished I was as sure as I sounded. Changing the subject, I asked, "Hasn't this been sent to the cold case division?"

He snorted. "Division? It's two guys, and they have probably 400 cases, lots of them newer than this. It's on the back burner for them." He saw the expression on my face and said, "I know, Kelly. And I'm sorry. But that's how it is."

I toyed with my veal, until he asked, "What's Martin Properties?"

It was my turn to shrug. "Darned if I know. I don't have any idea how to find out who was behind that. All I know is they're not in business today, nobody in real estate has heard of them, and I don't know where to go next. But I have a lot of questions."

"Such as?" He put down his fork and looked at me warily.

"Why would punks, as Anthony calls them, be interested in frightening me away from that house? Especially since it's already public knowledge that the skeleton has been found. I can see someone wanting to keep it a secret, but now…it doesn't make sense. Anthony says someone's paying them, but why?"

"He's probably right. Maybe if we knew more about Marie Winton, we'd know who's behind this."

"Like who killed her?"

"Well, yeah, especially that. But maybe there's something else in the house you haven't found yet. Letters, bank statements, some kind of paper trail."

My mind jumped to the diary that I was determined not to mention. "I can't take those plaster walls back to studs, and I'm not sure where else to look. But what if I found a diary?" I was sort of testing the waters.

"Kelly, leave it to the cops."

I pushed my pasta around. "I will. I'm scared now, for the first time, really scared." I paused a minute, the salad speared on my fork frozen in space. "Did you realize Tim already knew about the skeleton the other night when he tried to act so surprised?" Just because I wasn't digging into the mystery didn't mean I couldn't ask questions.

Mike lost his wary attitude and became my co-conspirator. "Yeah, I did. His expression was fake, and he talked too loud about it."

"And too long. What if it's the skeleton that brought him back to town pretending to fear for the girls' safety? I don't know who told him, but more important why did he make such a fuss about it the other evening?"

"Because I was there?" Mike asked.

"Maybe," I said thoughtfully, "or maybe to scare the Guthries away from buying my house."

"I don't follow. Why would a skeleton in another house scare them away from this one?"

She pushed her plate aside. "Or away from dealing with me."

"Kelly, don't get paranoid about this." Then, changing the subject, "Tell me about your new house."

I fell for the diversion, describing the wonderful details of the Hunt house.

"I hope I'll be invited to see it," Mike said.

"Of course," I replied, but I wondered just where this relationship was going. So far, I didn't feel a spark—or maybe with Tim newly resurfaced, I was scared off relationships. *But,* I told myself, *you're not twenty anymore. You know that relationships grow and develop. The days of instant head-over-heels love are over.* I thought fleetingly of Joanie, still searching for that kind of romance.

****

Tim actually brought the girls home before eight, but he didn't come near the house. Instead he let Theresa walk them in. Mike and I were in the living room, sipping coffee.

"How was dinner, girls?" I asked as they both hurtled themselves at me, landing in my lap and sliding to the floor in a jumble.

"We had pigs in a blanket, just like Maggie said," Em's voice was pitched high with excitement. "It was really good. But the service was soooooo slow"—she rolled her eyes for dramatic effect—"that Daddy said we're never going there again."

"And some friend of Theresa's that Daddy knew came and sat at our booth for a long time," Maggie chimed in. "He had a ponytail and real baggy pants, but he was fun. He teased us, and then he bought us those little balls they have in a machine there. His name is Joe."

I looked at Theresa. Long hair and baggy pants meant a gang member to me, just like those who were trying to scare me.

Quietly, Theresa said, "It wasn't anybody I wanted to see. I think he worked with Dad a couple of times, and that's how Mr. Spencer met him."

Mike and I exchanged long looks. And then I said to the girls, "Well, I'm sure it's not anybody your dad knows well. It was nice of him to buy you girls those little rubber balls. Did he let you put the quarters in the machine yourselves?" That was always a big deal when the girls went to Ol' South—putting quarters in the machine that spit out balls. Half the time, they both lost their balls on the floor under the table and ended in tears.

"He did," Em said triumphantly, "and I still have mine." Then she looked a little crestfallen. "It's my second one, because I lost the first one."

"I told you to be careful," Maggie scolded.

"Okay, girls, up to bed. No baths tonight. Maggie, did you finish your homework?"

"All but a little bit."

"I'll help her," Theresa said, shepherding them along. "Come on, girls, upstairs."

"Mom, will you kiss us goodnight?" Em's voice held a quaver.

"Of course."

The child turned and waved. "Good night, Mr. Mike. I'm sorry I couldn't have dinner with you."

"Me too," Mike replied, grinning.

After the girls went upstairs, Mike didn't linger long. I walked him part way out the sidewalk to the curb. "Thanks, Mike. I enjoyed the evening—and your choice of dinner and wine was perfect."

"I enjoyed it, too, Kelly. I hope we can do it again soon."

"Me, too," I said and turned before he could try to kiss me. Was it my imagination or was he leaning in for a kiss? It wasn't my imagination that I wasn't ready for that, was almost scared in fact.

I remembered another question. "Mike, wouldn't a body that was in a house long enough to be a skeleton smell bad, at least at first? So bad the neighbors would notice?"

He rolled his eyes and said, "'Night, Kelly."

But as he left I had a stab of conscience about the diary in my closet. No, I told myself, it wouldn't help them. It was a personal thing.

****

Two nights later, I was sound asleep when the noise started. Racing motors, up and down the street. Shaking my head to bring myself to consciousness, I sat up, listening. It was definitely cars racing up and down the street. I threw back the covers and padded barefoot to the window to peer out. At least three cars were racing down the street. They looked like low-riders, old cars fixed so that their back ends nearly dragged the pavement. As I watched, they raced past, then turned at the corner and whirled back. *They're going to defeat me by sleep deprivation.*

"Mom, I'm scared." Maggie stood in the doorway.

"Come get in my bed," I said. "You'll be safe. I won't let anything happen to you." Silently I cursed whoever would frighten my children.

Em stumbled sleepily down the hall almost immediately. "I hear a lot of noise," she said. "What is it?"

"Cars," I said. "Someone racing cars up and down the street. It has nothing to do with us." Even as I said it, I knew that was a lie.

Theresa. I told the girls to stay tucked in my bed and went to the guest room. Theresa stood staring out the window.

"Theresa, please get away from the window."

"Why?" the girl asked. "They can't see me. And they're punks. They won't really hurt anyone. They just want to frighten you."

"How do you know that?" Every fiber in me was on alert.

The girl shrugged. "I just know," she said. "I go to school with guys like them. They're all show, but they're really cowards."

"Theresa, come away from the window, please. They've shot up the front door once. I don't want to take a chance. Come get in my bed with the girls."

Theresa shook her head. "I'm not afraid. I'll sleep in my own bed." She turned her back on me.

I wondered from her words if Theresa knew more about this than she was letting on, but I didn't know how to question her, how to find out without making her clam up permanently. Belatedly, I thought to call 911. But, instead, I checked on the girls and then ran downstairs to fish Mike's card out of my purse and call his number. When I told him what was going on, the noise still roaring outside the house, he said, "We'll be right there. Why didn't you call 911?"

I didn't even answer.

The police came, sirens roaring, and, of course, the cars left before they got there. So a chase wasn't effective. The cars apparently separated and disappeared into the tiny back streets that lace Fairmount.

Mike came to the door. When I opened it, he said, "Kelly, have you seen this?"

I stepped outside. There was a large black bull's eye on my new front door, apparently painted with a can of spray paint. Granted, it was the most irregular bull's eye I'd ever seen since it had to straddle the many panes of glass and the wood between them. But there was no mistaking what it was.

I looked at Mike. "What does it mean?"

"It means what you already know. You're a target." He looked grim.

I summoned up all my bravado. "After I gave up investigating?"

"Did you tell them that?"

"No chance. But if they're watching me so closely, they should know."

"It's not," Mike said, "a chance I'm willing to take. Turn on your alarm, lock your doors, and call 911 before you call me if anything happens."

I looked long and hard at him. "Yes, sir, and...thanks, Mike. You make me feel safe." I wished I could hug him or somehow get closer to him to say thank you, but I wasn't comfortable with it. Maybe this was just the wrong time.

Upstairs the girls were huddled in my bed, clutching each other, and Em was crying.

"Hey," I said. "Mike says it's okay. We can go to sleep." Well, he didn't exactly say that, but I thought it was a good white lie.

Within minutes, both girls were asleep. But once again, I lay awake, wide-eyed, reviewing all that was going on in my life.

Next morning I was barely settled with coffee and the newspaper, the national news on TV, when the phone rang. I answered cautiously.

"Just what was going on last night?" Florence Dodson demanded. "It kept me awake half the night. I'm sure it had something to do with that girl you've taken in to live with you."

"Mrs. Dodson, I have no idea what was going on or why. It bothered me as much as it did you. And I called the police."

"Well, I see there's a bull's eye on your front door. They must have done that. So you're the reason the neighborhood is being disturbed." Her tone was accusing.

I was too exhausted to argue with her. "If I'm the reason, you don't have to worry much longer. I'm moving in a month." I hung up the phone before she could answer, but I knew a call from Mom would be next.

Within ten minutes, the phone rang again, and it was my mother. "What kind of teenage hooligan have you taken into that house with my grandchildren?" she demanded.

"Been talking to Florence, haven't you?" I didn't hang up on Mom, but I didn't give her a lot of answers either.

Chapter Eight

I read the paper distractedly—really only leafed through it, sipping at coffee, and mostly staring out the kitchen window. With a start, I realized I needed to get the lawn guy to clean up the yard, rake leaves, and pull out dead plants left from summer. I'd completely ignored what had once been a garden so charming that I was probably too full of pride. *Too busy,* I told myself. *Gardening would be good for me. I always enjoyed it. I'm trying to do too much.* Vowing I would take better care of the Hunts' garden, I went to wake the girls.

They, too, were dragging. "Can't we have a hooky day?"

"I think I'm sick and can't go to school."

I held firm. They just ·had a hooky day, and they were going to school. Theresa, on the other hand, was up, dressed, ready for the day, and text messaging on her phone.

I went back downstairs, fixed breakfast, and the morning moved along as usual. Anthony was cheerful when he came to get Theresa, until he saw the front door. "What happened? Someone give the girls spray paint?"

I shook my head and told him the whole story.

He swore softly, so the girls wouldn't hear him. "I have paint left. I fix today after I take Theresa to school. I'll have to scrape the windows. Take a long time."

And it will take him away from the Fairmount house again.

As if he read my thoughts, Anthony said, "Don't you worry, Miss Kelly. I'll finish that house."

"Thanks. I know you will. I just hope it's not jinxed."

He crossed himself. "Don't even say it."

The girls were still grumpy when I dropped them at their respective schools, and they pretty much ignored my pretend cheerfulness when I wished them a happy day.

"Can you come get me early, Mom?" Em asked. "I think I'll be tired."

I smiled to myself. "Miss Emily will see that you take a nap."

Em rolled her eyes and marched independently off to her classroom. But just before she went into the room, she turned and blew me a kiss. I returned the gesture.

Then I went to my office.

"Message for you," Keisha said, handing me a pink slip. "Call Anthony."

Then why did you hand me the slip? I checked myself—I was as grumpy as the girls. I dialed Anthony's cell phone, and he answered promptly.

"Miss Kelly, there's one of those things—what you call them?"

"What things, Anthony?"

"Like was painted on your front door."

"Oh, a bull's eye."

"Yeah, there's one on the front door here, too."

I sighed. "Okay. Do the best with it you can."

"That was a newly refinished door," he moaned. "Not as easy to fix as paint."

"Do what you can," I repeated, feeling defeated. "I'll come right over."

I went to the house, knowing there was nothing I could do. But I had a question for Anthony.

After I saw the door, I said to him, "I simply can't call the insurance company again. Do what you can. If we have to have a new door, so be it."

"I scrape and fix,' he assured me.

"Anthony, do you know someone named Joe, a young guy?" I repeated what the girls told me about the encounter at Ol' South.

"Yeah, I know him." Anthony spat off the porch where we stood. "He's no good. Doesn't want honest work for a living. I warn Theresa away from him."

"She seems to have believed you, said he was no friend of hers."

He shrugged. "I don't know if that's the truth or not. I think she likes him and just doesn't want me to know. He work with me some summers ago, when Mr. Spencer was still around. Lazy, steals little thing—you name it, he does it. But he's sweet on Theresa. I tell her no way. He's older anyway, too old for her."

Sweet on Theresa. Maybe the whole thing has to do with Theresa being at my house and not with me or the skeleton at all. No, they mentioned the house and the skeleton. "Do you think he's part of this bunch that's trying to scare me?"

Anthony nodded. "I think maybe but got no proof. Theresa says she didn't recognize him last night."

So Theresa talked to her father about last night's incident. I found that interesting because she hadn't said a thing to me this morning. In fact, she was unusually quiet and not even interested in helping Em.

Anthony went back about his work, and I stood on the porch, thinking how confusing everything was. Down the street an elderly woman, wearing an apron over a ratty sweater and wool skirt, swept her sidewalk. Impulsively I headed down the steps to speak to her. On my way I passed two nicely painted houses, one with a painted iron fence enclosing its front yard and the other with neat flowerbeds. Then a house badly in need of paint and shoring up, with an abandoned washing machine on the front porch and a yard almost bare of even crabgrass. The sidewalk in front of this house was cracked and dotted with holes, forcing me to watch where I stepped. I crossed the street and approached the woman.

"Excuse me," I began.

"Oh, dear, I just never buy or give to people who come to the house," the woman said, "even though you look a nice enough sort."

I hoped my amusement wasn't obvious. "No, no, I'm not selling or soliciting. I own that house down the street." I pointed. "I just wanted to ask you about one of the residents. How long have you lived here?"

"Since 1949," she said proudly, leaning a bit on her broom. "My husband, God rest his soul, bought this house when we married. Paid $4,000 for it, he did. I've lived here ever since."

"Do you remember Marie Winton who lived in the house from 1958 until 1967?"

She sniffed a little. "Never did know her name. She wasn't the neighborly sort, and back then, this was a real neighborhood. We all knew all about each other, walked in and out of almost any house almost without knocking. But I know who you mean. Pretty young thing. Dark hair."

"Yes, she wore it flipped up. Tell me about her— did she work, maybe teach school? Did she live there alone?"

"Now, I don't spread stories, but as far as I could tell she didn't work. And she lived there alone but there was a man there a lot. Drove a big black Cadillac, he did, and always parked it in back, so one of the neighbors told me. I'm not the prying kind myself."

"And he visited her often?"

"Most every day at noon. Stayed a couple of hours usually. Once in a while he came at night, but not very often. I don't know what she did the rest of the day."

For a woman who's not the prying type, you know a lot, and it's all most interesting. Marie Winton was what Mom would call a kept woman.

"Far as I could tell, she only lived there for two years. Then the house sat vacant for a lot of years."

The answer to the odor question. That whole time there was a corpse turning into a skeleton.

"During the years the house was empty, did any of the neighbors ever comment on anything about it?" I hesitated. "Like a bad smell?"

The other woman scoffed. "The only bad smell was from the rabbits the people next door raised. Must have been a thousand, before zoning laws made them move. Smelled worse than a barnyard. Nobody walked down that way if they could avoid it."

"You've been most helpful, Mrs....oh, I'm sorry. I forgot my manners. I'm Kelly O'Connell." I held out a hand.

The woman took my hand in her left hand and said, "Pleased to know you. I'm Mrs. William Glenn. My husband, he was a teller at the old Fort Worth National Bank, all those years. Now it's called heaven only knows what. Our children are grown and gone, but they're good to me."

"Mrs. Glenn, here's my card. I'm a realtor in the area. If you ever need anything, you just call me."

"Oh, dearie, I'm not gonna sell this house. They'll have to carry me out and then the kids can sell it."

"Oh, no, that's not what I mean. I mean if you yourself ever need any help, anyone to get groceries, or anything like that, I'd be pleased to help."

"Why, thank you, dearie. You're a sweet girl." A moment's pause, and then, "You'll let me know if that skeleton is Marie Winton, won't you?"

"Yes, ma'am, I surely will." I hadn't mentioned the skeleton, and I saw no need to confirm that it was Marie Winton at this point. But clearly Mrs. Glenn knew about it. So did everyone else in Fort Worth.

I nearly sang as I went back down the street. My cell phone rang, and I answered to hear Mike Shandy say, "They found Marie Winton's family. They confirm that she went missing and was never heard from again."

"When?" I asked.

"September 1959."

"Mike, have I got a story to tell you."

"Save it for the detectives, Kelly. They're on your trail."

"I'll be in my office the rest of the day," I said stiffly. If Mike was going to follow procedure, so would I. But I really wanted to call Mrs. Hunt and walk through her house. I'd put it off till tomorrow.

I called Keisha, who announced she wanted Chinese for lunch, so I stopped by Ho Ho next to the Grill—the name always turned me off the place but Christian insisted it was great for takeout. I got a beef and broccoli and sweet-and-sour pork, figuring we could share, which we did. Keisha claimed the office had been quiet except for some guy named Buck Conroy who called four times.

I called Mrs. Hunt first, arranging to walk through the house the next morning. "Mrs. Hunt? It's Kelly O'Connell. I wondered if we could set a time for me to walk through the house again and talk about what furniture you wanted to leave and so on. And also I didn't look at the guest house. It seems I will have someone living in it—the young girl you met the other day. Maybe tomorrow morning, either 9:30 or 10:00?"

"Of course," Mrs. Hunt said, "Anytime. Just come after you get your girls to school. I'll have the coffee pot on and a fresh coffeecake."

I could almost smell the coffeecake in my mind, and my mood brightened. "I'll be there," I said.

****

Afterward, I wondered if I was expecting Mike Hammer or Sergeant Friday from *Dragnet*. Buck Conroy was an ordinary man, probably in his late forties, mostly lean but a few more beers might push his belly over his belt. His hair was gray at the temples—distinguished, I thought—but his eyes were world-weary, as though it would take something big to surprise him. He flashed an ID at Keisha, who simply nodded in my direction.

"Ms. O'Connell?" he said as I stood to meet him and hold out a hand. "Detective Buck Conroy."

"I've been expecting you," I said, motioning for him to sit down, all the while wondering if I was about to get a lecture on meddling in police business.

"Hear you found out some information from a neighbor," he said. "Haven't had time to get around to that. Who was it?"

"Mrs. William Glenn, a sweet little old lady."

"I'm sure," he said dryly. "Address?"

I shrugged. "On the east side of the street, about halfway down the block. The house with the old-fashioned nandinas."

"Ms. O'Connell, if you're going to do police work for us, you'll have to be more precise with the details." Now those world-weary eyes were laughing, and I laughed too.

"Call me Kelly," I said. "And I am not going to do police work. This was just a neighborly visit." If Mike hadn't told him about the threat to the girls, I wasn't going to. "I hear you found the victim's family."

"We think so, but let's go back to Mrs. Glenn first."

So I repeated the encounter as I remembered it, which was almost verbatim. "She seemed to disapprove of Ms. Winton. I think my mother would call her a kept woman."

"Well, I know some that would like being kept, and some men that would like to have someone to keep—they just never seemed to mesh," he said philosophically. "Now we got to find out who was driving that Cadillac. I suppose license plate's too much to hope for."

"You won't get it from Mrs. Glenn—she claims never to have seen the car. She's not, after all, a gossip. Just heard about it from the neighbors."

"Any chance some of those neighbors are still around?"

"You can try, but I doubt it. That's a pretty fluid neighborhood or has been until recently."

He flipped his tiny notebook shut. "Well, damn, I thought you'd walk the block for us."

I didn't know whether to bristle or not, but when I saw he was smiling, I smiled too and said, "When I get around to it."

"Touché. Now about the family—they'd like to see the house, specifically the cupboard. It's kind of macabre to my way of thinking, but it's your call."

"When do they want to see it?"

"They're arriving this afternoon from Crawford, a small town outside Waco. I'm sure you've heard of it these days, president and all. Just a couple of brothers and, I think, one sister-in-law. Parents are long dead, of course. Brother tells me the mother died of a broken heart. Seems to think not only should I have solved this murder, I should have prevented it."

"So they're angry." It was an obvious statement.

"They're plain, small-town folk, and I think they're overwhelmed, maybe confused. We'll treat them nice."

"Anthony, the guy that's redoing the house for me, should be there tomorrow all day. I'll tell him to expect them. You'll be bringing them?"

"Nope. I got detecting to do. But someone from headquarters will escort them. Mayor likes us to treat people like this with kid gloves, so they don't make a stink." He rose. "Thanks for your help. If you run down Martin Properties, let me know. Here's my card. I expect we'll talk again."

I took the card and found myself saying, "I hope so," and then thought it was a wildly inappropriate comment. I didn't mean I wanted to talk to him necessarily. I meant that I wanted the case to move along.

Conroy just smiled, gave me a mock salute, and left.

I got out the phone book, turned to Martin, and stared in dismay. There were pages of Martins.

****

Next morning, the newspaper headline over the article read, "Skeleton identified; relatives arriving." A brief article rehashed the story of the finding of the skeleton, identified the victim as Marie Winton, and said the family was coming to Fort Worth from the small town of Crawford. Of course it played up President George W. Bush's connection to Crawford, which had absolutely nothing to do with the Winton family. I sighed. I hated to see the story in the public attention again.

After I got the girls delivered to their schools and told Keisha where I'd be, I headed for the Hunt house. *I must stop calling it the Hunt house and start calling it mine.* I parked on the street and got out to walk up that wonderful path to the front door. Only then did I notice that there was a bull's eye painted on the sidewalk in front of the Hunts' house. My first thought was, *At least they didn't disfigure the house and scare the Hunts.* The second was, *Damn. Whoever it is has made the connection. I thought once we moved here, we might be safe. How did they know?*

Mrs. Hunt greeted me warmly, but I was almost brusque as I asked, "Mrs. Hunt, have you seen what's painted on your sidewalk?"

"The bull's eye? Adolph found it yesterday morning when he went to get the paper. We heard more street noise than usual that night. I suppose it was just kids." She shrugged, apparently not too concerned. "We'll get it off before you move in."

"Oh, I'm not worried about that," I said. "I'm just sorry that it happened."

"Me, too. Come in and have some coffee and cake, and then we'll get down to business."

I spent over two hours there. The Hunts would leave almost everything in the living room and dining room, taking only two occasional tables.

They would take all the bedroom furniture, which suited me fine. I made scribbled notes as I went through the house, mentally placing the bedroom furniture we already had in this house, consigning living and dining room furniture to a garage sale.

"Now," Mrs. Hunt said, "you must go through the guest house. I fixed it up for our niece, who came to visit often."

The guest house had an L-shaped living area that wrapped around the bathroom. In the small corner, there was an efficiency kitchen, complete with a combination unit that was both stove and refrigerator and yet was still just counter-size, a sink, and a few cabinets.

"I'll leave the dishes," Mrs. Hunt said. "I already have too many."

There were plain white pottery dishes, a few pots— but good heavy stainless—and an iron skillet. "Most people don't know how to cook in these today," Mrs. Hunt said, "but I wouldn't trade mine for anything."

"Would you tell me how to cook with it?" I asked, mentally moving the skillet inside the house.

The whole place had bright yellow walls, royal blue woodwork—an odd combination that I might have thought would never work until I saw it—and blue-and-yellow plaid curtains. The comforter on the bed and the pillow shams echoed the blue-and-yellow color scheme, with an obviously cheery effect. A small writing table, a rattan chair, a bookcase filled the rest of the small room. I would add a TV for Theresa.

When I left, just before lunch, I was greatly cheered. I went by the office but nothing pressing had happened, so I went to the Fairmount house. Anthony was there. So were Marie Winton's brothers, David and George, and her sister-in-law, Phyllis, whom George introduced as "the little woman." Both men were, I guessed, close to seventy, their faces and hands tanned and gnarled by years spent outdoors. They called me "ma'am." A policewoman, out of uniform, accompanied them and introduced herself as Sally McLean. She called me "Ms. O'Connell."

"Ms. O'Connell, we appreciate you making the house available to us. Mr. Anthony here has shown us the…ah…cupboard in question and detailed how he found…ah…the remains."

Hard to be delicate, Sally. Why not say it like it is? "I'm glad to help," I offered condolences to the family. They were actually standing in the kitchen, looking at the charred wood. It went through my mind that I should tell these people about the diary. They would treasure it as a remembrance of their sister. But I couldn't bring the words out of my mouth. Someday I'd get it to them, but not now, not until the case was solved.

"Mr. Anthony said there's been a fire," the proper Ms. McLean said. "Vandals, I believe?"

"Why would anyone burn Marie's house?" Phyllis wailed.

I declined to point out that it hadn't been Marie's house in a long time. "Probably to cover up something they didn't want found—or couldn't find themselves." I thought Ms. McLean should have come up with that or a better answer.

"Poor, poor Marie," Phyllis said, wringing her hands.

"Marie couldn't wait to get out of Crawford," George said. "Too tiny to hold her. Didn't want to marry a farmer like her daddy or her brothers. But we never thought…." He shook his head in disbelief.

"Never thought," echoed David.

Phyllis broke in with, "The boys are somewhat ashamed. They hope this story doesn't get back to Crawford."

I was dumbfounded and had no reply, but Ms. McLean rushed in with, "No need for it to. We'll try to keep any more mention out of the paper." She neglected to mention it had already been in the *Fort Worth Star-Telegram.*

George warmed to his subject. "She used to write us letters, all about the man she was going to marry and how busy and happy she was, said sometimes they went to one or two small restaurants but mostly they stayed in. Thought it was odd. Marie was always on the go, never content to sit at home."

I thought I knew the reason: the man she was going to marry was already married and couldn't be seen with her in public. But I kept quiet.

George went on, "Then one day the letters just stopped. We finally notified the authorities, oh, 'bout six months later, but they couldn't find any trace of her. Nobody could figure it out." He paused and then added bitterly, "Guess now we know why."

"Did the authorities search the house?" *If the authorities were notified, why wasn't it in the cold case records? Buck*

Conroy should have found it, but I could see him shrugging his shoulders and saying, "Just slipped through the cracks."

"I believe they did, but they didn't find nothing."

I wondered what they smelled. "The man she was going to marry—do you remember his name?"

George shook his head. "Maybe the missus does," he said turning to his wife.

"Martin," she said clearly. "Martin something, but I don't remember what." She could, I thought, be an attractive woman but her boxy-cut suit—apparently her Sunday best—did nothing to flatter her, nor did the perm that added kinks to what might have been soft, gray hair.

Martin?" I repeated. "Are you sure that wasn't his last name?"

"Quite sure," Phyllis said. "She called him Marty. We never met him, of course."

"Did you ever see a picture?"

"No." She sniffed, obviously still indignant over the snub.

"But they were making wedding plans?"

"That's what she told us...."

George interrupted. "Why are you asking us all these questions? You're not with the authorities. They're the ones who are supposed to be solving this. We should talk to them."

"Of course," I said as graciously as I could. "Have you talked to Detective Conroy?"

"Who's he?"

I thought it wouldn't be tactful to answer, "Someone who's all tied up with other cases." Instead, I said, "Let me give you his cell phone number" and fished in my purse for the card. As I read it off, George said, "I don't know as I trust a man who has a cell phone and not a regular office."

And how could he function as a detective without leaving a "regular" office?

I was looking for a way to escape, but I knew I couldn't abandon Anthony, who stood silently by, looking distressed. Phyllis saved us. "George, it's dinner time. I saw a Denny's down by the motel. Let's go eat. The burned smell is making me slightly nauseous."

I always disliked that word—and people who used it.

For some strange reason, Anthony's favorite phrase went through my head, and I thought, *Mother of God, they're staying at the Clayton House.* The Clayton House was probably the cheapest, oldest, most run-down motel in our part of town. There was a nice Ramada down the street in one direction and a Residence Inn and Court-yard by Marriott in the other. But they were staying at the Clayton House.

They left without a "Thank you" or "Nice to meet you" or any of the polite vagaries. When they were gone, Anthony said, "I feel sorry for them, but I don't like them."

"Don't worry about it," I said, "you don't have to put up with them."

****

Halloween was a success—sort of. The girls went off to school, dressed in their costumes, Em feeling, she said, "like a princess" in a pink tulle tutu and pink leotard, with a silver crown on her head and a silver wand in her hand. Privately I thought Maggie's deliber-ately drab costume was less attractive, but Maggie was most pleased. I promised to take them trick-or- treating in the early evening, dropped them at their schools, and rushed to the Dollar Store to buy candy to give out at our house.

Mike Shandy called the office just before I left to get the girls. "You plan on taking the girls trick-or-treating?"

"Of course. I hate to leave the house, but they're set on it."

"Let me take them and you stay with the house. I'm not comfortable about the whole thing."

I knew I should listen to him, but I said, "Mike, they can't go trick-or-treating with a police officer—and even if you're off-duty, everyone in the neighborhood knows who you are."

"Okay, if you promise to stay on your block, I'll watch the house and you take them. I got off duty specially."

I started to bristle. He was treating me like a little child, but then I remembered how scared I'd been a couple of nights ago, and I agreed.

And that's how Tim Spencer arrived at what he still considered to be "his" house and found the door opened by the policeman for whom he'd developed a definite dislike.

"Trick-or-treating?" Mike quipped, as he later recounted the incident to me.

"I came to see my daughters in their Halloween costumes." Tim's voice was thick with offense.

"Oh. They're trick-or-treating, but Kelly said they'd stay in this block. You can go look or come in. I'm just minding the house, till Kelly gets back."

"Well, you can go now," Tim said dismissively. "I'll 'mind the house.'" His tone indicated that he was definitely mocking Mike.

"I don't think so," Mike said he told him. "I told Kelly I'd watch the house."

According to Mike, they sat in uneasy silence. Two or three trick-or-treat groups came to the door, and Mike greeted them cheerfully. In turn, they'd say, "Trick-or-treat, Mr. Mike," and he doled out the candy. Their cheerful greetings to him didn't improve Tim's mood at all.

When the girls and I came in, I clearly didn't expect to see those two men sitting there together, and I barely managed a civil hello to Tim. The girls greeted both with equal cheer, "Hi, Dad. Hi, Mr. Mike."

"I came to see you in your costumes," Tim said petulantly. Clearly he did not feel they were making enough of a fuss over him.

"Did you bring us treats?" Maggie asked.

"No," he said shortly. "You've got enough in that bag."

Without hesitation, she whirled around, "Mike, can I help pass out treats?"

"I think I'll turn that over to your mom, Maggie. I've got to be going. But I like your outfit—what's that character's name again?"

Pleased, Maggie said, "Hermione. I'm Hermione."

"You sure are," he said, hugging her.

Tim left hastily a moment after Mike, and I let the girls help give out treats until about eight, when I turned out the lights and signaled that the evening was over.

Upstairs I found Theresa watching from her bedroom window. "I wanted to be sure Joe didn't come," she explained. "He didn't."

****

I am a list maker, and the next day I sat at the kitchen counter, making a list of what had to do before the garage sale. I'd studied the calendar. If the girls and I were going to move November 15, I'd have the garage sale the next weekend. Too bad I'd already missed the neighborhood garage sale but there was no help for that. Then I listed:

Sort girls closets
Clean my closet
Go through kitchen cupboards
Tag and mark major pieces of furniture
Empty garage

The garage. I phoned the Worthington, and asked for Tim Spencer's room.

"I'm sorry. We do not have a guest by that name," the operator said.

Puzzled, I asked, "Can you tell me when he checked out? It must be within the last"—I thought a minute—"two days."

"Checking my records, I don't find a guest by that name the last month."

I scratched my head. If Tim wasn't at the Worthington, where was he? What if he'd kept the girls too long one night and I'd tried to call him there? Not being able to find him didn't particularly bother me as long as the girls were safe—I'd just as soon never hear from him again. But it was strange—and I'd get the truth before he took them anywhere again.

That afternoon, with both girls in the car, I asked casually, "Did your dad ever take you to the hotel where he's staying?"

They chorused "No," and Maggie asked, "Why?"

"I just wondered," I said vaguely.

I was not left to wonder for long. I purchased a pre-cooked roast chicken at Central Market, along with some mac and cheese. *An expensive way to feed them,* I acknowledged, *but healthy and they'll like it.* They did. Theresa went to have dinner with her family and spend the night—Anthony had described it as a trial visit. So I had the girls to myself and was thoroughly enjoying it, when the phone rang.

When I answered with, "Hello," Tim said casually, "Kelly, I thought it was only fair to tell you that I've filed papers for custody of the girls. My lawyer says it will have to go to mediation, of course, and I gave him your lawyer's name."

Surprised but not particularly upset, I told him he was wasting his money. "But Tim Spencer, if you drag those girls into this and make them testify or put them in an awkward situation, I'll have your hide!" Deep down, Tim probably knew it was a lost cause before he began, but he was punishing me. Tim had left the marriage and then blamed it all on me. And now he was punishing me. But I would not let him punish the girls.

"By the way, where are you staying? I tried to call the Worthington today, and they'd never had a guest registered under your name."

'Why did you call?" he countered.

"I need you to get your stuff out of the garage. I'm having a garage sale next weekend, and we're moving on the fifteenth."

"You sold the house?" He was aghast.

"Yes. You knew I would. I just found a buyer sooner than I expected."

It was Tim's turn to pause. There was a long silence, but at length he said, "Well, I don't know what you want me to do with the stuff in the garage. I have no place to put it, and I can't ship it to California. It's not worth the freight."

"I don't care what you do with it. Either it's gone by next Sunday night or I'll call Goodwill. And I'll have my lawyer officially notify your lawyer. This is my property, and you have no right to store your belongings here."

"Bitch!" he spat out.

I remembered when that would have broken my heart. Now it didn't faze me. "By the way, Tim, where *are* you staying?"

"Try the Days Inn on Highway 30 out in White Settlement," he said, naming a suburb to the west of the city, and slammed down the phone.

Maggie was watching me attentively. "Was that Dad?"

"Yes, sweetie, it was."

"I could hear him yell at you, Mom. That wasn't very nice of him."

"No," I agreed, "it wasn't. But he was upset. Always remember, he's upset with me, not you."

"I don't like him," Em said and ate another mouthful of mac and cheese.

****

I spent the week getting ready for the garage sale, with the girls' help. "Let's pull all your clothes out of your drawers and closet and see what still fits, what you want to keep and what we should get rid of," I said, trying to make it a game.

Maggie wanted to discard nothing. "This is too small," she said, holding up a velvet dress that she'd probably worn once to what occasion I couldn't remember. "But Em can wear it."

And Em will probably only wear it once too. But she put it in the "keep" pile. That pile grew much larger than the "discard" pile, to my dismay.

The same wasn't true of my closet. I discarded things with gay abandon and then remembered all those clothes that I'd once loved and now couldn't remember where they were. Gone, I guessed, to garage sales or Goodwill. I sorted the discard pile again and pulled out a few things, but I was pretty much heartless.

Tim called Saturday morning and wanted to take the girls to the zoo on Sunday. I agreed and thought that if it weren't for his lady friend I'd suggest we all go together. Fort Worth has a world-class, state-of-the-art zoo for a city its size, and it was always a joy to watch the girls run from one outdoor exhibit to another. They loved everything from elephants to meerkats, and Maggie particularly liked to ride the zoo train. We all avoided the herpetarium. But, given the girlfriend, I suggested he pick them up at 1:00 and hung up thinking I'd have to get back in the habit of taking them to Sunday school and church.

Then Mike Shandy called and asked if he could fix supper—at our house, of course—that night. "That'd be great, Mike, but I have the girls. They're going to the zoo with their father tomorrow afternoon—would that be a better time?"

"Nope, I have to work. And I'd love to fix dinner for all of you. I'll come up with something kid friendly."

I laughed. "Okay, but I really can cook. Next time it's my turn. Tonight I'll do dishes."

"It's a deal."

Chapter Nine

Mike brought the perfect dinner for the girls—soft drinks, hot dogs, potato chips, pickles, and ice cream. He even brought paper plates, grinning as he said, "I didn't want you to have to work too hard."

"Mike, the mind reader," I said. He really is something else, I told myself. But I wasn't ready to say that to him aloud. Instead, I said, "I really worked hard today, getting things ready for the garage sale. I think I've got a handle on it."

"Still need me to move furniture?"

"If you can, I'll be grateful. Theresa and I couldn't possibly get that sofa and the huge chairs outside. Let's just pray for a warm, clear day."

We ate in the kitchen, and Theresa joined us, seeming to enjoy herself and blushing when Mike asked her about boyfriends. "I haven't met anyone my dad approves of," she said. Then, to my surprise, she added, "I think maybe he's right."

"Probably is," Mike said. "Pretty girl like you must have guys swarming around." Then she really blushed to the roots of her hair.

"I think Joe has a crush on her," Maggie announced.

Just as Mike asked, "Who's Joe?" Theresa said rather sternly, "He does not. Just hush, Maggie," and Maggie subsided, her feelings hurt. Theresa saw that she'd hurt the child and came around the kitchen island to hug her. "I'm sorry, Maggie. Joe's a sensitive subject." She ruffled Maggie's hair, and within minutes Maggie was back to her happy self.

After supper, it took three minutes to clean up—mostly rinsing disposable plates and putting them in the recycle bin, although I did say I'd clean the grill later. We all went outside to enjoy one of the last of fall's mild evenings.

"Daylight savings ends in a week," Mike said. "We better play ball while we can still see." So he threw the ball for the girls—Maggie was pretty good at catching it, but Em let it bounce on the ground and ran squealing after it. Theresa proved to be really good at throwing it back to Mike, who whistled and said, "You got some arm, Theresa. You ever play baseball?"

She laughed. "Just T-ball when I was little. I'm not much interested in sports."

Sitting on the sidelines, watching, I wondered what Theresa was indeed interested in. I had yet to see the rebellious girl Anthony described, and if she was in love with Joe, she hid it well. For all I could tell, she was a happy teenager and a sweet girl, albeit with more knowledge of "punks" than I had.

Mike left early, feigning exhaustion from the ball game, and I read to the girls until they went to sleep. Theresa disappeared to her room, but not before she said, "Thank you, Miss Kelly. I had a good time tonight."

****

Sunday loomed as a long day. The girls and Theresa were gone with Tim, I'd done everything I could for the garage sale, I'd sworn off digging into Marie Winton's mystery—I was at loose ends, not something that happened often in my busy life. I called Joanie, who didn't sound quite as perky.

"Joanie, let's go to brunch. Maybe LaMadeleine."

"Oooh, Kelly. Don't even mention food to me until about noon. It…the idea makes me sick."

"That bad, huh? You eating dry saltines before you get up in the morning?"

"Of course not. Why would I?"

"Because they'll really help that queasy feeling."

"Now you tell me. Doctor says I should be past this any day now, but I'm still waiting."

"Joanie, get dressed and come over here. I bet moving around will make you feel better. Do your hair. Put on your makeup."

Joanie groaned, but she agreed. It took her an hour and a half but when she appeared, I thought she looked good. I exaggerated a bit. "Joanie, you look great. I'd never know you didn't feel good—or that you were pregnant."

"I've gained five pounds," Joanie moaned. "I'm going to be big as a house, I just know it."

"You tell your boss yet?" Joanie still worked in that high-powered ad agency, and I wasn't sure how they'd feel about a pregnant "associate."

"Yeah. She was really neat about it. Said we'd have to get me some really smart-ass maternity clothes. I just don't have to mention whether I'm married or not to clients."

Instead of going out, I fixed a cheese omelet—nice and bland, I thought—and toast. "No bacon," Joanie insisted. "I can't bear the smell."

I remembered that I couldn't stand bacon when I was pregnant either. "How about mushrooms?"

"Ooh, no. And I used to love them."

I laughed. "It will all go away," I said. "You'll love those things again."

Over brunch, Joanie asked, "That policeman still hanging around you?"

"Mike Shandy? Yeah, he brought hot dogs for the girls last night. We had a good time."

"Kelly, there's something you're not telling me."

I was thoughtful for a long minute. "Mike Shandy is almost the perfect guy—good, solid, reliable, likes the girls a lot. He's everything that Tim wasn't...I'm just not sure I'm ready for a relationship."

"Kelly, Tim's been gone—what? Three years? I don't see how you've stood being alone that long."

I sighed. Joanie and I were certainly of different minds about some things. I could not, would not flit from bed to bed, nor would I ever ever expose my girls to such a lifestyle.

****

The girls returned about five-thirty, saying they'd eaten at the zoo and were full up. By then, Joanie left, saying she had a date that night. "Nothing special," she said. "I'll behave."

"I didn't eat," Theresa said. "The food's nasty. May I fix myself a grilled cheese?"

"Of course." We all gathered in the kitchen. The girls giggled and recounted tales of the gorilla house, the lions, the Texas Village, and the generally good time they'd had. Theresa joined in, laughing at their antics as they imitated the animals.

****

The next morning, I opened the paper to find the Wintons on the front page. "Family Identifies Skeleton" read the headline. I skimmed the story—all the previously quiet details came out—the victim's name, her family's identity and a repeat of the hometown story emphasizing the presidential connection. I was sure Phyllis was mortified, and, to my own dismay, the name of O'Connell and Spencer Realtors was prominently mentioned. I flipped on the kitchen TV in time to see the Wintons being interviewed by a reporter. George was once again the talker, while Phyllis and David hung back. The reporter ended his story with, "The Wintons are asking anyone who has any information about this case to come forward. Of course, they'd particularly like to talk to the late Miss Winton's fiancé, Martin, whoever he is."

Wouldn't we all?

I woke the girls and Theresa and went back downstairs to fix breakfast and lunches. When Theresa came downstairs, she was an entirely different person from the cheerful teenager of last night. She looked like she hadn't slept. Her face was pale, her eyes puffy. She barely spoke, and when Em tried to hug her, she pushed the child away.

"Theresa, you okay?"

"Yes, ma'am. Just a little tired. I...I didn't sleep well."

Breakfast was a strained affair, with all of us giving Theresa furtive looks and wondering what was wrong. I couldn't imagine what could have changed the girl overnight.

When Anthony came to get her, Theresa walked out the front door without a word, didn't greet her father, and stalked ahead of him to the car. He looked at me and shrugged. I decided I'd go to the house on Fairmount later that morning to talk to Anthony.

I got the girls to their schools, checked in at the office, and then went to Fairmount. "Anthony?"

"In the kitchen, Miss Kelly," he called.

The Black Brothers people were gone and the walls were relatively free of soot and bright paint, though the smoke smell lingered. *Enough that it made Phyllis Winton sick,* I thought wryly. Anthony had opened the windows, letting the fall breeze freshen the house as much as it could. That meant he had pried off the plywood and would have to replace it at the end of the day.

"I don't know," he said, shaking his head. "I rebuild the cabinets, but I have to start from scratch." His voice took on an ominous tone. "It will be expensive, Miss Kelly."

"Insurance will pay for that—it was the first bit of vandalism, before I stopped reporting it," I told him. "Don't worry about it. I want to fix this house."

"That's good," he said, smiling. "I fix it right."

"Anthony, about that space…." I nodded toward the hidden space that once held the skeleton.

He scratched his head.

"I told you I put spice racks on the door."

He paused a minute. "You want a plaque in her memory?" He had just the hint of a grin.

"No, no. I just…well I guess you're right. Do it as you said." Then I shifted to the topic really on my mind. "Anthony, did you notice anything different about Theresa this morning?"

"Different? How you mean different? She was quiet, but she's that way with me a lot. I think it's her age."

"She was happy and talkative last night, and this morning, she was like a different person."

He shrugged. "Teen-agers, they're moody."

"No," I said, "something happened overnight. But what? She couldn't have left the house. I'd have known." A sudden thought. "Maybe she got a text message that upset her. I know she texts a lot."

"Sure. All the kids do. She begged for the phone, and I got it for her. Not many minutes. She uses them all—that text messaging." His tone dismissed it as a bunch of foolishness, but I could see deeper implications.

Text messaging. Theresa got a text message during the night that upset her. That was it! But how would I find out what the message was or what it had to do with? I left more puzzled than when I'd arrived, but Anthony seemed untroubled. He was tearing burnt wood out of the kitchen.

Anthony did not bring Theresa back by five, as he usually did. Instead he came by himself, with his sons, whom he left in the car as though he didn't want them to hear what was going on. "Miss Kelly, she not there at the school when I go to pick her up. I call and look and I can't find her."

I sensed his fear and frustration. "Anthony, let's call some of her friends. Do you have their numbers?"

He shook his head. "You know teenagers. They got secrets. She never brings friends around anymore, like she used to when she was young. I don't know." The head shaking continued.

"Okay," I said. "There's nothing we can do but wait. Maybe she went home with a friend and forgot to tell you. You take the boys home, feed them, and I'll wait here. If either of us hear, we'll call the other. And Anthony, don't leave your house." I had a sudden thought. "Do you have Theresa's cell phone number?"

He pulled a small spiral pad out of his overalls pocket and recited it to me. I immediately called but there was no answer. "I'll keep trying," I said.

After he left, I thought about calling Mike, but that seemed like calling in the heavy artillery before I had to.

When the girls asked about Theresa, over a meal of frozen chicken pot pies, I said she'd gone home with friends. But I knew I wasn't hiding my concern from them. Em was balky and didn't want to go to bed, and Maggie was short-tempered with Em, and I finally was short-tempered with both of them. By eight thirty, half an hour late, they were in bed, but I could tell neither girl was asleep.

I was almost in bed when the phone rang about eleven. "Miss Kelly?" The voice was scared, tentative, so soft I could barely hear it.

"Theresa?"

A sob. "Yes. Can you come get me?"

"Where are you?"

"A gas station on Northwest 28th Street. They...they beat me. Could you just come get me? I can't call my father."

I collected my thoughts. "It may take a bit. I have to find someone to watch the girls." There was no way I was taking the girls out late at night on an errand like this. "Are there people around you? Are you safe?"

"Yes, I think so."

"Okay, Give me the address and then stay right there."

I hung up and wondered who I could call to watch the girls. Not Tim. I didn't want to admit to him that I needed help, nor did I want to let him know how close his girls were to danger. I considered Mrs. Dodson and discarded the idea. Mrs. Dodson was the neighborhood's most incurable gossip. Mike would only order me to stay home while he went for Theresa—and I thought that betrayed Theresa's trust. And then I came to the last resort—Joanie.

"Joanie, I need you. Right now. I need you to come watch the girls. I have to go out."

Joanie just moaned in reply. "I can't. I've been throwing up all day. I am so sick. Besides, where do you have to go at this hour of the night?"

"I have to go get Theresa. She's in trouble." I said sharply.

"That girl you took in? Why don't you send her father?"

"I can't. That's all. Don't ask, Joanie. Just get over here."

"Okay. I'll try."

Try? I need you over here ten minutes ago. While I waited, I reviewed my options. I knew it was dumb to go after Theresa by myself. Should I call Anthony? Instinct told me that would make a bad situation worse. I wished I had a gun. Mike talked to me about it, and I'd said no, I didn't think I could use one. But now I thought I could. I checked my cell phone—plenty of charge. No, I'd go alone, but I'd be very careful. I went upstairs and kissed each of my girls, who finally were asleep, wondering if I'd see them again in the morning. *You're being overly dramatic,* I chided myself.

Joanie did look pretty washed out when she arrived. "I hurried as fast as I could," she said, collapsing on the couch. "Kelly, are you sure this is safe?"

"No," I said, my voice sharp again. "Here's Mike Shandy's number. If I'm not back in an hour, call him."

I sped up Sixth to Allen and onto I-35, then up to N.W. 28th Street as fast as I thought I could push the speed limit, my hand gripping the wheel, my eyes glued to the road in front of me. Once I turned off the freeway and headed west, I watched numbers—Theresa said 1400, which shouldn't be too far. When I got there, I found not a convenience store or a safe place where I thought Theresa might be but a house with a bunch of teenagers, boys and girls, milling around outside.

I tried to drive by slowly, figuring out the situation, looking for Theresa. Was that her in that dark corner? If so, someone was holding her back. Just as I decided I'd made a huge mistake coming here, a group of teenagers ran for my car and surrounded it. I'd made sure the doors were locked, so I was safely inside as I inched forward and they pounded on the windows and yelled threats. One waved a baseball bat as though he would smash the windshield in my face. Terrified, I realized my only option would be to actually run down two or three of these kids, drive over them to get away—and I wasn't sure I could do that. I froze, the car at a stand-still, and the kids began to rock it. Heart pounding, I clung to the steering wheel. Now I couldn't even inch forward if I wanted to. The rocking seemed to go on for an eternity, until I was sure the car would tip on its side.

Suddenly, lights flashed behind me, and dimly, I heard the wail of a siren. Police. How did they know? The boys rocking the car scattered as I sat perfectly still, afraid to move. More sirens began to sound in the distance, and then I heard a bullhorn. Cracking my window barely, I heard Mike Shandy's voice saying, "Everybody freeze. Hands on your heads." As I watched most of the teenagers complied, though two tried to run.

A second police car pulled up, two patrolmen jumped out and gave chase. Within seconds they were back, dragging the two escapees. Then a police wagon pulled up and the young people were herded into it. All except one. Mike Shandy came toward me, leading Theresa by the hand.

The girl had been beaten. She hid her face in her hands, but her hair flew in all directions, and an ugly gash, now covered by dried blood, streaked across on one arm.

I got out of the car, legs shaking beneath me. "Mike, how did you get here?"

"I followed you," he said grimly. "I happened to see you leave your driveway—okay, I drive by a lot when I'm on patrol and this time it was just lucky. I knew you shouldn't be going any place this time of night, so I followed you."

"And these others?"

"I called for backup. Here's your friend—she needs help, but she may also need a licking."

I eased Theresa's hands away from her face, but the girl refused to look at me. I tipped her chin up until I could see her face, puffy and swollen, bruises beginning to blacken, red scratches across her face. Then I saw scratches on her arms and a large bruise on one leg. I could only guess if the kicks Theresa received damaged her internally.

"They made me call you," the girl said softly. "They said they'd stop beating me...and I was desperate. I couldn't think of anything except to get them to stop. They said they wouldn't hurt you, just wanted to scare you."

"Hush," I said. "We'll talk later. We've got to take care of you." I looked at Mike for guidance.

"She needs to go to an ER," he said. "Does she have a relative you can call?"

A whimper escaped from Theresa's bruised lips. "Please, no, Miss Kelly. Don't call my father. He...he might beat me too."

"I won't let him do that, Theresa. But I won't call him."

Mike looked at me, puzzled. "There's a whole lot of this story I'm not getting. But someone needs to talk this girl to an ER—JPS, the county hospital, I imagine. And that will probably take the rest of the night. They'll want to do x-rays, the whole business. Who's with your girls?"

I clasped a hand over my mouth, just as Mike's cell phone went off. "Joanie, but she's sick," I said. "That's probably her. I told her to call you if I wasn't home in an hour."

"Okay," Mike said. "You go home to your girls. I'll get my patrol covered and take this young lady...."

"Theresa," I inserted.

"I know that," he said, out of patience, "I'll take Theresa to JPS, and then when they dismiss her...?"

"Will they treat her without a legal guardian?"

"How old is she?"

"I'm seventeen," Theresa said softly. "I have a driver's license."

"Yeah, they'll treat her if I tell them to."

"Then bring her to my house," I said. "I'll have called her father to tell him she's safe." I hesitated a minute. "Mike, I owe you an explanation. Come have dinner with us tomorrow night?"

"Let's talk about that tomorrow," he said and led Theresa away. Over his shoulder, "You're free to go, Kelly. Go home to the girls."

Mike led Theresa back to his patrol car, but the girl stopped, looked at me, and said, "Miss Kelly, I...I am so sorry I bring this trouble on you."

"You didn't bring it, Theresa. It's all mixed up in a knot I can't untie. But you go get those scratches and bruises taken care of."

"You go home *now*," Mike said.

And that's just what I did, knees shaking. I didn't even look again in the direction of the young people being herded into vans.

****

Joanie was asleep on the couch, so, knowing I wouldn't sleep, I sent her upstairs to bed, took the throw and settled myself on the couch. I may have dozed occasionally but I also tossed, turned, and worried during much of the night. Why would those teenagers want to scare me? What was in it for them? Anthony's obvious answer came back again and again: someone is paying them, but who? And what would happen to those kids who were arrested? Biggest question of all: what lay ahead for Theresa? Was I right not to tell Anthony right away?

I'd called him, of course, when I got home, and said, "Anthony, Theresa's safe, but she's been beaten. Mike Shandy has taken her to JPS so they can check her out."

Predictably, he said, "Mother of God! Who beat her? It was Joe, wasn't it?"

"I don't know. The police took a bunch of young people to the station house, but I came home. I bet they all bonded out and nobody talked."

"They're the ones messing with the house," Anthony said sagely. "You need to find out who's paying them."

"I can't," I said, "The police will have to find that out. Meantime you have to be extra careful." After this night, I was even more protective of my girls. I knew what lengths these people would go to.

Anthony grunted. "They don't scare me. I keep the tire iron by me. Punks."

"And the cell phone," I said. "I'll keep Theresa home tomorrow and let her sleep. Why don't you come see her in the late afternoon?"

"Okay, Miss Kelly. You know how to find me if you need me before that."

"I'm sure it's okay, Anthony. Try to sleep."

"Mother of God, who could sleep?"

****

Mike brought Theresa back about five in the morning. Bandages covered the worst scratches, but her eye could not be disguised—she had a huge shiner. And she looked dazed. "They've given her something to help her sleep," Mike said, "and here are some pain pills, only if she needs them. You keep them." And then he added, "Up high."

I put an arm around Theresa and guided her to the stairs. She didn't say a thing, and she was dead weight in my arms.

"Can you get her to bed or should I help?" Mike asked.

"If you could carry her upstairs, then I can handle it."

Mike deposited Theresa on her bed and said, "I'll be downstairs. We need to talk."

I knew that it was too much to hope that he would just leave without giving me a lecture. I took off Theresa's shoes, belt and other constricting clothes and then rolled her into bed, still essentially fully dressed.

Downstairs Mike made himself a cup of coffee. He sat in one of the chairs, and I curled on the sofa, hugging the comforter for warmth—and security. "What happened to the ones they arrested?"

Mike shrugged. "No idea. They probably made bond and are back on the street by now."

"That's what I was afraid of."

"It's the way our system works, Kelly."

"Then nobody found out anything from them, like why they're doing this or who's paying them…"

Mike looked surprised. "You didn't really expect to find answers tonight, did you?"

Yeah, I did. Aloud, "I suppose not. But I hoped."

"Kelly, I think Theresa's right. They didn't mean to hurt you tonight, just scare you. But they were serious enough about it that they didn't mind hurting Theresa."

"Won't they be prosecuted for that?"

He clutched the coffee cup in both hands, feeling its warmth. "Not unless she presses charges. And I guarantee you she won't do that. Her life would be hell if she did."

I felt like a small child. "Now what?"

"Leave it to us. Keep doing what you've been doing—finish the house, move out of this one…."

"They know where I'm moving," I said dully and told him about the bull's eyes.

"I'm not surprised. They're tapped into someone—we just don't know who at this point."

"Theresa?"

"No, or they wouldn't have beat her up tonight. What did you tell Anthony?"

"The truth." I could hear him shouting, "Mother of God!" "That she had been beaten but was okay and you'd taken her to JPS. And that she wasn't going to school today. I told him to come by in the afternoon and see her." I thought for a moment. "What I don't want is for him to go on his own search for vengeance."

"I'll go by and see him this morning," Mike said, "try to make him understand he must not take this up as his own fight."

"Good luck." I said. "Don't you need sleep?"

"What's that?" he asked with a lopsided grin. "What time does Anthony get to the Fairmount house?"

"About eight-thirty. It's six-thirty now."

"Okay, if I just wait here and go see him?"

"Sure."

I catnapped again on the couch, and Mike sat in a chair with his feet on the ottoman and looked like he slept a lot more comfortably than I did on the couch. I didn't sleep but just dozed—too close to time to get up. I'd sleep while the girls were at school. At seven—okay, a little after—I woke the girls and Joanie, and soon the house was moving into its routine, except that I told the girls Theresa was sick and they must be very quiet.

"Why is Mike in the chair?" Maggie asked.

"Mom," Em demanded, "did you and Mike have a sleepover?"

Tired as I was, I couldn't help but grin. "No, Em. He stayed because he got here early this morning, and he needs to talk to Anthony pretty soon."

When Joanie asked, "What happened last night? Mike didn't answer my call," I shushed her with a look at the girls and a mouthed, "Later."

Chapter Ten

Early Saturday morning, the day of the yard sale, was cool but blessedly clear. As I carried out boxes of clothes and toys and dishes, I thought that it had not been an easy week, to say the least. In fact, it had been damn difficult. Theresa was healing in body, if not in spirit. What she and Anthony said to one another, I would never know. But Theresa was once again helpful around the house and sweet with the girls, though she tended to retreat to her room whenever she could. Several times I caught her staring blankly out the window. *Time heals,* I thought, *and not much else does.*

Saturday morning, Mike arrived with two helpers about six-thirty, and they barely got the couch and chairs out onto the lawn when the first shoppers straggled by, braving the dark in order to find the bargains. I offered all three men coffee and rolls, but the two helpers declined. Mike accepted and said, "I'm staying all day. Hope you don't mind."

"I'm grateful," I said and meant it.

The girls wandered down a little before eight in their nightgowns, and I sent them back upstairs to change into jeans and sweaters. Theresa came down not much later, dressed and pale in spite of the fact that she'd put on makeup. Her hair was pulled straight back from her face, accentuating her rather stark appearance. She greeted Mike happily, though, and when he asked how she was feeling, she responded, "Much better, thank you." She seemed to mean it.

Sales were slow at first—a small item here, another there, but no takers on the big pieces of furniture. I wondered if they were overpriced, but Mike assured me he thought the prices were fair.

Anthony arrived and said he, too, would stay for the sale. He and Mike stood in the doorway, letting me handle sales and visit with people. Theresa mostly kept the girls indoors, though occasionally they came out and once Em wailed, "Oh, no, Mommy. You can't sell this" and pulled a bedraggled stuffed animal to her chest. I rolled my eyes, "Em, you haven't looked at that toy for a year."

"I know. I forgot about it. But now I remember."

"Okay, but only this one. Okay?"

"Yes, Mommy," and she trotted off happily, carrying her prize.

About ten a familiar-looking battered car drove up, and I watched open-mouthed as three teen-age boys in baggy clothes got out. I sensed Mike moving closer to me and almost reached out to squeeze his hand. The boys avoided looking at me and studied the goods. Then Maggie came out the door and went right up to one boy who had a pony tail. "Hi, Joe. How are you?"

That particular young man had a black eye, bruises on his face and arms, and clearly had been in a fight. He looked uncomfortable and glanced at me before he said, sort of awkwardly, "I'm fine, Maggie. How are you?"

"I'm okay," she said. "But you look awful. What happened to your face?"

He stammered. "I...I ran into a door by mistake."

She shook her head. "You gotta watch where you're going, Joe."

He just nodded, and Maggie went on, "I decided I don't like yard sales."

He grinned a bit then. "Me neither. Maggie, your dad been around this morning? We was supposed to help him empty the garage. He was going to come with a trailer."

Maggie shook her head. "Nope. We haven't seen him."

Joe looked perplexed but said, "Okay. Thanks. Maybe we'll come back later. If he comes around, tell him we was here."

As Maggie walked by Mike and me, she said, "That was Joe. His grammar's not very good."

They got in their car and left. Mike demanded, "How does Maggie know him? He looks like one of the ones that they arrested Monday night. I bet he was part of it."

Theresa came out to watch the boys drive away and was just in time to hear Mike. "Joe wasn't one of them," she said. "He would never hurt me." She turned on her heel and went back inside.

Lamely, I explained, "The girls met Joe when Tim took them to Ol' South one evening. He was there, and somehow he knows Tim."

Anthony grumbled, "He worked with me a little bit, when Mr. Spencer was still here. That's how he knew him, but I didn't know they saw each other since. Joe was no good as a helper. I let him go. But he's sweet on Theresa."

Thoughtfully Mike said, "I don't like that connection, don't like it at all. But I can't figure what it means."

Mrs. Dodson came by, cluck-clucking over new neighbors and whether or not she'd like them.

"I'm sure you will," I reassured her. "The Guthries are really nice people. I wouldn't sell my house to any other kind."

"We'll see," the older woman sniffed. "Don't much like change."

Or anything else. Aloud, I said, "I won't be far, Mrs. Dodson. You can call me if you need anything…and you can still visit with my mom when she's here."

The woman almost ignored that statement and began to prowl through a box of costume jewelry.

Around eleven, some TCU students pulled up and made an offer on the couch and chairs. It was about a third less than I'd been asking, but I was discouraged. I sold the set to them, and the students gleefully shoved them into a pickup. When you live in southwest Fort Worth, almost every third person has some connection to the university. I sort of hoped the girls would go there, but that was a long way in the future.

By noon, traffic died down, and I said, "I think we should call it a day."

Mike agreed and helped me cart the unsold things back inside. I hadn't really done too badly—I thought probably two-thirds of the things I put out were gone and when I counted, I'd made close to a thousand dollars. That would help with something special for the move.

Joanie appeared just as we carried the last box inside. "What? It's over? I wanted to shop."

I laughed. "You'll have to shop the leftovers inside." Joanie pouted and flounced inside where I followed her.

"I'm getting ready to order lunch. Want to stay?" Before she could answer, Mike, Anthony, Theresa and the girls all appeared, sort of one by one. After polling everyone, I ordered pizza, although Joanie swore she couldn't eat a bite of it (she ate two slices). Then one by one they drifted away—Mike to get ready for his shift, Anthony to check on his younger children that he'd left with an aunt, Joanie to run errands.

"Are we still having dinner tonight?" she asked as she left.

I said yes, and she said, "I'll bring a scrumptious dessert."

I arched an eyebrow. Apparently morning sickness didn't rule out "scrumptious" desserts in the evening.

****

I fixed a baked chicken casserole, a green salad with balsamic vinaigrette dressing. It was a meal bland enough for Joanie's stomach but also one the girls would eat. Theresa and the girls elected to have their dinner by the TV in Theresa's room, usually not allowed, but this time I gave in. Joanie and I ate in the kitchen, and as I poured myself a glass of chardonnay, I looked at Joanie and said, "Sorry." Joanie pouted a minute and then laughed—"in another couple of months the doctor says I can have an occasional glass."

"Only occasional," I said.

"You didn't sell any baby things today," Joanie said. "I was hoping to get some bargains."

"Oh, Joanie, I have the crib and everything. I just couldn't part with them, but you're welcome to borrow."

We ate dinner and chatted about this and that, mostly about the coming baby, which was clearly Joanie's favorite subject. She did manage to ask, "What about Mike?" and I shrugged.

"Status quo." *Joanie, do you ever have another thought in your head besides relationships with men?*

The phone rang about eight. I always answered it with some fear these days.

"Is this Kelly?" The voice was female but unfamiliar.

"Yes," I said hesitantly.

"This is Pam Spencer...uh, I'm Tim's wife."

I nearly dropped the phone. I'd been thinking dark thoughts about Tim exposing the girls to an illicit relationship and here he was married—why didn't he tell me? I managed to stammer, "I guess it's time that we talked."

"Past time," the woman said, "but Tim somehow never wanted me to meet you. That's not why I'm calling though. Have you seen him?"

"Tim? No, not all day."

"He left this morning to clean his things out of your garage, and he hasn't come back yet. He's not answering his cell phone, and I have no idea where he could be. He promised me a special dinner tonight. I think he said, ah, Del Frisco's—and I'm starving. I thought you might help."

Briefly I wondered if I was supposed to help find Tim or take Pam to Del Frisco's, a really pricey steak-house. Then I realized this could be serious. "Gosh, no," I said. "I don't have any idea. Wait a minute. There were some young men"—did my voice pause over that phrase?—"at my yard sale this morning looking for Tim. They said they were supposed to meet him here and help him with the garage. But he never showed up, and they left."

"I guess I'll just go to Taco Bell across from the motel. I suppose if he hasn't come by morning I'll call the police."

"I'd call if he's not back by, oh say, midnight. I hear they don't consider people missing until they've been gone twenty-four hours, but it wouldn't hurt to call. And, Pam... uh, let me know, will you? I'm a little worried. I won't tell the girls."

"Okay," she said.

That ended the conversation, and then of course I repeated it verbatim to Joanie, who immediately made a dark mystery out of it, connecting it to the skeleton and the fire at the house on Fairmount.

"Joanie, your imagination is running away with you," I told her. I somehow didn't want to admit to Joanie that I was worried. Aloud, I said, "Tim probably ran into an old friend...or thought of a money-making scheme."

"Since this morning?" Joanie asked skeptically, and I knew she was right.

We lingered in my bedroom after dinner—the only place that offered any comfortable seating since the living room furniture was gone. The girls were in bed, Theresa was apparently watching TV—I checked on her once—and the house was quiet and peaceful. I was sort of enjoying the success of my garage sale, and I put the worry about Tim out of my mind, along with the worry about the vandals who plagued me. Just sort of put everything on hold. Maybe it was that second glass of wine in my hand.

Any such feelings shattered when the doorbell rang. A quick glance at the bedside clock told me it was almost ten, too late for anyone to be calling. Joanie jumped from her chair and demanded, "Who is it?"

"I don't know," I said. *Does she think I have x-ray vision?* "But I guess I'll find out."

Dramatically, Joanie said, "Wait. We need something for self defense."

"What would you suggest?" I asked dryly, as the doorbell rang again, this time more insistently.

"A baseball bat?" Joanie said.

"The girls don't play baseball, Joanie, and if they did it would be with soft bats. You stay here."

But Joanie tiptoed down the stairs behind me, as though being silent might make her invisible—or safe.

For the first time, I damned the glass-paned door. I had no hiding place. Deciding boldness was the best tack, I strode toward the door with as much determination as I could muster but a quaking fear inside of me. I expected to see Joe with his baggy pants and ponytail. Instead, I saw Detective Buck Conroy.

Throwing open the door, I said accusingly, "You almost scared me to death."

"Sorry about that. Couldn't stand two deaths in one night."

Something clutched at my stomach. "What does that mean?"

"Ms. O'Connell, your ex-husband is dead." He said it flatly, without emotion. Officers aren't all good at delivering bad news, especially Buck Conroy.

"Tim? Tim can't be dead." The wild thought went through my mind that he hadn't cleaned out the garage yet, so how could he be dead? I just couldn't imagine a person walking around on the earth, perfectly healthy, one day and dead the next. The numbness of denial set in.

Buck Conroy didn't mince words. "He was shot. I have to ask this: where've you been all day."

Buck Conroy needed serious lessons in breaking news to concerned parties. I didn't cry, but I felt like I ought to, and then I didn't know what I felt. Suddenly, my knees seemed about to give way, and I looked desperately around the empty room, wishing even for a straight chair I could sink on to. I decided sitting on the carpet was better than standing with quaking knees. To my surprise, Conroy hunkered down so that he was at my level.

"I've been here. We had a garage sale and then Joanie was here for dinner...." I turned toward the stairs, but there was no sign of Joanie. "Joanie, come down here."

Joanie inched her way down the stairs. "Is Tim really dead.?" She had the weirdest look on her face that I'd ever seen, and I wanted to say, "Oh, come on, Joanie. You barely knew him."

"'Fraid so, ma'am. You are?" His appraisal of her was frankly top to toe.

"Joanie Bennett, a friend of the family." She smiled at him as though they had a secret.

Well, maybe Joanie had a secret, but I bristled. Was she placing herself as a friend of Tim's as well? "Joanie's been here since about six," I said, trying to sound businesslike, "and this morning Mike Shandy was here from six-thirty until, oh, maybe noon. You don't think I shot him, do you? I don't even have a permit...or a gun."

Conroy permitted himself a slight grin. "No, I don't think you shot him, but as I said, I have to ask. If Shandy was here with you, you've got a clear alibi. We figure someone shot him about eight this morning. What kind of a car did he drive?"

Behind me, Joanie said, "Oh, how horrible," followed by a kind of moan.

"Rental," I said. "A...oh, I don't know, probably a Camry like mine. Mid-size, nothing classy or remarkable, just a car."

Conroy nodded. "We found a Camry parked about a hundred yards away. No kind of ID in it, but a check of the VIN number showed it was a rental, charged to one Tim Spencer."

So that's why he didn't come meet Joe and the others to clean out the garage—he was already dead when they asked about him. "Have you notified his wife?"

"Wife? I thought you were the only wife in the picture."

I shook my head. "I thought so too. I thought he just had a girlfriend, but she called tonight because she couldn't find him and she was worried. Told me they're married."

"Where is she?"

"Days Inn. But I'm not sure which one. I think Tim said out on the West Freeway."

"You just saved me a bunch of trouble. We were going to have to search for where he was staying." Conroy picked a walkie-talkie from his waistband and spoke into it, issuing orders that had to do with the Days Inn and Mrs. Spencer. Then he lowered himself onto the carpet next to me. "They'll question her, dust the room, and see what they can find."

It all sounded callously cruel and heartless. *Would the officers show any compassion for the new Mrs. Spencer's loss? More compassion than Buck Conroy showed?* Before I could ask anything about that, he said,

"Let's talk about your ex-husband. Who hated him enough to kill him?"

I shook my head, still trying to grapple with how I felt. I'd hated Tim lately—no, not hated, just been so darned mad that he'd even think of taking the girls to California. But dead. No, I never wanted that, and now I didn't know how I felt—or how I should feel.

"Since he came back to town, I've found out a lot of people didn't like him, people that never told me when I was married to him, but none of them would have killed him. They just didn't like him."

"Like who?"

I didn't want to implicate people, so I said, "It doesn't matter."

"Yes, it does," he persisted. "You let me be the judge."

"Okay, Anthony, the carpenter who works for me, and Keisha, my office manager. You know, even Em, my four-year-old, said she didn't like him. And he's her father." Then it dawned on me. "Oh, God, I'll have to tell the girls."

"Yeah, you will." He looked a bit more sympathetic.

"Tell us what, Mom?" It was Maggie, standing on the landing, clutching Em by the hand. Joanie hovered behind them, doing nothing useful.

I held out my arms. "Come to me, girls," and they came. I gathered them in a huge hug. "Your father's dead," I said, thinking that I wasn't a bit more tactful than Buck Conroy. "We don't know what happened or why, but he's dead."

"He won't take us to Ol' South again?" Em asked.

Maggie shut her up with, "No, Em, and besides, he said he'd never take us there again." Then she looked at me. "Did someone hurt him?"

I stroked her hair. "Yes, darling, someone did." I turned to Buck Conroy. "This is Detective Conroy, and he's going to find out who hurt your dad, but…." I took a deep breath, "You'll be okay. Nothing in your life is going to change except that you won't be going out to dinner with him and Pam."

Maggie fixed me with a curious look. "How did you know her name?"

"I talked to her tonight. You could have told me her name—it wouldn't have made me sad. And you could have told me they were married."

Maggie stared at her bare foot. "I…I didn't feel right about it."

I hugged the girls again and said, "You go upstairs with Joanie, and I'll be up to tuck you in soon." *Joanie, do something useful. Get a little practice for motherhood. Put these girls to bed and read to them.*

Joanie must have heard the thought, for she said, "Come on, girls. I'll read to you." And upstairs they went. But Joanie threw Buck a long look as she went up and added as an afterthought, "Tim was scum, but he could be charming."

Buck looked at me and muttered, "What's that supposed to mean?" but I just shook my head. I was still thinking about the girls. *Poor Tim. His daughters didn't even cry. I suppose he'd been so little a part of their lives.* I still felt I should cry but there were no tears. Instead I just felt numb. I think I was more struck by the enormity of sudden, unexpected death, than I was by the loss of Tim. And I was curious. What had Tim gotten into? With all that was going on, it seemed impossible that this was a random mugging or something unrelated.

"Buck," I said, "don't you work cold cases? Why are you investigating this one?"

He shrugged. "I asked for it—because of the relationship to you and all that's been going on. I...I just don't think its coincidence."

"Neither do I."

Theresa wandered down the stairs. "I heard voices," she said.

Conroy looked at her and said, "I can't keep all the players straight in this game. Who's that?"

I explained and then told Theresa in simple straightforward terms about Tim.

Theresa looked right at us and said, "Joe wouldn't kill anybody. He's not that bad." She looked at me directly. "He was furious when he heard they'd beat me. He fought with a couple of them." And then she disappeared upstairs.

I remembered how Joe looked this morning. He had indeed been in a fight, and I hoped, for some illogical reason, that Theresa was right about why.

"What the hell does that mean?" Conroy stood up, stretching to ease his aching back. "Who's Joe?"

"Long story," I said. "Come on in the kitchen, and I'll fix coffee." I held out a hand, and he helped me up.

While I made coffee, I tried to explain about Anthony, Theresa, and Joe. Buck kept interrupting with questions. "This Joe is sweet on Theresa, so he arranges for his friends to beat her up? Won't wash, Kelly."

"I think...I don't think he arranged that. He may have arranged a kidnapping, thinking she'd be safe and I'd be scared. Kidnapping her was a way to get me out of the house and scare me. I don't know what would have happened if Mike hadn't followed me—although I didn't know he was doing that. But Joe surely looked like he'd been in a fight when he came by this morning. He was supposed to help Tim empty the garage."

"So Joe and Tim are connected? This gets more tangled by the minute."

I explained about Joe working with Anthony when Tim was still here but admitted I didn't understand the current connection any better than Buck did.

"I think you're giving this Joe too much credit for being a nice person, but how did Shandy know to follow you?" His tone clearly said this story was getting less and less believable.

"He was on patrol, saw me leave the house alone at nearly ten-thirty, and knew that wasn't right."

He spread his hands. "Okay, I give up. What we have to do is find out this Joe's involvement, right?"

"Yeah. Anthony says he's being paid, and that makes sense. But I can't imagine Tim was paying him— except maybe to help clean out the garage. Besides, if Tim was paying him, Joe wouldn't kill him. But, still, I don't think Tim had any money—he never paid child support."

"So I got lots to do: find this Joe and talk to him and find out who killed your ex. I got to talk to Anthony and Keisha, even though I believe you they aren't involved." He looked at me. "You okay with him gone? I mean...well, you know, I assume you were married several years and you got two kids together and...well, hell, I don't know about these things, marriage and all."

I studied him. "You ever been married?"

"Once. For about two months. Didn't last, but no regrets. And I have no idea where she is, living or dead. Long gone, out of memory. Different thing."

"Yeah," I said, "it is a different thing. I imagine I'll shed some tears for Tim...but not yet."

Upstairs I found the girls asleep in my bed, and Joanie sitting on the window seat staring out the window. "You okay?" I asked.

She turned, and I thought I saw some streaked mascara.

"It's just...well, you don't expect that to happen to anyone you know, even if you don't know them well."

"I know," I said. I didn't know what else to say to her, but she seemed more upset than I was.

"I gotta go," she said.

Some instinct welled up inside of me. "Joanie, how well did you know Tim?"

Her toe played with the carpet, and her eyes refused to meet mine. "He might be the father of my baby. I don't know. It's one of a couple of possibilities." She actually blushed, which was a good thing because I was at first speechless and then ready to slap her. Sleeping with your friend's husband—okay, ex-husband—was one of the biggest betrayals I could think of. How could she? I could see Tim's part of it—he was charming, and he may well have been pumping her for information about me. Besides, I realized too late that Tim had not exactly been faithful. But with Joanie?

And Joanie didn't even know for sure Tim was the father of her baby because there was more than one suspect. It reflected a lifestyle I couldn't understand—that desperate, late-thirties single state. What was the song? "Looking for Love In All the Wrong Places." I counted back to see when it happened, because three months ago, I didn't even know that Tim was in town. I thought he hadn't been here in—what? Over a year? He'd come to town and hadn't even seen his girls! Their absolutely unforgiveable behavior stunned me, perhaps more than Tim's death.

"Joanie, tell me. I thought Tim hadn't been here in over a year."

Her toe was really busy with the carpet, and she didn't raise her eyes toward me. Slowly, oh so slowly, she got the words out. "He came to town, I think to spy on you. He called me and, hey, I'm always up for a happy hour drink. Well, three drinks led to dinner and then…." Her voice drifted off, and I didn't need to ask more.

I didn't say anything but just sat looking at her, still stunned.

"It was just one night, Kelly, and it didn't mean anything. Too much wine. I…I never wanted this to happen"—she pointed to her stomach—"and I sure never wanted to hurt you." She was babbling now out of nervousness.

I held up a hand. "Stop, Joanie. I don't want to hear any more. Just go home. I'll call tomorrow."

****

The tears came in the middle of the night, and they were not for what I'd lost, but for Tim himself, for what he could have been, and what life should have brought him. I thought my tears were silent, but they woke both the girls.

"Are you crying for Dad?" Maggie asked.

"Yes, sweetie, I am. Nobody deserves to die suddenly and so young."

"I thought he was old, like you," Em said.

But Maggie was serious. "I…I think he was trying to be a good father, and that makes me sad. He…well, he'll miss a lot. And we'll miss having a father."

Em immediately began to wail, while Maggie sat with tears running silently down her cheeks. I checked my own tears to hug the girls. "Your dad will miss seeing you grow up, and that's very sad. But you can remember the good in him and, for his sake, be the best people you can be."

"For your sake, too, Mom," Maggie said.

They went back to sleep, but I lay awake, thinking about Joanie. Hers was the classic betrayal of one woman by another, and yet I thought I didn't really care. Would it change my feelings about her? I hoped not. I'd work to make sure it didn't. Joanie would need more support than ever in the coming months. Then the weird thought occurred to me that her baby could be a half-brother or sister to my girls. I was so tired I almost giggled. Then I wondered if Joanie expected child support from Tim. If so, she'd be sadly disappointed, but I don't think she'd thought that far ahead tonight.

Eventually I slept, huddled in a knot in the middle of the bed between my girls. But it was not a restful sleep.

Next morning, I was up early, tired but too restless to sleep. I scanned the newspaper. In the "Local Briefs" there was a short piece about the body of an Anglo male, thought to be in his forties—*Tim would hate that! He was thirty-eight*—found in Trinity Park. The man had been shot, and announcement of his identity was pending notification of relatives. The kind of thing you read in the paper all the time. Feeling ghoulish, I clipped it—the girls should have it someday. Meantime, I'd keep it, maybe laminate it, and hide it away.

But the local TV news had a different story. The victim as identified as Tim Spencer, formerly of Fort Worth and O'Connell & Spencer Realty. I felt a sense of foreboding when I heard that, though I don't know why. "Mr. Spencer had been back in Fort Worth for about two weeks, though the nature of his visit to the city is unknown. Police report no leads at this time. Anyone with information about Mr. Spencer is asked to call Fort Worth Police headquarters."

Not a call I'll be making, I thought. And then, some-how, I thought of Pam Spencer, sitting alone in the Days Inn on West I-30, the freeway. I should have called her last night. Imagine being in a strange town and learning that your husband, the only person you know in the city, is dead. Before the girls were up, I found the number to

the Days Inn on the west freeway, dialed it, and asked
for Mrs. Spencer. The voice that answered was leaden.

"Pam? It's Kelly."

"Oh,   Kelly."
"Are you okay?"

"I don't know. Surprised. Scared. Angry. I...I took
something to make me sleep, but it didn't really work."

That explains the thickness in her voice. "Pam, have you
eaten breakfast...or dinner last night?"

A pause. "I ate Taco Bell last night, but after I
heard, it didn't sit well on my stomach. And this morning, I...I couldn't eat."

"I'm coming to get you. We'll have breakfast."

"No. I couldn't eat."

"Eating and talking are what you need. You get
dressed," I said firmly.

I wakened Theresa and asked her if she could watch
the girls. "Don't let anybody in," I cautioned.

"I know. Not Joe. But my dad? Or Mike?"

I softened. "Only those two. And here's my cell
phone number. Tell the girls I've gone to take care of
Pam."

On Sunday morning, the freeway was empty, and I
was at the motel in less than fifteen minutes. Pam
Spencer was still fumbling with her clothes when I
knocked on the door. She opened it hesitantly and then
invited me in. The room was messy, with open suitcases
and clothes thrown about, the television blaring mind-
lessly, the curtains drawn against the daylight. I suspected
it would have been messy anyway but a police search
hadn't helped, and I could see traces of white powder
that I assumed were from dusting for prints. The room
also smelled strongly of stale bourbon, and I knew how
Pam Spencer soothed her fears and made the frightening
time pass. It wasn't medication—it was bourbon or, God
forbid, both.

Pam was dressed in jeans and a sweatshirt, no makeup, her hair roughly combed. She was younger than me by a good bit but not the pretty young thing I thought Tim would choose. Her eyes were red and her face puffy but that could have been from crying or bourbon, either one. *Be fair, Kelly. She hasn't fixed herself up. She probably usually looks a lot better.* Aloud I said, "How about Ol' South? I know you've been there with the girls, and the grease would probably do you some good." I always heard that grease helped a hangover."

I ordered a German pancake, with all its lemony goodness, while Pam ordered corned beef hash with eggs and two sausages. I tried hard to sit back and let Pam do the talking, but talk wasn't forthcoming.

"Pam," I said tentatively, "you'll have to make some arrangements. Have you called Tim's mother?"

She looked blank. "No. I thought you'd do that."

I'm not married to him. You are. "His mother blames me for the divorce. I think the call might come better from you." Tim's father had been dead many years, and his mother doted on her only son. Naturally since he could do no wrong, the divorce was all my fault and I stole the girls from him. Bernice Spencer criticized me when we were married, and no doubt the pattern accelerated after the divorce.

"I've never met her," Pamela said dully.

Incredulous, I asked, "How long have you been married?"

"Three weeks. This is our honeymoon...uh, was."

I wanted to ask the next logical question: how long have you known him? But I didn't. "Do you have family you can call to be with you?"

"My sister. I guess I can call Ellen."

"Why don't you do that? I'll call Tim's mom. I'm sure she'll want him buried in Arkansas. You don't object do you?"

She shook her head. "I wouldn't know what else to do."

In the end, it all worked out, though not in what I would call a pleasant manner. Pam perked up after breakfast and looked enough better that I took her back to the house. Pam called Ellen, and I called Bernice. It was worse than I anticipated. Bernice dissolved into great sobs and demanded to know what he was doing back in Fort Worth and why I was involved. Finally I assured her I would have the detectives call her and when Tim's body was released they would send it to the funeral home of Bernice's choice.

"Released? From what?"

"It was a violent death, Bernice. There will have to be an autopsy."

"Oh, my poor boy." More sobs, then a pause. "The girls will come to their father's funeral."

I took a deep breath. "No, I don't think so. It would be too hard on them, and Tim's been out of their lives for so long, except the last couple of weeks. I won't bring them, and it wouldn't be appropriate for me to be there. But Pamela will come." I prayed that was true.

"I don't know her," Bernice sniffed. "But I guess she can come."

When Bernice hung up—slammed the phone really—I wondered how great a sin it was to have a glass of wine before noon. The girls wandered downstairs and were sitting on either side of Pam, as though trying to comfort her. Their stepmother—odd term that—reached out an arm around each of them, but she apparently didn't know how to cuddle.

"My sister will be here by noon," she said.

"Noon? Where does she live?"

"Plano."

The sister lived an hour away, give or take, and Pam hadn't called her? I was dumbfounded.

Ellen, a bright, well-dressed woman who oozed capability, indeed arrived about noon. After a glance at Pam, she said to Kelly, "I'll take care of her. She'll be fine." I sensed that Ellen was the in-charge one and Pam was the black sheep of the family. Indeed, this might not be the first time Ellen had "taken care of" Pam.

I gave Ellen the information about Tim's mother and Buck Conroy's name and number, and Ellen gave me her business card, hastily scribbling the home address and phone number. Then she swept her sister out the door. Over her shoulder, Pam managed, "Thanks, Kelly. You're a...a good person. Tim was wrong."

What a note to leave on. I suspected that I'd never see Pam Spencer again, never talk to Bernice Spencer, and Tim Spencer was out of my life once and for all. But what a way to go. I hated the violence, but I felt a deep sense of relief.

Chapter Eleven

Monday morning early, Buck Conroy showed up at the office. Without a by-your-leave, he sat in the chair opposite my desk and said, in an almost accusing tone, "Pam Spencer has disappeared."

Disappeared?"

"Yeah. Guys talked to her Saturday night, then yesterday, late, we went back to talk to her again. She's checked out of the motel, left no forwarding address. I don't suppose you know where she is?"

Was that sarcasm I heard? "As a matter of fact I do. Her sister from Plano came to get her yesterday about noon."

"And you were involved how?"

"I went to get her because I was worried about her. Took her to Ol' South for breakfast—she didn't eat dinner or breakfast, and she'd had a bit too much to drink Saturday night to calm her nerves."

"Yeah, I bet," he said. "You got contact information for the sister?"

I dug out name, phone number, and address.

"What else do you know about your ex's wife?"

"Nothing. I told you I didn't think they were married. Oh, I do know they'd only been married three weeks, and this was their honeymoon. And she's never met his mother. I'm sure all of that is a big help." *I can be sarcastic too.*

"Well, the guys told her not to leave town, so I can't believe she skipped."

"She didn't exactly skip. She needed support, and she went where comfort was offered." I did wonder just how comforting the ever-efficient Ellen was.

"He was killed by a .38," he said, watching me.

"What does that mean?"

"It's a small gun—about six-and-a-half inches long. Fits in a lady's purse. And it's lightweight. Under a pound." His look was still calculating.

"Does that mean you think I did it?"

"You and the wife are the only ones on the list at the moment, but as I said, no, I don't think you did it."

"What kind of a gun killed Marie Winton?" I asked.

He smiled. ".38. Ballistics will have to tell us if it was the same gun. I kind of doubt it." He got up to leave. Then he stopped and looked at me. "Something going on between your ex and that friend of yours that was there Saturday night?"

"Joanie? No, of course not," I tried to laugh it off, but I don't know how successful I was. On the other hand, I couldn't see that it would do Buck Conroy any good to know that Joanie was pregnant and Tim might be the father. Joanie did not kill Tim—I knew that for sure.

"I wouldn't be so sure," Conroy said. "I thought her reaction was sort of funny. Interesting lady, though," he mused as he turned to leave.

"Nice fellow," Keisha said, after Conroy was gone. "I'd sure not be takin' him home to Mama."

Keisha was right. Buck Conroy was too rough around the edges.

****

Tuesday was closing day, ten o'clock on the Hunt house and two in the afternoon on mine. I was nervous about closing on the Hunt house four hours before the Guthries closed on mine. I knew a deal wasn't a deal until it closed, and if something happened—heaven forbid—in those four hours, I'd own two houses. Another thought I kept batting out of my mind. Claire Guthrie wasn't going to let anything stand in the way of owning the house in Fairmount.

Closing with the Hunts went easily. They were as always charming and almost touchingly grateful to me for buying their house. "We know you'll love the house," Mrs. Hunt said, "and all we ask if that you write us about it—and you and your family—from time to time."

I grabbed her hands. "Oh, you must come visit when you are in Fort Worth. I'll want you to see how much we love living in the house." I really meant it, and I didn't plan to change a thing about the house.

Mr. Hunt, more taciturn than his wife, grunted, "We won't be in Fort Worth much, if at all."

Mrs. Hunt patted his hand affectionately. "Adolph, we might just come to see Kelly and the girls…and our house."

"It's not our house anymore," he said stubbornly.

Mrs. Hunt smiled gently. "Oh, yes, it will always be my house."

"It really will," I said, "and I want you to feel that way."

The Hunts' movers were coming on Thursday, and they would be totally out of the house by Thursday night. "You're welcome to bring things over that evening," Mrs. Hunt said, even though I didn't officially get possession until Friday. I thanked her and said I just might do that. I thought I'd bring one significant item—I wasn't sure yet what—to put in the house and signify possession. Maybe my grandmother's soup tureen that I kept on a high shelf so it wouldn't be broken. Now it would go on the top of the built-in buffet, with the mirror behind to reflect how lovely and ornate it was.

Closing with the Guthries was not nearly as pleasant. "I suppose you'll leave the alarm system on," Jim Guthrie said.

"Only for a week. I notified them of the change a month in advance or else I'd pay for the full year. I've transferred service to my new house, but they'll allow a week of doubling up."

"Then you'll have the code to our house" he asked, while his wife laid a gentle hand on his arm and said softly, "Jim."

"I have to look after my family," he said curtly.

"You can change the code any time you want, but there is a charge," I said just as curtly.

Then he asked, "What if something goes wrong? Say the hot water heater breaks down Saturday night?"

By now, I was fed up. "Then it's your hot water heater. Mr. Guthrie, the house was inspected by one of the best in the business, and it got a perfectly clean report. None of us can predict when an appliance is going to suddenly go on the blink, but it's unlikely in this case and if it does happen, it won't be because of poor maintenance."

He signed without saying another word, though he cast a glowering look at his wife, who smiled and said, "Jim, you're going to love living there. And we'll have room for the children to visit in years to come."

He looked like maybe that wasn't an advantage.

The Guthries would take possession on Sunday, and I knew there was no leeway in him. I would have to be out by Saturday night. Goodwill had been called to empty the garage, the movers were coming Friday, and, the Lord willing, it should all go smoothly. By Saturday night the old house would be sparkling clean and ready for new owners. I even hired a cleaning crew to go through it, freeing me from that chore and allowing me to concentrate on the move. I knew without a doubt that

I would find a clean house on College Avenue. By Sunday night, I hoped to have Theresa and the girls fairly well settled and be able to get back to work on Monday.

I was a ghost in the office the next few days. "You really work here?" Keisha asked as she handed me a sheaf of messages on Wednesday afternoon when I breezed by about three, on my way to get the girls.

"I have to get us ready to move. Is there anything urgent?"

"Some woman who gives her name as Mrs. North—I guess she don't have a first name or it's something awful she don't want to admit—keeps calling. I told her you aren't likely to be around much this week, but she said she really wants to talk to you."

I grabbed the message. "Okay, I'll call her. Anything else?"

"Nope. Anthony came by for an advance to buy...oh, I don't know what, but the receipt's on your desk."

I called Mrs. North. A maid answered the phone and said that Mrs. North was unavailable. I told her that I was returning a call but would not be in my office. If Mrs. North needed to reach me urgently, she could call my cell. I left the number. The maid dutifully said, "Yes, ma'am," and wrote the number down, repeating it back to me.

"Thanks," I said and hung up the phone. "I'll be at home if you need me," I told Keisha. "Unless you'd like to come pack dishes."

"No, thanks. My mama moved so often I've done enough of that to last a lifetime. But you have fun. I'll just stay here and run your business for you."

I just smiled at her. "Thanks."

I spent most of Wednesday and Thursday packing boxes. Twice I went back to King's, the local liquor store on Berry Street where you could go to buy Thunderbird, if you really wanted, or to ask for sophisticated advice for the best wine to serve at a dinner party. They had a huge selection and were free with advice. They were also free with wine boxes, but you had to pick carefully through their discard pile because many were too dirty to use. The clean ones were a good size. *Kelly, why don't you just break down and buy movers' boxes? Because old, penurious habits die hard. Even habits from the poverty of college and newlywed life.*

I showed the girls how to pack their clothes in boxes and made each one pack a suitcase with enough clothes for three days. Each had a bright printed satchel kind of suitcase on wheels, and they thought the whole thing was great fun. The kitchen almost stymied me. I had no idea I owned so many dishes and pots and appliances. *I should have sorted better before I had the garage sale. I could sell half this stuff at a second garage sale. Maybe I should donate it to Good Will and take a deduction.*

****

Buck Conroy interrupted my packing on Wednesday; his first words were an accusing, "You're not in your office."

I stared at him. "No, I own the business, and I get to set my own hours. Right now packing to move is a lot more important. What can I do for you?"

"You know Pam Spencer has a record in California? Maiden name's Martin."

My ears perked up, thinking of the M.W.M. initials and the lover named Marty. *Surely that's a coincidence.* "No, I didn't know any of that. Why would I?"

"What kind of people was your husband running with in California?"

"I'm sure I don't know that either. We weren't in communication very often."

"Well, so far, it looks like he was dealing with some pretty shady people. I want to check out who he was in touch with here. Subpoenaed the phone records from the motel, but they didn't tell us much. Couldn't find a cell phone."

"He had one," I told him. Then, "Find out where he was getting money," I said, "and you may unravel the whole thing, though I don't know what that would tell you about Marie Winton."

He shrugged. "Maybe nothing. But you're right, that might lead us to today's murderer. Then we can worry about forty years ago." He sighed in exasperation and turned to leave. "Oh, by the way, the new Mrs. Spencer possessed a .38. We found it in a drawer of undies she forgot to pack. No license, of course, because of her record."

After he left, I sat for a long time staring at a stack of dishes and wondering about the mystery of who Tim Spencer really was.

****

By Thursday night, I had everything packed except, I swore, toothbrushes. When the girls were asleep, I took Marie Winton's diary down from its shelf and packed it beneath a box of my underwear, where no one but me would ever find it—like Pam's gun, I suddenly thought. That diary was a thorn in my conscience. I knew I should tell someone, but I somehow just wasn't ready.

That evening we took my grandmother's tureen to the new house, wandering through the sparkling clean empty rooms, marveling that this was now our house.

"Well, girls, how is it?"

Maggie, who'd harbored all those doubts but now had her own room, said, "I love it, Mom. I'm really going to like living here."

"Miss Kelly," Theresa said, "the guest house…it's so neat and private. I…I thank you."

I still wondered about the wisdom of putting a seventeen-year-old in a free-standing building. But instead of voicing that, I asked, "You won't be afraid?"

"No, not at all."

"We'll get you some kind of alarm, just to be sure."

Theresa looked long and hard at me. "Joe's not going to bother me. Neither are his friends."

I wondered how she could be so sure. Theresa's feelings about Joe were a real puzzle. Surely they were too young for the classic love-hate relationship, and yet she sometimes scorned him but always jumped to his defense when someone said something negative about him. Except Anthony—when Anthony scorned Joe, Theresa turned silent.

****

I spent Friday packing up the kitchen and went to bed exhausted. A strange noise pulled me out of a sound sleep. Something went plop against the house. I listened and heard it again. Something definitely hit the front of the house—not a big something but enough to make a sound. Cautiously, I threw back the covers and felt for my slippers. Before I could get to the window, though, I heard the sound of sirens, that strange peculiar sound police cars make when the sirens are turned on for just a minute, as they close in on whoever it is they want to stop. The sirens stopped as quickly as they'd begun.

I looked out the window and saw Joe's car, with a police car on either side of it, lights still flashing. Puzzled, I just stood there while the doors to Joe's car were pulled open and the occupants pulled out and put against the car, their hand on the roof, their feet spread. Police officers searched them for weapons. Fascinated, as though I was watching a stage play in which I was not involved, I stayed rooted to the spot.

Ever watchful, Maggie came up behind me. "What is it, Mom?"

"It's Joe and his friends. The police have stopped them, but I don't know what they've done." Something in me didn't want to know, didn't want to go downstairs and out the door. But when the doorbell rang insistently I went, Maggie, by now joined by Em, padding behind me.

Mike Shandy was at the door. "Bad news," he said. "Come on outside."

I wanted to ask, like a child, "Do I have to?" But I went. Mike took me by the hand and led me halfway down the sidewalk. Then he turned me toward the house, and I gasped. Two huge spots of bright yellow paint discolored the house—the plopping noise I'd heard. They covered brick, windowsill, and window, one even creeping down over the front door, which made me think how furious Anthony would be. I was speechless, even though I kept opening my mouth to say something, ask a question, to try to grasp what happened.

"They used a paint ball gun," Mike said. "We found it in the car."

"Why? I thought the vandalism ended. Nothing happened...." I remembered. "Nothing since Tim died."

"That's only six days, Kelly. And clearly, it has happened again." He was as patient as he would be with a child.

"The Guthries." An unladylike thought went through my mind about what Jim Guthrie would do if he saw this. "I have to get it off before they take possession. Anthony! I've got to call Anthony."

Mike put out an arm. "Not in the middle of the night. You can't do anything until tomorrow."

Unnoticed by either me or Mike, Maggie walked to the street, where Joe and his friends were still lined up against their car, guarded by two officers. "Joe," she said with determination, "why did you do that to our house?"

The young man looked at the ground and didn't answer her.

"Joe, that was a bad thing to do. I thought you were my friend."

I noticed only then and screamed, "Maggie, you come back here this minute. Em? Where are you?"

"Kelly, calm down," Mike said. "Both girls are fine. Nothing will happen to them. There are six policemen here, and three unarmed punks." He'd picked up Anthony's word.

Em was indeed standing right next to me. Feeling foolish, I reached for the child and waited as Maggie came up the walk.

"I'm disappointed in Joe," Maggie said. "He's not my friend anymore."

I hugged her and turned toward the house. As I did, I saw the curtain in Theresa's room flutter. She watched but did not come outside. So much for her prediction that Joe wouldn't hurt her. Maybe not her, but he hadn't sworn off me yet.

"We're booking them," Mike said, "and we won't let them make bond quite so fast this time. Kelly, take the girls upstairs. You're safe for the night. Try to sleep."

I knew I wouldn't sleep.

As Mike left, he said, "I'll be here early in the morning, with doughnuts."

"Thanks." I put an arm around his shoulder. He was so good. "Mike, there's no way I can thank you for all you do for me."

"Part of it is my job, part of it is that I like you a lot, and part is that I think you're getting a rotten deal."

For the first time I smiled. "That's quite a mix. But thanks."

As the girls and I walked upstairs, both girls headed for my room, their usual pattern of late after something happened in the night. But tonight Theresa stood in the hallway.

"What did they do?" she asked.

"Hit the house with a paintball gun," I said wearily. "I'll have to call your dad first thing." I looked at the girl. "You said Joe wouldn't hurt you. I guess that didn't include me?"

"I thought it did," Theresa said, "I really thought it did." She buried her hands in her face, and I could tell that she was crying. Telling the girls to get in my bed, I went to Theresa and put my arms around her. She hugged me almost desperately and sobbed on my shoulder.

"Theresa, it's not your fault. Or is it?"

"No," the girl said, "but maybe I could have stopped it. I don't know. I might have, before they beat me. Then I was scared."

"Could have? How?"

But Theresa turned and went into her bedroom, closing the door firmly behind her and leaving me standing speechless in the hallway.

****

Sleep didn't come, and I was up even earlier than need be the next morning. The coffee pot was packed, and my only real choice was a drink of water. I brushed my teeth, tried to put on a little makeup and combed my hair, but the result was an exhausted-looking woman in jeans and a baggy sweatshirt. *Maybe I'm really bi-polar. I go from high joy to real lows from day to day. Yesterday I was so happy about the new house and everything. It looked like it was all working out—except for finding out who killed Tim and Marie Winton. But the day-to-day stuff should have been alright.*

Mike arrived at six-thirty with the doughnuts he'd promised and Starbucks coffee.

Trying to brighten up, I said, "You're a lifesaver."

"I try to be," he said.

There really wasn't anything for us to do, so we sat on the living room floor with coffee and doughnuts, speaking little. Finally I asked, "What did you find out from Joe last night?" I was almost past the point of caring.

"Me? Nothing. I had to get back on patrol. Turned it over to the detectives."

"Oh."

Coffee finished, we got up, and Mike asked, "What needs to go in my car?"

I pointed to boxes, some of which contained precious, delicate china; others held things we needed immediately, but I marked each box carefully.—kitchen, bedroom, girls' rooms, dining room. Mike began to load, and I went to waken the girls.

"We're moving today," Em shouted as she jumped out of bed. "I have to hurry. I have a lot to do."

"Like what?" I asked with a smile.

"I don't know, Mom, but I bet I do."

Maggie got up more slowly and said tolerantly, "What we have to do, Em, is stay out of the way. But I heard Mike say he was bringing doughnuts."

"Then that's the first thing I have to do—eat a doughnut."

The movers came promptly at eight, and as soon as I saw them started, I called Anthony and told him about the paint splotches. He cursed under his breath, not meaning me to hear, and said, "I come right away. But you need brick people. I can call."

"Please," I said. "Tell them it has to be done today."

"You'll pay," he warned, but I just sighed and said, "I know."

My cell phone rang about nine. "This is Kelly.

"Ms. O'Connell? This is Mrs. North."

Keisha's right. The lady without a first name!

"Yes, ma'am. I knew you called, and I returned your call." *Why was I already intimidated by this woman?*

"I was out of town briefly, but now I'm back, and I'd like to look at some houses in Fairmount today."

"I'm sorry. I'm afraid I can't show you houses until at least Monday. My family and I are moving today."

"Oh." The displeasure was evident. "I really wanted to get busy with this."

"I'm sorry," I said, leaving the dutiful tone behind. "I have two young girls, and I absolutely cannot leave on moving day."

"Yes, yes, I understand." The tone implied that she did not understand at all. "Will you be available first thing Monday?"

"Yes, ma'am. I could meet you at nine-thirty."

"No earlier?"

"No. I have to get my girls to school." This woman really bugged me, and I hadn't even met her yet. Not a good way to start a relationship with a client.

"Alright. Nine-thirty at your office. I know where it is."

"I'll look forward to seeing you," I said with what I hoped was a cordial tone. The words were not true.

Mike took one load to the new house, came back, and said, "Kelly, unless you need me, I'm going home to sleep. I'm dead on my feet."

"Mike, you've been such a help. And I know you're tired. Go on and sleep. I can handle things here."

"OK. I'll check you when I wake up."

"Sweet dreams."

He looked at me with an ironic smile on his face. "Yeah."

Anthony arrived while the movers were still loading. Looking at the damage, he cursed under his breath again and didn't even apologize. "The brick men be here ten o'clock. I start on the wood now. By tonight, it be okay."

"Really?" I thought he'd say it was impossible, he'd get it done next week, and so on. I wasted lot of time anticipating Jim Guthrie's reaction.

"I promise."

The movers finished. I loaded my car, locked up the house, and followed the movers to the new house, leaving Anthony in charge of paint removal. There, I began directing the movers where to put what pieces of furniture. As I stood in the living room, pointing this piece to the bedrooms and that huge box to the kitchen, Buck Conroy knocked and entered without waiting for a by-your-leave.

"I got news," he said.

He seemed to have no notion that I might be busy with something. "What news?" I asked.

"Your friend Joe talked last night."

I put down whatever I was holding and sank into one of the overstuffed leather chairs. Almost afraid, I asked, "What did he say?"

"Your ex was paying him to vandalize your house and the one on Fairmount, but he claims that he had nothing to do with the fire at that one. And he claims he didn't kill your ex. He also claims he wasn't there when the girl was beaten—and he got uptight about that one."

I tried to absorb this and fit it into the puzzle. "I thought the vandalism stopped when Tim was killed—until last night. So that doesn't make sense. Why would they disfigure my house after Tim was dead and couldn't pay?"

Conroy smiled. "He had a credit balance, and they thought it was something to do out of respect for his memory."

"A memorial tribute? They shot paint at my house as a tribute to Tim?" I teetered on the edge of hysterical laughter.

"That's the story I got from the young man. Okay, young ruffian. I suspect they all had some beer, and it seemed like a good idea at the time."

"So now?"

"They didn't bond out this time, because it was a second offense for the other two, close on the heels of a first, and even though we can't tie Joe to that night of the beating, he has a prior."

"A juvenile detention center won't help them, will it?"

He shrugged. "Maybe, maybe not. Might just teach them some new tricks. But Joe's twenty-one, too old for juvvie, and the state pen would teach him new tricks. The rest are under age and will go to juvvie if they don't plead out."

"Will I have any say on what happens to Joe?"

"You can decide whether or not to press charges. If you do, no; you can make an appeal at the sentencing hearing, but it's up to the judge. Sort of depends on the luck of the draw—which judge he gets."

I thought about that. "I'll let you know."

"You ought to send the little twerp to jail," Conroy said. He pulled out a cigarette and would have lit it, except that I waved my hands in a negative gesture. "Your ex paid him handsomely. But that doesn't mean he's not a suspect in my mind for either the fire or, more important, Tim Spencer's murder."

"But why would Tim pay him? And where'd he get the money? He claimed he couldn't even pay child support. We're back to what I said—find out where Tim was getting the money."

Conroy shrugged. "We found his cell phone—sloppy detective work. It was in the car, fallen down between the seat and the console." He looked disgusted. "We traced some calls. He's been in touch with some less than honorable men here in town. I don't yet know the nature of the business, but he was mixed up in something not good."

"Did you ask Pam where he got money?"

He got a funny look on his face. "Yeah, but what she said didn't make sense. She said he'd found out who was Martin Properties."

Martin Properties! "The owners of Marie Winton's house," I exclaimed.

"Well, yeah, but whoever they were, they've sure disappeared. We've tried everything to find them."

"I know. So did I."

He looked angry that I'd beaten him to the investigation.

"But why vandalize the houses? What was in it for Tim?"

"I asked Joe about that, but he said he didn't know. Just said something about scaring you away from the skeleton house."

If Tim were alive, I could hear him saying something about how stubborn I was. Aloud, I said, "But then Joe didn't kill him, did he? Why would he kill the person who was paying him? And he wouldn't kill him and then give him a memorial, even if it's a twisted one."

"You're probably right. Joe doesn't make sense as a suspect, but maybe he could have suspected Tim would double-cross him. But then, why the memorial tribute, as you call it, a week later? I won't take him off what I see as a rather short list." He looked at me a long minute. "There's always the possibility that you hired someone to do it. I don't believe that either, but I got to put it on my list of possibles. Pam Spencer is looking better and better to me. And then of course there's your ex's connections here and in California—he may have double-crossed someone, and the murder isn't related to Marie Winton at all. Worst thing is we still don't have any idea who killed that Winton woman. Neither case is closed, and, in

spite of everything, I got a strong feeling they're connected."

I stared at him. "Are your instincts usually right
on?"

"Yeah," he said, "they usually are."

I didn't know whether or not to worry. Maybe relief
was most appropriate.

"Got to go," he said. "Got a hot date tonight." He
leered at me, sort of laughing, and then left.

****

The girls and I spent Sunday unpacking—no church
again, though I sent a quick apology to God and hoped
he understood. The girls hung dresses in their closets,
folded PJs and shirts and jeans in drawers and by early
afternoon had their rooms neat. Struggling with the
kitchen things, I wished my part was that simple.

Theresa came in for lunch, and I made everyone
grilled cheese sandwiches. Looking around at the still-
unpacked boxes and the stacks of dishes, I decided I'd
wash them later. Theresa asked, "Miss Kelly, can I help
you with this?"

"Don't you need to unpack your own things?"

"I've pretty much done that, but I...I want to talk to
you."

I looked at the girls, but Theresa said, "No, they can
stay." She reached an arm for Em who came for a hug.
"I think it's time for me to go home. My dad, he'll try.
He knows now the strap isn't the answer. And my
brothers, Stefan and Emil, they need me. My dad needs
me." Then in a rush she added, "I wouldn't want you to
think I'm not grateful...it's just I think it's time to go
home."

Em began to sob and wail about missing Theresa,
and Maggie went to Theresa's other side and asked
solemnly, "Will you come back for a sleepover?"

Laughing, Theresa said, "I sure will."

I pushed the girls aside so I could hug Theresa. "I think that's a wonderful decision," she said. "Have you told your dad?"

"No. But I know he'll be glad."

"I know he will too. Let's invite him and the boys to dinner tonight, and you can tell him and then go home with him. Can you repack your clothes that quickly?"

"I never unpacked them," Theresa said with a slight smile.

So it was done. A puzzled Anthony accepted the dinner invitation and said they would be there at six. After he talked to Theresa, she handed the phone to me. "He wants to tell you something. About the paint on the house."

I looked at the phone as though it might bite me. "Anthony?"

"Good news. Well, sort of good news. I wasted your money calling the brick people. Its water-base paint and came off easily. But I don't know that I could have done it alone in one day. Now you can't even tell it was ever there. Brick didn't change color, wood doesn't need repainting."

"Oh, Anthony, that's wonderful."

"They only there three hours. Not too much cost, I hope."

I was so relieved I didn't care. I might even file an insurance claim, now that I could assure Dave Shirley that the vandalism was over.

After I thanked Anthony, probably one too many times, and hung up, I looked at my watch. Too late to do a pot roast. I'd have to do chicken. I left Theresa watching the girls, while I ran to the store and got chicken thighs to roast with lemon and butter and herbs, makings for a salad, and baking potatoes to which I'd add sour cream, butter, and cheese. Then I bought two bottles of wine and a big bottle of Coke—a special treat for the girls who were usually only given 7-Up or Sprite. When Mike Shandy called to ask how the move-in was going, it was no problem to add him to the dinner party—I had plenty of food.

While I was at the grocery, Theresa made huge leaps in unpacking the kitchen, and the girls were drying the dishes she washed.

"Theresa, I don't know if I can let you go or not," I said. "This is wonderful."

"Well, we have to eat dinner tonight, and I didn't think you wanted to serve on disposables."

"Not for our first dinner party in the house," I said.

Dinner was a huge success. With Theresa's help, Maggie set the table—place mats on the wonderful oak dining table the Hunts left, my best heavy pottery, cut glassware, and the good stainless flatware—okay, it wasn't my grandmother's sterling, but that had to be hand-washed. This was a wedding gift, one of the things Tim used to gripe that he should have had in the divorce because it came from someone on his side. *Well, he doesn't need it now—what an awful thought.*

As we sat down to dinner, Mike raised his wineglass and proposed a toast to the new house. After everyone toasted and said, "Here, here!"—with Maggie and Em looking a bit puzzled—I raised my hand for silence. "I think Theresa wants to make an announcement."

Theresa looked uncertain, then raised her glass and said, "To my dad, the best dad ever." As everyone clinked glasses and repeated, "Here, here," she said, "Dad, I'm ready to come home."

Speechless for a minute, Anthony blinked and looked at her. "You sure?"

"I'm sure."

"You…"

"Dad, don't ask. Joe won't be a problem and neither will his friends. You and Stefan and Emil need me."

"Ah" he said, "we do." He got up and walked around the table to hug his daughter, who rose to return his hug. "When?"

"Tonight."

Nine-year-old Emil said, "Does that mean she can boss me around again?" His father assured him it did.

The meal dissolved into loud chatter and happy laughter. The girls helped clear the table, and everyone cheered when I brought out the frozen ice cream cake I'd kept hidden after my grocery-store trip.

Someone knocked on the door while we were eating the cake, and Mike jumped up with "I'll get it." He came back, with a strange look on his face, leading Buck Conroy and Joanie. "Look who dropped in and brought champagne to christen the new house."

Buck Conroy waved the bottle, while I thought he'd just stirred it up and made popping the cork all the more perilous. Joanie stood with a satisfied smile, but it didn't escape my notice that she was holding on to Buck's hand, the one that wasn't waving the bottle. *Oh, Joanie,* I thought, *what have you done now? No wonder you haven't called me about morning sickness or other pregnancy problems. You've got Buck Conroy.*

I got plastic cups for everyone—sorry, no flutes available. I owned maybe two—hmm, Mike and I could have champagne some night. But this night even the girls had tiny sips, and so did Theresa's brothers. Everyone raised a glass in response to Buck's almost too-jovial toast for health, happiness, and safety for the occupants of this home. I was amazed at the transformation in him. He seemed...well, less crude, less ready to rub me the wrong way.

While Theresa went to get her things, with her brothers trailing along to help her, we sat and talked about the move, the house, the paint on the old house. "We haven't solved the murders," Conroy said, "but it looks like you should be safe now, Kelly. Mike can stop worrying about you and get back to work."

Mike took the jibe good-naturedly and said, "It's more fun to worry about Kelly."

Trying to keep it a light moment, I said, "I didn't like the vandalism, but it's kind of nice to have someone watching over me." Mike was staring at me, and we exchanged a long look. Joanie didn't miss a thing. She saw the look and smiled, but all the time her hand was on Buck Conroy's thigh. That was one more thing I couldn't worry about.

Before Theresa and the boys came back, Anthony pulled me aside. "Miss Kelly, you give me my daughter back. I...I don't know how to say thank you."

"You just did," I said, hugging him. "But send her to visit me often."

"I will," he promised.

They left, over Theresa's protests that she should help with dishes and my assurances that I could handle it.

The girls went off to get ready for bed, and Mike and I sat around talking to Joanie and Buck. I suspected Mike wished they'd leave as much as I did. It wasn't too long before Joanie said, "Buck, I've got to work tomorrow. We should be going." Buck jumped up, and they left amid profuse thanks for the champagne and hugs all around. I was astounded—I was hugging Buck Conroy?

Mike and I sank back down into the living room chairs, both silent for a long time. After a while he asked, "What do you make of that?"

I shook my head. "Joanie is Joanie. If anyone can turn a sow's ear into a silk purse, she can do it."

He shrugged. "I don't know what the hell you just said, but I think I get the idea."

When I got up to do the dishes, Mike said, "I'll help," and he did, proving efficient at washing dishes.

"You going to miss having a dishwasher and disposal?" he asked.

"Probably," I said, "but I don't care. I'm too happy in this house."

"It suits you," Mike said, "it really does."

The girls came out in nightgowns, smelling clean from their baths, and demanded good-night hugs. Mike and I tucked them in together, kissing each girl and wishing her sweet dreams. A thought flickered across my mind that it was like being a family again.

Mike left as soon as the dishes were done. When I walked him to the door, he wrapped his arms around me and whispered, "Kelly, I hope I'm not out of line saying this, but I feel at home in your new house."

Our kiss was prolonged and anything but platonic.

More tired than I could believe, I took a hot bath, decided I couldn't read, and fell into bed. But just before I drifted off, I remembered that I had that early appointment with Mrs. North tomorrow and apprehension crept over me. *Why does that woman make me nervous, just on the phone? What will she be like in person?*

Chapter Twelve

When I got to the office Monday morning a little after nine, a woman sat in the visitor's chair opposite my desk. I stopped just outside the glass door to study her, and the hackles rose on my neck for no explainable reason. She wore an expensive, well-tailored pinstripe pant suit—even at a distance I could tell it was a St. Johns—with a cream silk shirt, the whole outfit brightened by a scarf draped around the collar of the jacket. I never could drape a scarf so that it looked anything but silly, and I felt a moment's jealousy. Her jewelry was large, clunky, and pure gold. She was about fifty, with artful blonde hair, variegated enough to make it look natural, though of course it wasn't. Her hair was cut just at her chin level and swung about her face when she dropped her head for a moment. I was staring at money and privilege, and I looked with a tinge of regret at the wool flannel pants, corduroy jacket, and practical loafers that I wore.

Mrs. North was tapping the arm of the chair impatiently.

Pushing through the door, I said "Morning" to Keisha, who didn't reply but just cast her eyes toward my desk as if to say, "Watch out. This one will bite." *Thanks, Keisha.*

Brisk and businesslike as I crossed the office. "Mrs. North?"

She stood and held out her hand. "Good morning, Ms. O'Connell. I know I'm early but I'm anxious to get started. Shall we go in my car?" And she picked up her purse as though ready to leave.

Take control now or lose it forever, I told myself. "I like to drive clients in my car," I said as easily as I could. "I know where the different houses are and don't like sitting there, saying 'Turn left here,' and the like. You can understand that makes for an awkward tour around the neighborhood. My car isn't fancy, but it's clean." I'd seen the sleek Hunter green Jaguar in the parking lot.

"Fine," Mrs. North said. "Let's go."

"Whoa," I held up my hands, trying to make a joke of it. "Let's sit first and talk about what you want, what you're looking for. You've got to give me some idea of which houses to show you." As we both sat down, I took in the Louis Vuitton purse and the diamond on her left hand, large but again tasteful.

Mrs. North looked startled, but she settled back into the chair. "Of course. I guess I expected you to read my mind."

I pulled a new client form out of the drawer and said, "I ask clients to fill this out, but why don't we do it together. Your full name?" I hoped for a first name, but all I got was, "Mrs. Jerry North."

"And where are you living now, Mrs. North?"

"In Westover. But that doesn't matter. The house is for my parents, not me. They're in the Rivercrest area in a huge house that's too much for them these days."

Her foot was tapping in the air, either from impatience or nervousness, but I pushed on. "And what are you looking for? Single story, small yard?"

She nodded. "Most definitely. My mother's in a wheelchair and unable to care for herself. She has nursing care twenty-four hours a day. My father is fine....It's just that he's getting frail. He's eighty-two this year."

"I understand," I said sympathetically. Then, as diplomatically as I could, "Mrs. North, Fairmount is at best a changing neighborhood. Nicely fixed-up homes are next to houses that look like they may fall down. My question is why Fairmount for your parents? Why not a smaller home in the Rivercrest area? Or have you considered Berkeley or Park Hill?" I named adjacent, upscale neighborhoods.

Mrs. North, it seemed, had her answers planned to all questions. "My parents lived in Fairmount when they were first married, and it's a sentimental thing for them. They'd like to come back."

Somehow that answer didn't sit well with me. You didn't move to Fairmount from Rivercrest. You moved there because you wanted an older, charming house instead of tract housing in the suburbs or wanted to be closer to town. I looked down at the form and saw that I filled in very few of the spaces. Something was off here, but I couldn't tell what.

"Your phone number," I said, again trying to be businesslike. She gave me home and cell numbers. "Now, what are your requirements in the house?"

"Requirements?" She seemed puzzled.

"How many bedrooms, baths, etc.? Do you need handicapped facilities for your mother?"

She waved an impatient hand in the air. "We can remodel to suit Mother's needs. And bedrooms? Why I guess just two—one for the nurses and one for my parents. A modest kitchen will do—the housekeeper cooks for them."

I began to wonder if the parents even knew that their daughter was considering moving them. "Let me pull a few descriptions from the file," I said, turning to the cabinet behind me and extracting descriptive sheets of the five houses that came to mind.

"Shall we go?" Mrs. North asked.

Maybe she has another appointment and has only allotted a certain amount of time to this venture. Just as we headed out the door Keisha took a phone call and held up a hand to Kelly.

"District attorney's office. You better take it."

Mrs. North gave an obvious sigh of impatience, but I assured her, "This won't take a minute. Please have a seat." I waved a hand at the visitors' chair by Keisha's desk, and Keisha gave me a long and not pleasant look. I went back to my desk, picked up the phone, and said, "Kelly O'Connell."

"Ms. O'Connell, Larry Ashford, D.A.'s office. I want to talk to you about Joe Mendez." It flashed through my mind that I never knew Joe's last name. "When do you plan to come in so we can press charges? He's admitted to the vandalism, and the hearing's scheduled for tomorrow but if we don't have anything from you, we'll have to let him go. Somehow this slipped through the cracks. I should have contacted you right after he was arrested."

I was quiet so long that Larry Ashford said, "Ms. O'Connell? Are you there?"

"Yes, I'm here. But I don't know what I want to do. I'm not sure I want to press charges."

"You're not sure? How can you not?" His voice was so strained that I pictured a young man in his late twenties, new to the district attorney's office, who paled even as he heard my words.

"It seems to me the difference between introducing a young man, who's basically okay but hasn't been given any guidance in life, into the criminal justice system or offering him a chance for rehabilitation. Does he have a record?"

"No. Just one other minor violation—also for vandalism."

"What I want for him is probation with community service, but I understand you can't promise me that. And

I want a chance to talk to him privately, before he appears in court."

Larry Ashford sounded nervous. "I can arrange for you to see him. Hearing's at two tomorrow. But the sentence—we can speak for you, and you can speak yourself, but it's up to the judge."

"Let me know when I can see Joe."

He sounded a little calmer. "City jail. Ten o'clock tomorrow. That okay?"

"That's okay."

"Good, we'll want to talk to you too."

As I approached Mrs. North, the other woman stood. "I hope we can go now." Impatience was clear in her voice.

I didn't care to parade my personal life before her and didn't mention that my house had been vandalized and my ex-husband killed. In her scheme of things, since they hadn't happened to her, they were probably insignificant. I just said, "Yes, of course." *But do you read the paper, lady? Did you see the piece about the man who was found shot in Trinity Park? Oh, I'm being dumb. She has no reason to connect that with me—different last names and all.*

I showed her a charming frame Victorian house with gingerbread trim, a picket fence, and a lovely garden. Inside were well-tended hardwood floors, a modernized kitchen, three bedrooms, and a bath and a half. "No, it just doesn't look like them."

So we went to a brick cottage on College Avenue where the street edged down into the more exclusive Ryan Place addition. This one had larger rooms and a more airy, open feel. It also had a St. Charles kitchen that must have dated back to the '50s but seemed serviceable for anyone who was not a gourmet hostess who wanted a cooking island for friends to gather around. The bathrooms had those tiny tiles that mark older homes, and the master bath had a built-in dressing table with a long mirror over it, flanked on either side by built-in drawers. Many houses in Fairmont had that configuration, and I always loved it.

"I'll put this on my list as a possible," Mrs. North said, folding the description and putting it in her purse.

And so it went with the next three houses—two were "just not right" and the third, "a possible." I couldn't detect a pattern in the way Mrs. North made her choices, and I was baffled.

As we got in the car, I said, "I'll try to think of some others. I know you're in a hurry, but you just can't always find exactly what you want on the market when you"—I started to say when you are so inflexible but changed it—"when you have such a definite idea what you want."

Mrs. North laughed. "I realize I'm difficult to please. You know, I drove by a house the other day, on the corner of Fairmount and Allen. It had your sign on it and looked like you're renovating it. Could we look at that one?"

The skeleton house. I shook my head. "It is being renovated and has had several setbacks"—I saw no need to elaborate—"so it's not ready to show, won't be for at least six months."

"I'd like to see it anyway," Mrs. North pushed.

I was reluctant. Why would she be so determined to see that particular house? Again, I smelled a rat—or was it a decomposing corpse? Still, I didn't want to lose a client. "Okay, but I warn you, it's a mess right now."

We parked in front, and I led the way up the walk. I opened the door and called, "Anthony?" thinking to give him fair warning, though nothing I could say aloud would do that.

"In the kitchen, Miss Kelly. Working on the skeleton closet."

Oh, swell. Of all times, why did he have to say that now? I looked at Mrs. North, but if she'd heard, she gave no sign.

"Anthony, I have a client with me."

"Oh, Miss Kelly, I'm sorry. I go outside and you can look around."

"There's no need for that," I said, unsure just how to handle the introductions.

"No, no. I need a break. I'll sit in the sun and warm my bones. It's cold in here."

It was cold in the house, the kind of cold that settles in an empty house. I made a mental note to get the heating system worked on so that it could be used. A freeze could come at any time now that it was November, and there was no sense taking a risk on the pipes and plumbing.

Mrs. North headed straight to the kitchen, where lumber was scattered about and cabinets pulled out. If you weren't used to looking at construction, you would see nothing but a mess. "What do you plan for the kitchen?" she asked.

I explained that the original configuration would stay. "There was a fire—happens too often during remodeling, you know" —that was my attempt to dismiss the fire— "and Anthony, my carpenter, is redoing it yet again."

"What about that cabinet?" She pointed deliberately to the skeleton cabinet.

"Spice shelves that will swing out and reveal storage behind them," I said. "It was Anthony's idea. There was… uh, dead space…behind there before."

"Very clever," Mrs. North said. "Is this the house I've read about in the paper? The one with the skeleton?"

I stared at nothing. "Yes, it is."

Mrs. North waved a dismissive hand. "That wouldn't bother my parents. I want to buy this house."

I seemed unable to keep my tongue in my head. "You haven't seen the rest of it." This was getting stranger by the minute.

"You're right. Let's go." And the client led the realtor through the house. If I hadn't known it was impossible, I would have thought Mrs. North had been here before. "I'm particularly interested in the fireplace," she said, adding, "They do enjoy a fire at night."

As if by rote, I recited, "The fireplace is the original tile, with decorative tiles inserted. It's flanked by the traditional bookshelves on either side, but this one has a more decorative mantel than most of this era—the mantel is oak and carved, and the bookshelves, as you see, are a matching oak. Usually in these houses, they're painted pine."

"Yes, it's quite attractive."

"This is not a wood-burning fireplace and can never be," I cautioned. "It's not deep enough. But it can hold a gas stove, which is what it did in the old days, or a small set of gas logs. If you don't want to carry out ashes, that's an advantage."

"Certainly." A slight pause. "Ms. O'Connell, I'd like to buy this house."

You haven't even asked the price, and I don't know what I'm going to ask for it when I'm done. Aloud, I said, "I can't sell it in this state. I have to finish the renovation." *Her imperious manner brought out my stubborn streak.*

"I'll have my people finish it."

My people. I hated the phrase. "Mrs. North, I want to sell this house. I want very much to sell it. But I won't, until I'm satisfied with its appearance. I'm sorry. If you can wait six months…."

"I can't."

"Well, then we'll just have to keep looking for other houses for you."

Mrs. North gave me a black look, and we rode back to the office in silence. When she left, my client said, "Let me know if you change your mind. I'll give you $400,000 for it." And she was gone.

I gulped. The most I could hope for from the house was $250,000, if Anthony was as magic as I thought he could be. I went inside and sat at my desk for a long time, staring into space, thinking about the strangeness of the morning. Why would Mrs. North be willing to pay so much for a house in Fairmount? Why did she want it so badly, if it was for her elderly parents? It had to have something to do with the skeleton, but what was the connection?

Keisha looked over at me and said, "You thinkin' deep thoughts?"

"Not deep. Puzzled."

"That woman was something else. Came in here like she owned the place." Keisha was quick to add, "I was polite. But I didn't like her."

I didn't either. Doesn't she have any identity besides Mrs. Jerry North? There was a lot about Mrs. North I didn't know…and I knew just the person to ask.

I picked up the phone and dialed the *Star-Telegram*. "Martha Blackman, please." I met the feature writer at several social events, and we'd hit it off. Still, I felt impertinent calling her.

"Martha Blackman." The voice was businesslike.

"Martha? It's Kelly O'Connell. I'm in real estate and we've met…."

"Kelly, of course. How are you?"

"I'm fine, and you?"

"Fine. What can I do for you?"

"I…well, I have a question about someone you might know. I just met a woman who introduced herself as Mrs. Jerry North and never gave me a first name. And there were several things about her that were puzzling. I thought you might know her."

At the other end of the line, Martha Blackman chuckled. "So you've met Jo Ellen."

"That's her name?"

"Yeah, and don't quote me, but she's a dragon lady."

"Well, I thought so, but I wasn't sure. She wants to move her parents to Fairmount."

"Why ever?" The voice was incredulous. "I don't know who her parents are, but Jo Ellen has a huge home in Westover—she could move five families in there and not be crowded."

The initials M.W.M. flashed into my mind. I was sure it was a wild guess, but she asked, "You don't know who her parents are?"

"No. Jo Ellen and Jerry support all the right causes—Jewel Charity Ball, Zoo Ball, all that stuff, but they're very private. They don't give parties themselves or any of that."

"You suppose she would have been a deb in her day?"

"Probably."

"How would I find out?"

A great sigh. "You'd have to go back through old newspapers—thirty years ago, give or take, and watch for articles about debs. The Assembly probably keeps records, but they might not want to release them. Or you could look in wedding notices. Either one would take you a long time."

I paled at the thought of endless hours of research. "Okay. Thanks. You've been a help."

Martha laughed. "You going to tell me the whole story?"

"When I figure it out. But I don't think it will make a feature for you. Thanks." And I hung up. *Maybe a feature for the local crime pages.*

I went to see Anthony, tomorrow's dealings with Joe Mendez much on my mind. Anthony was at work but still on the kitchen. I wondered if the kitchen would ever be finished so he could move on to the rest of the house.

As if he read my mind, he said, "I have plasterers coming tomorrow to work on the walls in the rest of the house, restore the original plaster. And the painters are scheduled. We'll get there, Miss Kelly, but I don't know how soon." He shrugged. "The kitchen? It's the most difficult. You order new appliances?"

I said yes. I didn't even want to think about the dollars ticking away. If I was going to break even, I should sell this house within a month, and there was no way that was going to happen. "Anthony, I need to talk to Theresa tonight, absolutely must."

"I bring her to your house."

"Anthony, I have to talk to her in private."

He gave me a long look, but he worked for me for several years, and he trusted me. "Okay. I bring her and leave. Come back when you tell me."

"I can come get her...."

"You got the kids to worry about, and you shouldn't be in our neighborhood alone after dark. I bring her. What time?"

"Six? I'll give her dinner."

"Okay. The boys and I will get a hamburger while you talk. They'll like that."

I smiled. "Thanks."

Theresa arrived at six. I fixed chicken piccata, buttered noodles, and broccoli. I'd noticed already that in this house I felt more like cooking. As I dished out plates for the girls, I said, "Why don't you eat in front of the TV in my room tonight? Special treat."

They whooped with delight, though Em said, "Theresa, will you come kiss me goodbye before you leave?"

"Yes, Em, I will. And I'll get a hug from Maggie, if she'll give it to me."

Maggie just smiled, suddenly shy, and they were gone down the hall.

"Theresa, I need to talk to you."

A guarded look. "That's what Dad said."

"Tomorrow I am meeting with the prosecutor and then going to the sentencing hearing for Joe. He's admitted to the vandalism. The kidnapping charge is not involved, since you didn't press charges."

"Are you going to press charges?" Her look was even more guarded, edging, toward hostility.

"I don't know." I spread my hands in a gesture of uncertainty. "I need you to tell me the truth about Joe. What kind of person is he? How do you feel about him? Is he just rotten through and through, or is there…oh, you know, some hope of turning him around?"

"Did he tell you why he did the vandalism?"

"Yes. My ex was paying him."

Theresa nodded. "Joe told me. He bragged about it, and I told him he was dumb to do it and mean to frighten the girls." She looked stricken for a moment. "And you too, of course. But I was more worried about the girls."

"What did he say?"

"He said it was harmless, and nothing bad would happen. But then that's what he said the night he persuaded me to go with him to North Side."

"He didn't kidnap you? You went willingly?"

She hung her head. "Yeah, Miss Kelly. I went with Joe, but then he left—and that's when I got scared. He promised me it would be all right, but he was wrong. It wasn't guys that hurt me—it was girls, but their boy-friends cheered for them. And Joe later got into a fight with two of them."

I remembered Joe's black eye and bruises the day of the garage sale.

"I know Joe has a lot of faults, and he needs to straighten up, but I love him. My father would be furious if I said that to him."

It was just what I'd suspected. I thought it would do no good to ask how she could love someone who would do those things. "Don't say it for a while," was all I could say to her.

"Joe's never had a chance," Theresa went on. "He didn't have a dad like mine, who taught him right from wrong. His dad disappeared when he was little, and his mom, she works all the time, and she's tired, and she doesn't pay any attention to what he does. He's grown up without rules."

"Do you think...is he basically a good person?" *What a dumb question.*

Theresa chewed on her lip. "I'm not ready to give up on him yet. If he gets worse, yeah, I'll move on. But for now, Joe's what I want."

"Okay. I think I know what I'll do, and you've reas-sured me. But I won't give him a total pass. I'll help in the way I think is best."

Theresa looked at her. "Miss Kelly, I'm like my dad. I trust you."

"Okay, eat your dinner. It's getting cold."

****

The Tarrant County jail was a grim place, in spite of its modern construction and sleek red brick exterior walls. I found myself in a waiting room with tiled walls and concrete floor, telling the receptionist at a barred window why I was there. She directed me with a bored wave of the hand to one of the stackable dull grey plastic chairs that lined the room. I waited for about ten minutes—*Okay, I'm ten minutes early because I'm uncertain about this whole thing and want to get it over.*

A young man rushed in, and I recognized Larry Ashford, even though I'd only talked to him on the phone. He had the same harried air about him that I'd heard in his voice. He was older than I'd thought, maybe early thirties, but he wore the requisite blue suit, light blue chambray shirt, and red tie with a small pattern. "Ms. O'Connell? Kelly? I'm sorry if I've kept you waiting. I just couldn't get out of the office, the phone…."

I cut off his wandering apology, rising and holding out my hand. "It's okay. I was early. Let's go see Joe Mendez." I thought I showed a bit of bravado I didn't feel.

We rode an elevator to the fifth floor, where, he explained, there were offices and "meeting" rooms. The jail cells were above. We stepped off the elevator into drabness—hallways painted an institutional color somewhere between gray and green, offices with windows covered by blinds. Larry Ashford led the way to a receptionist desk, where we signed in and were told what room to go to. He seemed to know his way around and took me to the proper room. He knocked on the door, and I heard a gruff, "Come in."

"I'll stay, if that's all right," Larry Ashford whispered.

I nodded. I couldn't have said no at that point, if I'd wanted to.

Joe sat at a scarred Formica table, wearing the orange jumpsuit of an inmate. His hands were cuffed, which made me want to cry out that wasn't necessary. Joe's head hung down, and he didn't look at me. A burly sheriff's deputy stood at one side of the room, his hands clasped in front of him. He nodded at us, and I guessed he was trying to look inconspicuous.

Ashford held a chair for me, and I sat opposite Joe. Ashford sat at the end of the table and leaned back, as though he were an observer.

Okay, you asked for this meeting, and now it's yours to handle. "Joe, could you look at me?"

He raised his head, and I saw that his bruises were faded, his black eye much better. "Why'd you come here? Theresa send you?"

"No. I came because …oh, I don't know why I came, to tell the truth. I think you did some awful things—to me, my girls, to Theresa—but I don't think you're that bad a person, and I don't know that I want you to go to Huntsville or wherever."

He stared at me, clearly amazed. "I thought you'd want me locked up for years. Thought that was why you'd come."

"No, I came to talk to you, to ask you why? You know Theresa won't press charges for the kidnapping, but it's up to me to decide what to do about the vandalism. It's not as serious a charge as kidnapping, but you'd still go to jail. And right now you're under suspicion of murder, which at the least would send you to Huntsville. None of that is as awful to me as the threats that were made to my girls."

"That was the other guys talking. I wouldn't have done that, and I wouldn't have let them do anything." He kept his eyes fixed on my face, and, looking at him, I didn't see evil or malice. Instead I saw, perhaps, confusion. *What are you now? A psychiatrist?*

I plowed ahead. "I'm not sure I want that to happen. I think maybe you'd come out a worse person than you'd go in." I saw a flicker of interest at that. "But I believe actions have consequences. I think you need some punishment."

"So does my mother," he said, the words mumbled to the point that I wasn't sure I'd heard them correctly.

"Your mother?"

He nodded. "Yeah, she's really mad at me." He sounded like a child who'd been punished.

I turned to Ashford, "Can we talk outside for a minute?"

He nodded and followed me out of the room.

"Seems to me our friend Joe hasn't gotten a fair shake in life. No one's taught him about being an upstanding citizen and all that. He was probably beaten when he misbehaved, but no one showed him the right way."

Ashford nodded, though I could tell he was wondering where this was going.

"If he were given…what do you call it? Deferred adjudication? Would he or could he be required to have some counseling?"

Larry Ashford rubbed his chin with his hand. "It's not usual, but I suppose it could happen. Once again, it's up to the judge. But to do that, Joe's lawyer would have to agree to a plea of no contest. As it is, we've got a guilty plea. And, frankly, Kelly"—he didn't even notice that he'd slipped into using my name—"my head will roll if the plea changes to a lesser one." He thought a minute. "But under deferred adjudication, he might be required to do community service, and you could request counseling. I don't know where the judge would go with it."

"Perfect. Your head can stand to roll a lot better than his," I told him. Then I turned and went back into the room. "Joe, who's your lawyer?"

"Some dude…uh, guy…the court appointed. I can't afford no lawyer."

Exasperated, I said, "Do you know his name?"

He thought a minute. "Mc...something like that with a Mc in front of it. Uh, McGill, that's it." He looked as though he expected approval.

I looked at Ashford. "You know him? Can you get him on the phone in the next fifteen minutes?"

Ashford nodded and left the room, pulling out his cell phone as he did.

Turning back to Joe, I said, "Joe, you need to promise me a couple of things. I'm going to press charges because, as I told you, I think you have to understand the consequences of the things you did to my property—two pieces of my property—and to my life. My sanity, if you will. But I don't want this to ruin your life. So, if you plead 'No Contest,' which means you did it but you aren't exactly admitting it—I'm no lawyer and I'm on shaky ground here, but I think that's what it means—the judge will give you, oh, say, six months probation, during which you'll have to check in with a probation officer, do some community service, and, at my request, get some counseling."

He stared at me again, and I wasn't sure he understood all of it.

"Joe, do you understand?"

"I think so, Miss Kelly. Why you do this for me?"

"Because I don't like to see us add another criminal to our population." And then I added, "Because you tried to help Theresa. And I'm afraid she loves you."

His face changed, and he said, as softly as I spoke, "I love Theresa. But she don't have nothing to do with what I did."

"I know that." Then, rising, "I'll see you in court," and I left.

I was drained. I rode down the elevator with Ashford, who was silent. When we reached the main floor, he finally spoke. "I...we need to talk before the hearing. I assume you'll be there?"

"Oh, yeah, I'll be there."

"Where can we talk?"

It was after 11:00 and my stomach was grumbling. "I'm going to La Madeleine and have a Caesar salad, a potato cake, and a glass of wine. Want to come?"

He loosened just a bit. "Yeah, for all of it but the glass of wine. I don't dare do that."

"Too bad."

After we went through the line, got our food and were settled at a table, Ashford said, "Okay, usually I tell the victim what to do. In this case, I guess you're telling me what you're going to do."

"Did you reach Mr. McGill?"

"He's supposed to call me any minute."

"Well, you gave me a quick lesson in the law in the hallway, but I told Joe I thought he should plead no contest, with his lawyer's agreement, of course," — Ashford put his head in his hands— "and that I wanted to speak both on his behalf and for what I thought should be recommended. Can I do that?"

"Yeah. But I see my career as a D.A. going down the tubes."

I took a sip of wine. "It can't be all that bad. You're saving society from another hardened criminal."

"We believe in punishment," he said righteously, and I resisted the urge to laugh.

Chapter Thirteen

The courtroom appearance wasn't as intimidating as I expected. The room itself was everything a courtroom should be—paneled walls, padded leather seats for spectators, the traditional wooden railing polished to a shine, the two long tables for the defense and prosecution, and of course the judge's wooden bench.

Ashford ushered me to the prosecutor's table on the right and showed me a seat, but when black-robed Judge Sullivan entered, we all stood. I thought it went pretty much like TV shows, with the judge calling for the plea—"No contest." But then the judge turned to Ashford and asked, "Does the prosecution wish to speak?"

Ashford said, "The complainant wishes to make a statement," and he nodded at me. "Ms. Kelly O'Connell," he said.

I wished I had planned in advance what I wanted to say. My palms were sweaty, my face going red. "Your honor" —I knew that part was right— "I know this young man only slightly, and that's a long, complicated story that you don't have time for."

"I appreciate that, Ms. O'Connell," the judge's tone was dry.

"But I don't think he's a hardened criminal, and I don't want to see him become one. I want"…I stumbled over the words… "deferred adjudication."

"Do you realize we dismiss a great number of vandalism cases?" Judge Sullivan asked. "Especially juveniles and I understand that Mr. Mendez is not a juvenile, but still…."

"I talked to Joe this morning and told him I thought actions have consequences, and he needs to learn that. But I also think he needs some counseling, and he needs to learn to help others, like community service…."

"Have you considered standing for the bar?" the judge asked, a smile flitting across his face. "Thank you, Ms. O'Connell."

It went pretty much as I hoped. Six months of deferred adjudication, after which, if Joe behaved, the charge would be dismissed, and he would have no record. The judge assigned a probation officer and a counselor, and Joe would begin community service the next week. The judge told him to get a permanent, fulltime job. Then he banged his gavel, said, "Next," and we were out of the courtroom.

"You happy?" Larry Ashford asked.

"Yeah. Call me if you lose your job."

He smiled as much as he could, and we parted. Just as he turned away, Joe and his mother caught up with me. Joe hung his head and didn't look at me, but his mother said, "Thank you. Joe and me, we're going to make it right. I'm…I'm going to pay attention to him." I didn't tell her I thought it was too little too late. But I did put a hand on Joe's arm, almost forcing him to look at me, and I said, "Take care of Theresa."

He nodded, and I had the feeling he would.

It was time to get the girls, and I hurried to my car, feeling maybe a bit too smug until a small voice inside me warned, *that's when you always get in trouble.*

****

Wednesday morning I was at my desk, trying to catch up on paperwork. I thought briefly of calling Mrs. North, "Mrs. Jerry North," and decided against it. I usually hated to pressure clients, but even though I thought one or two of the houses we'd looked at would fit, that wasn't what stopped me from calling. It was the uneasy feeling Jo Ellen North gave me. I wished I could just forget about her, but she was a pretty determined lady, and I knew she'd call again.

Keisha answered the phone, gave me a long look, and said, "Interesting phone call for you."

What's that supposed to mean?

"Kelly O'Connell."

"Ms. O'Connell, my name is Mark Smotherman. I'm with *Unsolved Mysteries,* the TV show."

I sensed trouble coming. "Yes?"

"The Winton family of Crawford, Texas—guess we all know where that is, these days"—a slight chuckle—"has contacted us about a segment on their murdered sister, and we're interested. I…well, truth is, would you cooperate? Could we film at the house, interview you? We've got to make Fort Worth part of the story or it won't fly."

I remembered how appalled I'd been when the *Star-Telegram* wanted to do a feature. But this was different—this was Marie Winton's family grasping at straws, hoping that a national television show would uncover the killer of their loved one. I knew the show had a strong success rate, but I didn't see how it could help in this case. Still…I sat, silent, thinking.

"Ms. O'Connell, are you there?"

"What? Oh, yes, sorry. I was thinking. When would you do this?"

"We schedule months ahead, so probably not till, oh, maybe March."

March? I expect Buck Conroy to solve this long before March. "Yeah, I'll help to a certain extent. Depends on what you want when the time comes." She paused. "What happens if the crime is solved before then?"

He sighed. "We cancel the segment and move on to other things. Happens a lot, which I guess is a good thing. I mean, crimes being solved." Then, his voice defensive, "But we do have a good crime-solving record."

"Yeah, I know. And the Wintons contacted you? Did they say the Fort Worth police weren't doing enough?"

He cleared his throat. "They said the investigation wasn't moving along as they'd like it to."

"Well, I think the police are doing the best they can"—*after ignoring the case for years*—"but I'd like to help the Wintons. I know they're suffering. So, yes, I'll do whatever you need." I added, "Well, almost whatever. Within reason."

"Thanks. We'll be in touch."

I put down the phone and stared into space.

"What was that?" Keisha listened to my one-sided conversation with curiosity.

"I may be on national TV," I said and told her the whole story.

Keisha shook her head. "I think you're gonna find out who did it before that. I got faith in you, boss lady."

****

My next phone call was from Buck Conroy. Before I could tell him about the television show, he said, "Well, your husband sure married himself a piece of work. We tracked her down at her sister's and went out to see her. Decided not to pull her in...yet." He added that last word ominously.

"What do you mean?" I could picture him, cigarette drooping out of his mouth, phone cradled between his shoulder and his ear while he did something else on his desk. In fact, I thought I could hear computer keys clicking. With great restraint, I didn't ask him how Joanie was—I think I was afraid he'd twist the reply.

"This is her third marriage. The Martin name came from her second husband."

There goes the connection to M.W.M. and Martin Properties.

"She used to be a stripper in LA, cut quite a swath. Don't know much about her first marriage—she clammed up about it. But Martin was in real estate, and that's how she met your ex. She left the husband for Tim Spencer. It was a messy divorce, two-year-old kid that the husband got custody of."

So Tim became a home breaker—not only his home, but somebody else's. "She say why she left a husband and child for Tim? If it was passion, don't tell me. I don't want to hear."

He laughed. "No. She's a gold-digger. She thought he was a real estate mogul. She just began to figure it out when he whisked her to Vegas for a quickie wedding and then brought her here. Said his fortune was here. But he also said something funny to her, that it was significant that her name was Martin because that was the key to his future. I doubt there's any connection to her ex and Martin Properties."

I thought about that for a long minute. "So he knew before he came here that the house was owned by Martin Properties? I know someone here told him about the skeleton—I just haven't figured out who. But how did he know about Martin Properties?"

"No idea. And I wish you'd figure out who shoveled information to him. It wasn't Joe. He came into the picture after Spencer planned the dirty work."

I sighed. "I agree. I don't know what difference it would make if we found out who first told him. If he knew about the death, could he research the history of the house online? I never thought of trying that."

"I don't know, but I'll find out."

"If you do, don't tell me. It would have saved me hours away from the office and home." I almost laughed but couldn't quite. "And that's the woman my ex-husband exposed my children to—a stripper who's been married three times. She didn't seem that bad…well, I don't mean bad…but you know what I mean."

"Aw, come on, Kelly. Happens to the best of us. Strippers can be good people. I don't think she's a bad sort. Life's dealt her some bad hands, and maybe she'd didn't handle them well. Sister's something else though—a real hard nose who doesn't cut Pam any slack. Kept saying she came from a good family and should have known better. Had the new Mrs. Spencer in tears."

"Do you think she loved Tim?"

"People like that? I don't think they know about love in terms of commitment—I don't think I know that—or at least I didn't think I did until recently. But, yeah, I think she loved him. And I think she cared about him and about your girls and was good to them—she talked about them."

"Thanks," I said. "That means a lot. So is she off your list?"

"Not by a long shot. Neither is Joe. But I got some other leads." With that enigmatic statement, he hung up without saying goodbye or anything.

The gossip in me came to life, and I called Joanie at work, something I almost never did. "Joanie, you in the midst of something?"

"No, just sitting here trying to plan a campaign, but my mind keeps wandering."

"In what direction?" I asked, as if I didn't know.

"Well, Buck Conroy of course," she giggled. "I can't keep my mind off him."

Or your hands, I thought. "Joanie, does he know about the baby?"

"Oh, yes. He says it doesn't matter at all. He kind of always wanted children—isn't that sweet?"

"Yeah, sweet," I mumbled. After asking how she was feeling, to which she answered she thought she was walking on air, and a few other questions to camouflage the nosy nature of my call, I said, "Well, come by and see the girls sometime."

"I will, and I'll bring Buck."

"Swell." I was afraid I banged the phone down. Keisha gave me a long look. I was worried about Joanie, afraid she was in for a big letdown at just the wrong moment when Buck decided he didn't find a woman seven or eight months pregnant attractive any more. Not my problem, I decided. Besides, what did I know about romance? I wasn't too successful at it.

****

A woman who lived in one of the grand mansions on Elizabeth Boulevard called, wanting to list her house for sale. With visions of a sale of at least $600,000, maybe close to $700,000, I was delighted to make an appointment to see the house that afternoon before the girls got out of school. Then I danced around the office until Keisha said, "For a woman who owns a house with a skeleton in the closet and whose ex-husband was just shot to death, you sure are happy."

"Got to look on the bright side, Keisha," I said. "This may be the sale that makes this company." I was back in my manic phase.

Elizabeth Boulevard was "the" address to have in Ryan Place, a wide street with huge trees and stately homes. Never mind that the ground shifted all the time, and those homes all had cracks in their old plaster. It just meant constant maintenance, and most of the owners could afford it.

The house was a classic, red brick with a long, wide porch across the front and large white pillars, evenly spaced windows, the front steps edged with red brick. Landscaping was good. I appraised the curb appeal and found it—well—wonderful. The downstairs windows were curtained with light, gauzy material that seemed unobtrusive, as was the bevel-paned front door, and when I rang the doorbell, I heard sonorous chimes. An attractive woman, probably in her early sixties, answered the door. *No maid here,* I thought with a certain amount of relief. The older woman was shorter than me, her hair cut fashionably short in a casual, almost windblown look, her makeup unobtrusive but perfect. She wore a velour pantsuit—comfort more than style. "Ms. O'Connell?" she asked.

"Yes, Mrs. Wright. I'm Kelly O'Connell."

"Come in," she said and welcomed me into an expansive entry hall with wide-planked, pegged-oak floors and two staircases that met on a large landing and curved upwards into one.

"I know you'll want to see the house," Mrs. Wright said and led the way on a brisk tour. The formal living room, with arched windows, old pulled plaster, wall sconces, and the same wide-planked wood floors, lay to the right of the entry hall and featured a large fireplace. Mediterranean tiles lined the circular firebox, and a beautiful, gilt mantel topped it. Beyond that room was a sun porch with a red tile floor, wicker furniture, and lots of windows. To the left of the entry was a formal dining room and a breakfast room and, to the back, an updated kitchen with a cooking island, Sub-Zero refrigerator/freezer, JennAir gas stove with a grill, a griddle, and a warming drawer.

"It's wonderful," I said, almost breathless.

Upstairs I toured four large, airy bedrooms, surrounded by windows, each with its own updated bathroom. Off the master bedroom another sun porch offered a wonderful space for reading the morning paper and sipping coffee.

"Come downstairs, and we'll have a cup of tea," Mrs. Wright said. "I always think that's so civilized in the afternoon."

I followed and found myself seated at a round cherry table, the distressing subtle enough to show that the table a genuine antique and not something bought at store that featured faux antiques. The tea was English, and with it Mrs. Wright served wafer-like chocolate and vanilla cookies. I decided I'd like to live this way.

"How much did you want to ask for your house, Mrs. Wright?"

"My dear, you tell me. But you must call me Barbara. I'm not used to such formality. As for the house, we've lived here since 1960. Raised four children. But now it's time for us to downsize. My husband isn't able to keep up the yard and all—he's a lawyer, and he's tired, ready for an easier life. We'd like to stay in the neighborhood—another reason I called you. I've my eye on a house you're redoing at the corner of Fairmount and Allen. One-story. I think that just might suit us, and it looks comfortable, substantial. I'd like to see it."

I swallowed hard. "It's still being renovated and we've had some setbacks. It's not ready to show." *That house is jinxed. How can two rich people want to buy a house where a skeleton was found?*

Mrs. Wright waved a hand. "That's not a problem. We're not in a hurry. We're just thinking ahead. But back to this house. We bought it for a song, and I don't know what it's worth today. If I don't like what you say, I'll get a second opinion."

I love meeting easy clients. "I think you should. I would put this house on the market at $795,000."

The other woman raised her eyebrows. "You would? That much?"

"Well, then you could be prepared to come down a little, but, yes, I'd start there."

After another sip of tea, I glanced at my watch and saw that it was time to get the girls. "Mrs. Wright, I have to run get my daughters from school, but I'll run comps on sales on Elizabeth Boulevard, just confirm my price estimate. Then I'll draw up a realtor's agreement and bring it by tomorrow morning, if that's all right. I generally ask a client to stay with me a minimum of three months. I wouldn't want you to expect the house to sell the first day I put a sign up—this house is special and will need just the right buyer, who can also afford it."

"I know, dear," she said, patting my hand. "We're not in a hurry. Now run get those girls. How old are they?"

As I crossed that huge entry hall, I told her about Maggie and Em and that I was a single parent.

"Oh, my," she said. "Well, I hope their father helps out some."

It was on the tip of my tongue to say, "He can't. He got shot last week," but I thought better of it.

Her last words were, "Think about showing me that house."

The idea of showing Mrs. Wright the house scared me, and I knew why—I was afraid of Mrs. North. That instinct came from deep within me. I'd met other society women who perhaps intimidated me, made me feel shabby or awkward or something but never anyone who made me afraid. I was afraid of Jo Ellen North for myself and, even more, for my girls. I drove a little faster to get Maggie from school.

Of course, Maggie was perfectly safe, waiting impatiently for me. Once she was in the car and we headed toward Em's day-care facility, I asked how her day was.

"Actually," she said in a matter-of-fact tone, "it was pretty dull. I can read better than anyone in the class, and I get bored listening to them."

The corners of my mouth twitched. "Perhaps you could ask Miss Benson to give you extra work... or maybe you could help some of the other children. Why don't you talk to Miss Benson about it?"

Maggie stared at me. She expected reproof; instead she got encouragement, and she was a bit uncertain what to do next.

Em claimed her day was wonderful. "Look," she said, waving a large piece of paper, "I drew our new house."

She captured some of the feel of the house—the pillars on the porch, the curving walk, and the bushes, all of course in primitive terms.

"Why, Em, that's wonderful. I'll put it on the refrigerator."

"No, Mom. It's so good it needs a frame," she declared.

"Of course," I murmured, vowing to hang it in my bedroom.

The girls didn't ask about my day, which was good, because I didn't want to tell them about going to court with Joe. The thought of Joe made me rethink Tim's California connection. Joe could have called Tim. He knew him from working with Anthony, but why would Joe call?

That night I called Theresa, ostensibly to ask how she was.

"I'm okay," she said. "Joe told me what you did today. Thanks."

"Is Joe okay with it?"

"Yes, ma'am. He's grateful to you, says he's going to make you proud of him and glad that you did what you did."

"I hope so," I said. Then with a guilty feeling of using Theresa I said, "Why don't you bring Joe to supper tomorrow night? Just to show that there are no hard feelings and get us off on a better footing."

She hesitated. "I don't know...I can't tell my dad I'm doing that."

This time I was honest. "Theresa, I'll tell your dad. It's time you stopped hiding your relationship with Joe. I'll explain the whole thing to Anthony tomorrow."

And I did. I lectured that sweet old man up one side and down the other. When I said Theresa loved Joe, he put up his hands in protest, but I talked right on. I told him what Theresa had told me about Joe being ignored as a child, and what I'd done in court.

"I don't care," he said. "She ain't goin' to see him."

"Yes, she is, Anthony. If you don't approve, she'll sneak. Why don't you try inviting him to dinner, getting to know him? Maybe he's changed since all this trouble." I took a deep breath, "Anthony, when you were young, did anyone ever give you a second chance?"

He looked surprised, and then his face softened. "Yeah," he said. "My pop did. After I'd done everything in the book wrong, he told me he loved me and had faith in me."

"And it made a difference?"

He looked at me. "Okay, Miss Kelly. You win. She can go out with Joe. I may not be ready for dinner with him yet, but I'll work on it."

"They're coming to my house for supper tonight," I said and turned away before he could roar.

"Who's coming for supper?" Maggie asked as I set the table for five.

"Theresa and Joe."

"I don't like Joe. I don't want him to come to our house anymore." She was determined. "He did bad things."

"I don't want him either," Em chimed in.

"Girls, he'll be a guest, and you will be polite. Joe is sorry for the things he did, and he's making up for it. And he's special to Theresa. You love Theresa, don't you?"

They nodded.

"Then for her sake you'll give Joe another chance, won't you?"

"Okay," Maggie said, "but if he ever does anything bad again...."

"Okay," Em echoed.

I decided to do oven-fried chicken, mashed potatoes, and make a salad. On the way home I'd bought a half-gallon of cookies 'n cream ice cream, the girls' favorite. "If you're pleasant and polite, you can have ice cream with chocolate sauce for dessert." I didn't even feel bad about bribing them.

Joe and Theresa arrived right at six, and Joe was a different person already. The pony tail was gone, and the baggy pants were replaced by well-fitting jeans over which he wore a plaid, cotton shirt. I stared just a minute and then winked at him. I swear he smiled.

Since I wasn't about to offer them a drink before dinner, as I would have Mike, we went right to the dinner table. They were both quiet, but I'll give Maggie credit. She tried.

"So, Joe, how was your day?"

Joe looked a little nonplussed. "It was okay," he said. "I went looking for a job."

"What kind of a job?"

He shrugged. "Just about anything I can do."

"Would you work at McDonald's?" she pursued.

I groaned inwardly.

"If I had to," he said, looking down at his plate.

It went through my mind to offer him a job working with Anthony, but then I dismissed that as one of the worst ideas I'd had for a long time. I'd already meddled enough.

"Joe likes kids," Theresa said. "I thought he might apply to the YMCA or something like that, maybe the Boys and Girls Club."

"Good idea," I said.

Joe seemed to get more in the spirit of things. "So, Maggie, how was your day?"

"Bor-ing," she said and told him how bored she got listening to others read.

Joe had no idea what to say to that, but Theresa said, "Be patient, Maggie. I was never good at math, and I appreciated it when some of my friends helped me."

Maggie looked at her. "I'm no good at math either."

Em didn't want to be left out. "Joe, do you want to see the picture I drew at school today? Mom's going to frame it."

"Sure I do," he said, and he was appropriately enthusiastic about her art. I could see that Em changed her mind about Joe, and Maggie was beginning to.

After dinner, they both pitched in to help clean the kitchen, and it was done in no time. "Theresa," I said, "would you take the girls to the back? I want to talk to Joe."

Joe looked like a deer caught in the headlights as I led him to the living room and motioned for him to sit in one of the big comfortable chairs. He perched on the edge of it, not enjoying its comfort.

"Joe, don't worry. You're not in more trouble, and I'm not going to get angry. I just need to figure something out."

He looked at his hands.

"Before my former husband came back to Fort Worth, he knew all about what was happening here, and I want to know how he knew."

Joe looked at me and took a deep breath. "I called him. He paid me to tell him."

"How did you know to call him?"

"Some guy I know up on Jacksboro Highway, he asked me to do it. He knew where Mr. Spencer was and that I knew him from having worked for him."

This was getting confusing. "What guy? What's his name?"

Joe shook his head. "I can't tell you that. There are some mean people around, and I don't want them to think I ratted on them. But I'll tell you that they said a Mr. Martin wanted your ex to let him know what was happening with that skeleton house."

Martin. Bells pealed in my brain in a wild cacophony of sound. "Who's Mr. Martin?"

"I have no idea," Joe said. "All I know is the name. Does that help?"

"Yes, I think it does. And Joe, this is between you and me. I'll never tell where I learned that name. As a matter of fact, it's a name I already know, but you've sort of tied it together for me."

"I don't understand, Miss Kelly, but you be careful. You're messing with some people who won't stop at nothing."

"Anything," I corrected before I thought. I looked at him. "You be careful, Joe, if you're involved with these people."

He grinned. "Not me, not anymore. I gotta show Theresa's father I'm good enough for her. I think my wild days are over—and I'm glad. I thank you, Miss Kelly, for what you did for me, in spite of everything."

Part of me wanted to reach out and hug him; the other part wondered if this was like a three-month conversion to religion. "I'm proud of you," is all I said, "and you let me know if I can help. I want you to make it."

I almost thought he I saw a tear in the corner of one eye. I don't think anyone ever believed in him before, except maybe Theresa.

After Joe and Theresa left, I kissed the girls and tucked them in, then ran for the phone book, turning to the pages for Martin, remembering that there were pages and pages of Martins. But now I started with the M listings, looking for M. Martin or Marty Martin. There were at least twenty-five people whose first initial was M. It was hopeless.

Now what, Kelly? I sat at my desk for over an hour, my thoughts tangled. Marty Martin was bound to be M.W. Martin or "Marty" of Marie Winton's letters home—I was convinced of that, but I had no proof. And he was older than Marie—judging from the picture in the locket he was maybe mid-thirties in the late fifties, which would put him in his early eighties now.

That Mr. Martin would want to know what was going on at the house was believable. Probably he hadn't worried all the years it was in private hands, but once someone—specifically me—began to tear it apart for renovation, he knew the secret was out. And then, of course, it was indeed out—in the newspapers, on TV. He couldn't do anything, but he must have known it would start an investigation. I guess no one is ever sure how safe their secrets are.

My mind spun out a tale. Martin wanted Tim notified because he thought Tim could stop me. Tim, knowing me too well, knew he couldn't stop me by asking—or ordering—so he employed Joe, who was eager for an easy dollar.

The right thing, I knew, was to tell all this to Buck Conroy, but I also knew I wasn't going to do that. He'd laugh at me for spinning theories in the air. I could hear him say, "Conjecture, Kelly, all conjecture. We can't go anywhere with that. Doesn't prove Martin killed Marie

Winton." And, of course, it didn't. It just meant I was getting closer.

Maybe I should tell Mike—but he'd lecture me again about getting involved where I shouldn't and putting myself in danger. In a way, if Martin was that desperate and had such bad friends as Joe implied, I really was in danger. That thought sent me down the hall to check again on my sleeping daughters.

I didn't get much sleep that night. About three o'clock in the morning I sat bolt upright in bed. M.W.M. wasn't Marty's initials—it was a wishful monogram on Marie's part. It stood for Marie Winton Martin. It hadn't dawned on me before. Mr. Martin was called Marty as a nickname from his last name, not his first, like my uncle who was called Mac because his name was MacBain. Sure didn't help solve the mystery though.

****

Next morning I went to the office but couldn't keep my mind on what I was doing. I was drawing up the papers for Mrs. Wright, when Jo Ellen North called. "I just wondered if you'd changed your mind yet about selling me that house yet," she said, her voice cold.

I might be afraid of her, but I wasn't going to let her bully me. "No, Mrs. North. I'll let you know when that house is finished. In the meantime, I have some other houses to show you...."

"I'm not interested," she cut me off. "You'll change your mind." And the phone went dead.

Was that a threat? It sounded enough like one that, acting on impulse, I called Mrs. Wright. "I'll have the papers done in about an hour," I said, "and I'll bring them by if that's convenient. And, Mrs. Wright, if you want to see that house on Fairmount, in its current condition, I'd be glad to show it to you—perhaps tomorrow? I have a couple of others for you to look at too."

"Lovely, my dear. My husband can look at the papers tonight, and I'll get them back to you tomorrow. Then you can put your sign in our yard—I'll feel like that's real progress."

"What time would be best for you tomorrow?" I asked.

"Let me just look at my calendar—oh, dear, I have a long boring luncheon to attend tomorrow. I suppose two o'clock makes it difficult to pick up your girls."

"I can have someone else pick them up, I think," I said. "I'll check tonight and let you know."

The papers were ready, but I thought it best to give an hour's notice. So there I was, an hour on my hands, and nothing but the mysterious Mr. Martin on my mind. Just to get my mind on something else, I decided to call Claire Guthrie and see how they liked the house.

"Oh, Kelly, I'm so glad to hear from you. We love the house. We haven't done a thing to it; you left it in such perfect shape. We have some remodeling plans on down the road, but we're very happy. Can't you stop by for coffee?"

"Now?" I squeaked.

"Well, sure, if you have the time."

"I have an appointment close to you in an hour, so yes, I'd love a cup of coffee," I said.

"The pot's on. Come right over."

It was weird to walk into the house I'd lived in for so long and see someone else's furniture and paintings and, well, just everything. The house even smelled different, maybe Claire's perfume, who knows? It was, subtly, a different house—and being there didn't make me sad at all.

We settled at the kitchen counter with coffee, and Claire asked how the real estate business was going. I told her about the house on Elizabeth Boulevard and my hopes for a big sale.

"Well, we like it here so much, I'm telling all my friends they should move to Fairmount," she said. "And I'm recommending you as an agent."

"I appreciate it," I said, hoping she meant it and that it wasn't just empty talk.

As the conversation lagged a minute, I asked, "Do you know a woman named Jo Ellen North?"

Claire laughed. "I know who she is, but she wouldn't know me from a fly on the wall. She's way above me socially—or thinks she is."

"You mean she has pretensions?" I asked with a grin.

"More than that. She *knows* she's better than anyone else. And I've no idea why. I hear there's something funny in her family background, like her father was in jail for tax evasion or something." Then she laughed again. "Listen to me, I'm nothing but an old gossip."

I filed her gossip away in my mind, even as I said, "Well, definitely not old." I hesitated. "Do you know an older man named Marty?"

She shook her head. "Never heard the name. Who is he?"

"I'm not sure," I said. "I'm still trying to figure out the skeleton business about the house on Fairmount, and his name came up. Mrs. North wants to buy that house. In fact, she wants it so much that it's scary—and suspicious."

"Why, Kelly, it sounds like you're in the midst of a mystery." She laughed again, and I tried to laugh with her.

We chatted on, exchanging news of each other's daughters—hers were in high school, and she was dreading the next year when the oldest, Megan, went away to college. "I'm hoping she'll go to TCU. She might be in the dorm, but at least she'd be close by, and I wouldn't be as frightened as if I left her on that huge UT campus."

"I can't even imagine the day," I said. "I'm still dealing with day-care, for heaven's sake."

"It'll go by before you know it," she warned, and I knew she was right.

As I left, we promised we'd get together for lunch soon. Driving the short distance to Elizabeth Boulevard, I realized that neither of us mentioned her husband. I wondered if he liked the house as well as she said he did.

I handed Barbara Wright the papers without going past the front door and then promised I'd be back at two the next afternoon, unless she heard otherwise from me.

I looked at my watch. It was noon. I went to the Grill, ordered a cheeseburger, and then before the check was written changed that to a Caesar salad with chicken. Keisha would be so proud. I ate my salad at one of the tall tables in the front room, where you sat with your legs dangling from chairs that are barstool height. It is a great place for watching the people who come in, but nobody I knew came that day.

Chapter Fourteen

That night I called Theresa to ask if she and Joe could pick the girls up from their schools the next day and stay with them until I finished an appointment. "I can do it, Miss Kelly, but Joe, he has a job interview tomorrow afternoon. He's going to the YMCA in Wedgwood, where they have lots of after-school programs and such for young kids."

"Theresa, I know you can take care of the girls alone, but how will you get them from school without a car if Joe's busy?"

"I'll take Joe to his appointment and then get the girls. Joe can take a bus—or wait for me, his choice. He won't mind."

"Are you sure?"

"Yes, Miss Kelly, I'm sure. You go on to your appointment, and don't worry."

"I'll leave Em's car seat at the office for you and tell Keisha to expect you."

I told the girls Theresa would pick them up, which elicited from Maggie the comment that Theresa was more likely to be on time than I was and from Em a question: "Isn't Joe coming too? I want him to. I like Joe now."

Fickle woman. "Joe may come by later."

****

Anthony called the next morning, but I wasn't worried. The days of Anthony calling to report bad things were over. Wrong.

"Miss Kelly? Someone broke into the house last night."

I thought I might cry, just put down the phone and sob. Had Joe been playing me for a fool? And Theresa? "How bad is it?" I asked and almost put my hands over my ears so I wouldn't hear the answer.

"This was something different," he said. "This was a professional, someone looking for something. He picked the lock on the back door and was methodical about going through the house. Pried panels off the fireplace, left the spice rack swung out so I know he looked there. But it wasn't vandalism—it was a deliberate search."

The diary. Of course, someone was looking for the diary. Before I could say anything, Anthony asked, "You still got that diary?"

"Yes. It's in my closet. With the move and all, I just sort of moved it and forgot about it." Well, I didn't forget, but I tried not to think of it because I didn't know what to do with it.

"You should have given it to Mike," he said sternly.

"I know, I know. But it's such a personal thing. I hated to hand it over to the police and have it tagged as evidence and thrown in a bin. Now...well, if I give it to them now, Mike will be furious. And, honest, Anthony, there's not one helpful thing in there."

"I'm afraid, Miss Kelly. Whoever wants that diary, wants it bad. And they might come after you next."

"Or you, my friend," I said. But it was a disturbing thought. As I hung up, I remembered Jo Ellen North's extreme interest in the fireplace. It all fit together, but I wasn't getting the picture. I was missing something, and I didn't know what.

I went home to check that the diary was still hidden and considered putting it in a safe deposit box. I'd think about that tomorrow.

At two that afternoon, I picked up Barbara Wright. She was dressed in stylish pantsuit, brightened by a floral silk scarf that I knew came from Neiman Marcus. Her shoes were Ferragamo and her bag, Louis Vuitton. Barbara Wright may have been comfortable in sweats, but she knew how to dress right when the occasion called for it. I was glad I had worn a bright red embroidered jacket from Coldwater Creek and sueded silk taupe pants, even though I still had on my serviceable loafers.

We started with the other two houses, both of which I'd shown Jo Ellen North—the charming Victorian with three bedrooms, a modernized kitchen, and that English garden, although in November the garden didn't show well; and the brick cottage on College with its open, airy rooms and its '50s St. Charles kitchen. "I like the feel of the house," she said, "but I'd need a newer kitchen. St. Charles was the thing in its day, but I cook too much—and entertain in the kitchen. We'd have to do major remodeling here."

Both houses, she said, interested her in one way or another, and she was glad she didn't have to decide that day. "Now let's go to Fairmount."

I told Anthony I'd be bringing a client through, and he straightened as much as possible. The house was still in the early stages of renovation. "We've had some setbacks," I said, not wishing to be specific.

"I've read about the house in the paper and heard the neighborhood gossip," Barbara said. "It doesn't bother me, and I can see beyond a mess."

As we toured from room to room, she was quiet, thinking, assessing.

"I know it's hard to tell now," I apologized.

"No, no, it's fine. I can see you're doing a good job of renovation, doing many of the same things I'd do myself. I think it would fit us. Let's go back again and talk about plans for the kitchen—that's probably most important to me."

So we stood in the midst of the kitchen, and I showed her, without a pang, Anthony's pull-out cupboards and the spice door.

"Is this where the skeleton was?" she asked.

I gulped, said yes, and tried to move on.

"It would make such wonderful dinner party conversation," she said. And then immediately, "How heartless of me. What is it they say on emails? Barbara Wright would like to recall that last message."

I liked this lady a lot.

We discussed counter tops and color schemes, and she made some good suggestions. I'd end up, I thought, tailoring the house to her—but she wasn't pushing me.

I let her take her time, but after about forty-five minutes, she turned to me and said, "Thank you, Kelly. I'll go tell Glenn about this, and we'll talk and think. Meantime, keep an eye out for other houses for us. We won't buy until we sell ours—no bridge loans for us in this economy—but we'd like to have some ideas."

"I'll do it," I said.

As we walked out the front door and down the steps, I saw a green Jaguar pull away from the curb and round the corner onto Allen Street far too fast.

My heart jumped into my mouth. Was Jo Ellen North stalking me or keeping watch on the house? Either way, it scared the living you-know-what out of me.

When I got behind the wheel of my car and reached to start the motor, my hands were shaking so that I struggled to put the key in the ignition.

"Kelly? Are you all right?" Barbara's face showed real concern, but I didn't want to tell her the reason I was shaking.

"I think I should have eaten lunch," I said. "It just came over me all of a sudden."

"You young people just don't pay attention to your bodies," she said. "Come in and let me fix you something."

"Thanks, but I have to get home to relieve the babysitter. I'll eat some peanut butter at home." Okay, I crossed my fingers at the white lie, but by then the shaking stopped. I was still scared.

I drove Barbara back home. When I got to my house, Joe was there, and they were all working jigsaw puzzles. Joe worked on a simple one with Em, letting her place the pieces and praising her when she got it right, helping her when she didn't. She crowed with delight every time a piece went into place. Theresa and Maggie were bent over a much more difficult puzzle of a mountain scene and barely looked up when I came in. The tranquil scene made me forget Jo Ellen North for a minute.

"Joe, how was the interview?" He still wore a starched white shirt, tie, and nice slacks. His sports coat was thrown over a chair.

"I think okay. They said they'd call in a day or two. They need someone from two-thirty until nine at night, which suits me fine."

Theresa added, "I could drop him off and pick up the girls for you every day if you want." She hesitated. "I'd like to do that."

"Theresa, I'd have to pay you. I wouldn't let you do it for nothing."

"No, Miss Kelly. You have done so much for us. I want to help, at least for a while."

"Well, we'll see if Joe gets the job. Then maybe we could do that two or three days a week. You still have to take care of your family, Theresa."

"I know. I can juggle both."

After Theresa and Joe left, I got the girls fed, worked on homework with Maggie and more puzzles with Em, and got them to bed. Then I got ready for bed myself, but of course sleep wouldn't come. It was too early for one thing, but I didn't know what else to do with myself. I couldn't settle down to read or even think about the office. And every time I shut my eyes, Jo Ellen North appeared in front of me, like the Wicked Witch of the West. Something was out of whack—Mr. Martin was the villain here. He killed his lover, Marie, and yet I had no inkling of a threat from him. But I was terrified of Jo Ellen North, and I wasn't sure why.

About nine-thirty I called Mike's cell phone. He answered with a curt "Officer Shandy."

"Mike? Are you on duty? It's Kelly."

I could hear the grin in his voice. "Yeah, Kelly, I know it's you. Aside from your voice, which doesn't sound like you tonight, I have caller ID What's up?"

I hesitated, stammered, wasn't sure what to say. "Oh, I just...well, I wanted to talk to you, but if you're on duty..."

"I can take a break in about ten minutes. How about you put the coffee on and I'll come over."

"Great." Mike wasn't going to solve my problem, and I knew it, but I was happier that he was coming over than I thought I would be. I put the coffee on.

"What's up?" Mike asked again when he was settled with his coffee.

"I don't know how to begin," I said. "I...you can't tell this to Buck Conroy."

"Kelly, you can't tie my hands like that. I could face charges for withholding evidence if you tell me something and I don't report it." He looked stern, and I was for a moment sorry I'd called him. But I had to tell someone.

"I don't have anything concrete, any evidence, anything you could prove."

Now he was impatient. "Kelly, tell me the story."

"I know who owned Martin Properties and who M.W.M. was. His name is Martin, and I think M.W.M. was the monogram Marie thought she'd have when they married."

He looked skeptical. "How do you know about this guy named Martin?"

"Well, we assumed Marty was his first name, but it must have been a nickname.

Joe told me about Mr. Martin. Honest, Mike, I think he has changed, and when I asked he told me everything he knew."

"But he doesn't know anything more about Martin than his last name, right?"

"Right. I figured I could look in the phone book, but there are lots of M. Martins. No way to tell who it is."

"And, that's Buck Conroy's job. But you're right—you don't have enough to go on yet. Still you need to call Conroy first thing in the morning. Promise?"

"Okay," I said, knowing that I hadn't told the whole story yet.

"I gotta get back on patrol," he drained his coffee cup and stood up.

"Mike, there's something else."

He turned and looked at me, waiting, his posture clearly impatient.

"This woman that wants to buy the Fairmount house, Jo Ellen North...I think she's stalking me or something."

"Why?"

"Well, she's been pressuring me to sell her the house right away, as is, and I've said no. The other day she made it sound like a threat. Last night, someone broke into the house again, but Anthony said it was a professional—they picked the back door lock and didn't vandalize but tore out some things that made it clear they were looking for something."

"What?"

"I don't know." Okay, I lied, but I just didn't figure telling Mike about the diary would do anything but make him furious at me—and I didn't want that. *Could I be prosecuted for withholding evidence?*. I rushed on. "And today, when I came out of the house, after showing it to someone else, Mrs. North drove away really fast. But I recognized her green Jaguar."

"Kelly, the break-in is serious, and you have to tell Conroy. But that business about this Mrs. North—it's odd, but it's nothing you can report. Tell Buck, but don't expect much. If it happens seven or eight times, yeah, you can. But right now you don't have anything. Just call Conroy about Martin."

"Okay." I walked him to the door and just sort of stood there while he gave me a good-night hug. I wasn't sure if he'd helped me a lot or not.

I called Buck Conroy the next morning first thing after I got to the office.

"Martin?" he said skeptically. "How do you know?"

"I just know. From Joe."

"Oh, yeah. That punk. As though you'd trust him."

"At this point, I trust him," I said, trying to convey my displeasure with his reaction.

"I guess we can have someone check all the Martins in the phone book, but for what? To see who has the nickname Marty?" He paused a moment. "You got time to do that?"

"No." Now I was angry. "I don't. And it's not my job. Mike keeps telling me that. But if it's any help, this man has connections on Jacksboro Highway."

"Isn't exactly the den of thieves it used to be, but there still some rough types out there. We'll keep it in mind. Meantime, you listen to Mike. He's right."

I almost slammed the phone down.

I was working away when the phone rang and Keisha got that funny look on her face again. "For you. You better take it."

By now, I never knew what that meant, so I answered with as perky a "Kelly O'Connell" as I could manage.

"Ms. O'Connell, this is Jo Ellen North."

I started to say hello, but she cut me off. "I see that you showed that house to someone else. I thought I had an exclusive on it." Her voice was stone cold.

"I have a client who wanted to see it, and no one has an exclusive. The bidding wars can begin when the renovation is done." I struggled to sound in control. "Besides, the situation on the house has changed. We've had another—ah, setback." Well, that wasn't true since this latest break-in didn't do much damage.

"Don't you dare sell that house to anyone else," she said and hung up the phone.

Another threat, albeit vague. I wondered what Mike would say now.

Late that afternoon, I was at home with the girls when Buck Conroy appeared at the front door. "Got any coffee? I got news, and I'll trade," he said.

"Give me a minute." I made him a cup in the single-cup coffee maker.

When I brought it back, he said, "We found your guy."

My guy? "How'd you find him?"

"I got contacts on Jacksboro Highway too. Your guy did time for tax evasion, has some shady connections."

Something clicked in the back of my mind—Claire Guthrie told me she thought that Jo Ellen's father did time for tax evasion.

"Name's Robert Martin, lives at 1305 Rivercrest Drive—pretty upscale address. And he admits to an affair with Marie Winton but swears he did not kill her. His story is that one day he went to the house, and she was gone. But she didn't take anything with her."

I was impressed. "That's pretty fast work," I said. Meantime I was writing down the address, though I had no idea what I'd do with it.

"Yeah, we can do it when we get a lead. And that's thanks to you. You buy that story?"

"That he thinks she left and didn't take anything with her? No. No woman does that, and every man knows it."

"I didn't think so either. I'll keep you posted." He gulped down his coffee and said he had to go.

After he left, I wasn't sure what to think. We'd solved the Marie Winton murder—or at least were close. Why didn't I feel what psychologists call "closure?" Because it wasn't solved. Something was still very wrong.

The next morning, impulsively, I drove to 1305 Rivercrest. It was one of the stately old mansions, probably built in the 1920s, almost southern antebellum in style—white pillars marching across the front, a verandah with French doors on either side of a double front door. It was three stories, with evenly spaced windows, now sporting plantation shutters but probably once draped in heavy fabric. As I drove by I could see the house stood on two lots and beside it was a large garden, with a pool, a greenhouse, and a cabaña—an estate, I thought, not just a house. I circled the block to come around and take another look. I had no idea what knowing where Robert Martin, Marie Winton's lover, lived would tell me, except that it would satisfy some deep curiosity. On the north side of the house, a drive-way led to what looked like a four-car garage, with guest—or servants—quarters over it. Okay, I told myself, one more pass by—and I circled the block again.

This time, as I approached the house from the north, a dark green Jaguar, coming from the south, cut in front of me to turn into the driveway. No signal, no courtesy of the road, no friendly wave. As the car turned, the driver looked at me—and I found myself staring right at Jo Ellen North.

Stunned, I picked up speed to get away, but after a block I slowed down and spun the story in my mind. Robert Martin killed his pregnant lover. Jo Ellen North must be his daughter, and she was trying to save her social position by protecting her father's reputation. Or something like that.

It made me so tired I wanted to go home to bed at ten o'clock in the morning, I drove with hands so shaky and breath so short, I kept wondering if I could make it home. My instinctive fear of Jo Ellen was right, but I had no idea what to do next. I knew, though, that I had to talk to someone, to have someone tell me it would be all right. Buck Conroy wasn't that person. Instead, I called Mike and woke him up.

His voice was thick with sleep, and I thought it sounded kind of nice, except I wasn't in the mood for that kind of nice. I blurted out my story, pausing every once in a while to take a deep breath.

"Kelly, slow down. I can't follow what you're saying. Where are you?"

"Driving home from Rivercrest."

"Okay, first thing. Pull over and put the car in park. Then we'll talk."

I felt like a child who was being chastised, but he was right. I was on Crestline Road, a residential street, and it was easy to do as he said. "Okay. I'm parked."

"Now, tell me slowly. You saw Jo Ellen North where?"

"At Robert Martin's house. I think she must be his daughter. And all along she's been so frantic to buy the house because she wanted to keep his secret hidden."

"Whoa? Who's Robert Martin, and how does he fit into this?"

I realized that I hadn't seen him to tell him all that Buck had told me, so I filled him in on the details.

"So what's his secret? The skeleton?"

"Yeah. He told Buck he did not kill Marie, but who else would have done it?"

"You'd be surprised. How old was Jo Ellen?"

"Too young. Maybe six, seven, eight. I think she's trying to protect him. But what will she do now that the police have questioned him?"

I could see Mike shaking his head, trying to wake up enough to puzzle this out. "I don't know. But don't make any more appointments with her. And you've got to tell Buck Conroy about this. Where are you going now?"

"To the office. I was so upset I thought I'd go home and crawl in bed, but I'm calmer now."

"Okay. I've got to get some sleep. I'll come get you for a late lunch."

"Thanks." I did feel better. In fact, I had done such a mood swing, I thought I could handle anything. It turned out I was wrong.

I had not been in the office five minutes when the phone rang and Keisha forwarded the call to me, though I noticed she was watching me carefully. When I said, "Kelly O'Connell," I was greeted with, "You've now sent the police after my father. This is too much. You'll be sorry."

I managed a weak, "Mrs. North?" My heart was pounding, and my hand got so sweaty I almost dropped the phone.

"You're damn right," she said in the coldest voice I ever heard and slammed down the phone.

With trembling hands, I dialed Buck Conroy's number. When he answered I told him I had to talk to him right away.

"Kelly, it's gonna have to wait until about four this afternoon. I do have other cases, you know, and I got a break on one that I've got to follow up on."

"Four? I have to get my girls at three, and I don't want them to be around when we talk."

"Get someone else to pick them up. Maybe your assistant. Do whatever you can. I'll be at your office at four."

"Okay." I hung up the phone and turned toward Keisha, but she was on the phone again. "Theresa," she said, pushing the button that sent the call to me.

I managed a cheerful attitude, though I felt anything but. "Hi, Theresa."

"Miss Kelly, I have good news. Joe got the job. We want to celebrate. I'll pick the girls up this afternoon, so you can work, and about six or so, I'll take them with me to get pizza and then pick up Joe. Then we'll come back to the house and we'll all celebrate."

Relief washed over me. There was my solution to the problem Buck Conroy presented. Sometimes I think the Lord really does look after me. "That'll work great. I have a four o'clock appointment and wasn't sure what to do about it. I should be home by five."

"Perfect," she said. "I have my key. And I'll come get the car seat."

"Theresa, if we're celebrating, do you want to ask your dad to join us and bring the boys? I'll buy the pizza."

She hesitated. "No, not yet. One night soon, though. I have to take it slow with Dad."

I could understand that. "Okay, I'll see you when I get home. And thanks. Oh, I'll still pay for the pizza."

It was not a good day. I fiddled, and I paced, and I twirled my hair—a habit that irritated Keisha. "Did you ever hear that poem by Gwendolyn Brooks about 'White girls be always fiddlin' with their hair'? That's what you be doin' right now."

"Well," I snapped, "I could sit on my hands."

"Maybe you should," she said blandly and turned back to whatever she was doing. Trust Keisha to keep me in balance—or at least try.

Theresa called about 3:30 to report that she and the girls were at the house and baking cookies. "For dessert," she explained. I thanked her, but I couldn't think about cookies at that moment.

By four o'clock, I had built a hundred stories in my mind, all of them bad and Jo Ellen North the villain in all. When Buck Conroy breezed in, I was ready to jump at him. The minute he hit the door, Keisha said, "Kelly, I got to leave a little early. That okay with you?"

I nodded. "See you tomorrow."

Buck sprawled in the visitor's chair by my desk. "Okay, what's this big news?"

Just as it had in the morning when I called Mike, the story tumbled out of my lips too fast, but I managed to get him to understand that Jo Ellen North was Robert Martin's daughter, she was so insistent on buying the house because she wanted to hide her father's secret, and she had threatened me. As close as I could, I quoted the threatening phone calls.

He squinted at me. Then he lit a cigarette—I normally didn't allow people to smoke in my office, and I sure didn't have an ashtray. I pushed the wastebasket toward him, hoping he wouldn't start a fire.

"You may be right. She may be dangerous. Mike's right. Don't make any appointments with her. And watch yourself and your girls. I'll go talk to Mrs. North tomorrow."

Tomorrow. I wanted him out the door in hot pursuit of her now. "Okay," I gulped.

He must have seen the look on my face, because he said, "Anything frightens you, call 911. I'll get the call, and so will Mike." And with that he was gone, cigarette still dangling from his mouth. *How could Joanie kiss someone who smelled of cigarettes all the time?*

I closed up the office and headed home, feeling somehow defeated, and, more than that, vulnerable.

Theresa's car was on the street. I parked in the driveway and used my key in the front door, so as not to disturb them. When I pushed open the front door, Jo Ellen North confronted me—holding a small blue revolver.

My stomach rose to my throat, my heart pounded, and my knees shook so that I was sure that they would buckle and I'd end up face down on the floor. But I gathered myself by thinking of the girls. "Mrs. North, I didn't see your car." *Why was I trying to be pleasant, as though this was a social call?*

"That's because I didn't park it near your house" Her voice was stone-cold.

"Where are my girls?"

"In the back with the sitter. I told them to stay there."

I'd have told her she had a lot of nerve telling my girls what to do, but then, she had the gun, and I figured that changed the balance of power, even in my own home. I was sure she could hear my heart pounding against my ribs from where she sat, which, to my mind, wasn't near far enough away.

"What can I do for you?" I asked, making a real effort to keep my voice strong.

"I want Marie Winton's diary," she said. "Beyond that, you can't undo the trouble you've caused. My father will be charged with murder, and it's your fault. We're going for a ride. Just you and me."

I remembered the conventional wisdom that said if you ever get in a car with a kidnapper, you're dead. I vowed she'd have to shoot me right on the streets of Fairmount before I'd get in her car. Of course, it was winter, and the late afternoon light was fading fast. If she didn't hurry, she'd have the cover of darkness. Still, I wasn't about to hurry her.

"Where?" I asked, ignoring the question about the diary. I'd bring it up again if I still could stall for time. I wondered if Theresa would think to call 911, but she had no way of knowing I was being held at gunpoint. And I couldn't quite call out to her.

She shrugged. "Trinity Park. You might as well die where your ex-husband did."

I think the word "die" didn't register. I didn't believe or my mind couldn't process that I might die that day—but my body reacted, and I thought I might throw up. "Tim? You killed Tim? Why?" And I thought he'd been shot over a deal gone wrong, gambling debts, something to do with lowlifes from Jacksboro Highway. Instead, this sophisticated—or supposedly so—country-club type killed him.

"He knew about my father and Marie, and he was blackmailing me."

"You shouldn't have paid," I said. Seemed a sensible reply to me, but it infuriated her.

"Don't you tell me what I should or shouldn't have done. I should have killed you too about two weeks ago. Then the cops would never have found my father. And I should have found that diary. I sent someone to look for it."

That last break-in to the house on Fairmount. And her intense interest in the fireplace—she thought it was hidden behind one of the tiles. Stalling for time, I said, "The diary wouldn't help you. Marie had a locket with the initials M.W.M. on it, she told her family about Marty who was going to marry her, and the house belonged to Martin Properties. How hard is that to put together? The police would have discovered that your father killed her sooner or later. I just pushed them into sooner."

Her face turned purple with rage, and it occurred to me she might have apoplexy—whatever that was—or a stroke or something before she could try to force me into the car. "My father did not kill that woman," she screamed.

Keeping my voice soft, I asked, "No? Then who did?"

She was out of control—a frightening thought. "My mother,' she screamed. "She found out he planned to leave her, and she killed the bitch. I was there. Six years old, and I saw the whole thing. I helped put her in that box. It's haunted me all my life." She took a deep breath and calmed down. "Now, it's time for us to go."

I was searching in my mind for another stall, something, anything. Just as I was about to say, "Wait. Let me get the diary for you," Em appeared in the archway that led to the bedrooms. Before I could scream, she said, "Mommy, is that bad woman yelling at you?"

It was just enough. Jo Ellen North turned, distracted, and I lunged and kicked, maybe given strength by desperation to protect my child. I don't know where the strength came from, but in that fleeting moment I wished I'd studied tae kwon do. The gun flew from Jo Ellen's hand, as I screamed for Theresa. Jo Ellen lunged for the gun, but another kick that caught her in the face prevented that. She went down on her knees, and I was on top of her.

Out of the corner of my eye, I saw Theresa take in the situation and grab the gun. Meantime, Jo Ellen and I were embroiled in a macabre wrestling match, first one of us on top, then the other. I fought desperately, for myself and for my girls. Even though I was fueled by rage and anger, she too was strong and she too was filled with rage. If I'd had time to think about it, I'd have realized we were like two primitive animals, not a sight for my girls to see. But I had no time to think, only to fight back with what strength I had. For a moment the world around us didn't exist. I felt her fingernails rake across my face. I grabbed her hair and pulled back hard, so that she was forced off me, and I rolled to sit on top of her. But her weight—she did outweigh me, which was slim consolation at that point—threw me off balance, and she was soon on top of me again, this time with her hands around my throat, squeezing—hard. I couldn't breathe. How long is it before unconsciousness came from cutting off breath? And now death seemed all too real to me. I fought back with more strength than I knew I had, bringing my arms up under hers and forcing hers apart with all my might—and desperation. Her hands flew apart, but she was too quick for me, or I was too weak by then. She had me by the throat again. I fought to get a breath. Spots danced before my eyes, against a backdrop of black. The more I struggled, the harder Jo Ellen squeezed. I just didn't have the strength left to fight back.

Suddenly, Jo Ellen North went limp, sprawling on top of me. I lay still for a moment, breathing hard. Then I pushed her off and saw Theresa standing over us, holding the gun by the handle.

"I hit her," she said. "Did I kill her?"

Rubbing my throat, I whispered, "I don't know, and I don't care. But give me the gun, and go get the cord from my bathrobe—it's in the bathroom." I saw my girls, standing wide-eyed and pale in the doorway. Maggie was sobbing and Em just stared in amazement.

Jo Ellen was out but who knew for how long—as I rolled her onto her stomach and pulled her arms behind her—convenient for a hammerlock, if needed. She began to stir and moan. "Maggie," I said, "call 911. Right away. Give them the address. Tell them whatever they ask." I had no idea how I could think that rationally, and I knew the minute that a cop came through that door, I'd turn into a blithering idiot. But until then, I hung on. "Em, go unlock the front door and open it."

Theresa returned with the cord—it was silk, like the bathrobe, and I knew I'd never wear it again, but it would be strong and wouldn't stretch. We tied Jo Ellen's hands behind her back, just as she began to stir and move about and threaten—loud and long. "You can't do this. I'll kill you and your children. Let me up this instant."

"Jo Ellen," I said, "feel this? It's your gun, and it's pointing at the back of your head. I were you, I'd lie still."

She collapsed in a heap. Of course, she had no way of knowing I didn't know from square one about guns. Did I have to cock it or whatever, or could I have just shot her? I didn't want to do that, and I prayed she would stay still.

She did. She began to sob, great wracking sobs from deep within. When she managed to speak, she cried, "My father…he's everything to me. My mother has Alzheimer's, and Dad's protecting her. But I can't let him go to jail. He's too old and too frail. Damn you." She began to get her grit back, and I nudged the gun against the back of her head, hoping against hope that it wouldn't go off by accident.

"I never had a happy family life. My parents hated each other after that, and I blamed everything on that woman. I know she kept a diary. She taunted Mom with it, just before Mom shot her. I…I had to find it. Protect my father."

The girls still stood in the doorway. It wasn't a scene I wanted them to see or hear—their mother holding a gun on another woman who was confessing to all sorts of horrid things—but I couldn't put down the gun and go to comfort them. "Girls, go to the front door and watch for the police. Maybe Mike will come."

It seemed an eternity that I sat there, listening to Jo Ellen North sob on and on about how Marie Winton ruined her childhood, how she'd resented her mother and loved her father. *Was I a therapist? I didn't want to hear this.* Although it seemed hours, it wasn't more than five minutes before I heard sirens.

Mike was not the cop that burst through the front door. It was Buck Conroy. "Okay, Kelly," he said. "You can get up. And give me that gun, handle first." His gun was trained on Jo Ellen, but she lay still.

Other cops stormed in, got Jo Ellen to her feet, removed the cord (I saw one of them grin), and cuffed her.

Then Mike burst through the door, made beeline for me, and enveloped me in a huge bear hug. I was never so glad to see anyone in my life. I sort of sank into his hug and would have fallen to the floor, if he hadn't held me up. He led me to one of the huge chairs, sat in it, and pulled me onto his lap, oblivious of the looks he was getting from his fellow officers.

"Tell me about it." His voice was ever so gentle.

And it all spilled out, how frightened I'd been, her confession, how enraged I became when I thought Em was in danger. I looked for the girls. They stood a few feet away, staring at us.

I held out my arms. "Come here," I said. "You are both the heroes of the day. I am so proud of you."

Maggie was still sobbing, though softly now. "Is it okay? Is the bad lady going away?"

"Yes, she is. We don't have to worry any more. Nothing's going to happen to us, our house, the house on Fairmount. It's all over." I felt the relief wash over me, and then the tears came. My sobs were as wrenching as Jo Ellen's.

"Don't cry, Mommy," Em said solemnly. "You were very brave too."

I thought about it for a minute and then, through tears, said, "Yeah, Em, I was, wasn't I?" I didn't know that I could ever do it again, but I'd been brave. I was alive, and my girls were alright.

Buck Conroy came into my line of vision. "Gun's a .38," he said. "I'm betting it's the same gun that killed Tim Spencer."

"She told me it was," I said.

He looked at me. "I should have listened to you this afternoon," he said. "Sorry."

That was all? I was astounded.

"I'll question her at headquarters and let you know what we find. Oh, and I'll call Joanie and tell her what happened."

You do that. Not high on my priority list right now.

The police took Jo Ellen away, though by then she'd recovered her usual spirit and was trying to order them around, threatening them for manhandling her, swearing her lawyer would have each of them kicked off the force.

"I'm calling in to take the rest of the shift off," Mike said. "What's for dinner?"

Theresa yelped. "Pizza. I forgot. And Joe will be waiting at the Y."

"Find my purse for me, Theresa, can you? I'll give you money for pizza." I did, and she left, with no mention of taking the girls with her.

I sat in the chair with Mike, and the girls clustered about us, but none of us said much. We were content to be safe and quiet. Mike ran his hand through my hair and softly touched the scratches on my face. I found that comforting. The girls clung to me, each holding a hand tightly. I forecast nightmares for some nights to come, but I couldn't worry about that.

Joe and Theresa came back in about forty-five minutes. Joe was full of bluster about what he'd have done if he'd been here, but Mike quieted him with, "I'm glad you weren't. It wouldn't have sat well with your probation officer. And Kelly proved very capable."

We ate pizza almost in silence. There just wasn't much to say.

Epilogue

Jo Ellen North confessed to killing Tim Spencer and attempting to kidnap me. After a long trial, she was sentenced to twenty-five year to life for first degree murder—she still didn't seem to realize she could have gotten the death penalty—and to ten years for the attempted kidnapping, served concurrently. If she lived that long, she'd be in her eighties when she got out, I figured, at the least.

Her mother, Elizabeth Martin, was beyond confession or charging. The court decreed that she be put into an Alzheimer's facility, and she went to the best, most expensive facility in Fort Worth.

Robert Martin was a broken man. Frail to begin with, his health went downhill during the court proceedings. By the time his daughter was sentenced, he needed full-time health care in his home. I knew the past would haunt him for whatever days he had left.

Marie Winton's family did not come to the trial. Phyllis Winton served as spokesman and told me the family was content that justice was served. They saw no need to put themselves through a trial, and I applauded them for that. I sent them Marie's diary, along with a note explaining that I hid it because I felt it was too personal to turn over to the authorities and contained nothing that would benefit the investigation. To my surprise, Phyllis wrote me a gracious note, thanking me for my consideration.

****

The rest of us went on with our lives. Maggie and Em did have nightmares, and they slept in my bed more nights than not. Mike was around the house a lot more, seeming to sense that he almost lost someone he valued. Whether he too wanted to spend the night in my bed was not discussed, but I knew it would come up eventually.

Theresa began to invite Anthony and the boys to dinner with Joe and my family, and Anthony, after some bluster and a lecture from me, began to accept Joe. Anthony finished the house on Fairmount, and it was a beauty. When I put it on the market, Barbara Wright was one of the first to see it and to make an offer. But that is another story.

The End

Author's Note

The Fairmount Neighborhood in Fort Worth, Texas, is very real, as are several places mentioned—The Old Neighborhood Grill, Nonna Tata, Lili's Bistro, and others. But the plot of this novel never happened, to the best of my knowledge, and the characters are fictional. This is a work of the imagination.

I was inspired, if that's the word, by a dead space in my own kitchen—a narrow spice cabinet between a deep pantry and a deep oven and storage above and below—and by a house under renovation in Fairmount that suddenly gave me the idea of a skeleton in a dead space. I now am pretty sure there's an old brick chimney behind my dead space—it may be holding the roof up for all I know. But there's no skeleton there. That's from my imagination.

About Judy Alter

Judy has written fiction and nonfiction for adults and young adults. Her historical fiction titles feature such strong women as Elizabeth Bacon Custer, Jessie Benton Frémont, Lucille Mulhall, and Etta Place, of Hole in the Wall gang fame.

Skeleton in a Dead Space is her first mystery and is the first in a projected series.

Recently retired as the director of a small press, Alter raised four children as a single parent and has seven grandchildren, with whom she spends as much time as possible. Judy lives in Fort Worth, Texas, with an Australian shepherd, an aging but affectionate cat, and a brand new Golden Doodle puppy.

http://www.judyalter.com/
http://www.judys-stew.blogspot.com/

Watch for more Kelly O'Connell Mysteries,
coming from Judy Alter in 2012

No Neighborhood for Old Women

If you enjoyed Judy Alter's *Skeleton in a Dead Space*, you might also enjoy these mystery/suspense authors published by Turquoise Morning Press:

Bobbye Terry, author of The Briny Bay Mysteries

Lynn Romaine, author of *Night Noise*

Cat Shaffer, author of *No Safe Place*

Thank you!

For purchasing this book from
Turquoise Morning Press.

We invite you to visit our Web site to learn more about
our
quality Trade Paperback and eBook selections.

www.turquoisemorningpress.com
www.turquoisemorningpressbookstore.com

Turquoise Morning Press
Because every good beach deserves a book.
www.turquoisemorningpress.com

~~~~~

Sapphire Nights Books
Because sometimes the beach just isn't hot enough.
www.sapphirenightsbooks.com

CPSIA information can be obtained at www.ICGtesting.com
Printed in the USA
LVOW040258290911

248386LV00001B/28/P